TOGETHER IN PARADISE

"Let me go!" Kristy commanded, but his arms only tightened. Suddenly made aware of how defenseless she was against this powerful man, her eyes widened. They were completely alone up here. Wedged between his thighs, her arms pinned flat by his grip, she was caught fast, helpless to move unless he willed it.

Looking into glowing sapphire eyes, Kristy was acutely conscious of his tensing body. Her heart began a slow, langorous beat as it began again, that throbbing sensuality she had sensed last night. The warmth of him flowed through her body like wildfire, and she could not breathe, nor unlock her gaze from his. Warm, caressing hands slid deep into her hair.

"Do you really want me to let you go, Mermaid?" Jason murmured huskily.

Her mind screamed *yes!* but her body softened against his unyielding chest.

Jason was kissing her hair as though savoring its texture. Kristy shivered. She felt his breath on her face, the slow, burning touch of his mouth on her cheek, caressing down to the corner of her lips. She shivered again, and his body intimately knew it. A throb of desire beat in her blood as she waited, caught in electric suspense. . . .

(Cover photograph posed by professional model.)

BLUE WILDFIRE

Faye Ashley

Leisure Books  *New York City*

A LEISURE BOOK

Publshed by

Dorchester Publishing Co., Inc.
41 E. 60 St.
New York City

Printed in the United States of America

Chapter One

She was locked into the throng milling around Air Hawaii, her five-foot, three-inch frame sandwiched between a female Amazon and some basketball coach's dream. On her right, three attractive women chattered incessantly, their entire conversation centering around the men they would meet at the parties they would attend in the smashing new clothes they had bought. On her left, a short, fat man in an atrocious red and blue, hibiscus-splashed shirt gesticulated wildly with a hand that contained a lit cigar.

Kristin withdrew as far as possible from the cigar-wielding hand. Irritably she displaced the camera prodding her shoulderblades, wondering, not for the first time, if she had taken leave of her senses. What had seemed so eminently right this morning had begun to take on aspects of madness.

Self-amusement curved her softly set mouth. No one but Kristin Loring would consider a month in Hawaii madness. The air around her hummed with laughter and excitement, and this holiday ambience was thick enough to slice! *Always out of step, Kristy*, she chided, dodging as the cigar danced her way again.

The cigar paused, its owner taking notice of her reflexive movement. "You all right, young lady? Look a little green around the gills! This cigar not bothering you, is it? How long you gonna be staying on Kauai?" he whooped, his expansive gestures creating glowing red laser beams around Kristy's face.

"I'm staying a month or so," she said faintly. This produced another whoop, astonishment this time. Keenly aware of the attention they were drawing, Kristy expertly flexed a shoulder threatened with cremation, replying softly, "My uncle Alex owns a hotel there, and yes, that cigar *is* bothering me. Can you see if they've opened the boarding gate yet?" she appealed.

They hadn't, but the cigar's attention was attracted to another young lady looking green at the gills. Hoping she did not appear as green as she felt, Kristy repaired her carefully vague smile. She was the recipient of several compassionate looks, and she had developed a severe allergy to compassionate looks. *There was no reason for them; she was young, attractive, fairly healthy, and this vacation*, she thought defiantly, *was the culmination of a lifetime dream.*

Then why was she feeling so dismal! It had all worked out so beautifully—really, it had, Kristy assured herself. She had narrowly avoided what would

6

have been a disastrous marriage; the interior design school she attended had taken its annual sabbatical; her job had vanished on the winds of relocation; and what better way to convalesce from a serious illness than in hot, tropical sunlight? She ought to be dancing on air. What she would really like to do was lie down somewhere—anywhere—and sleep for a solid week.

A concerted surge of movement coincided with the loudspeaker's strangled squawk. Borne along by the force of her sandwiching companions, Kristy breathed a sigh compounded of relief and reluctance. Ten hours of trans-Pacific flight had left her so exhausted, the last thing in the world she wanted to do was board another plane. However, this final leg of her journey would be mercifully short; twenty-six minutes, according to the beautiful Eurasian stewardess whose eyes glinted with amusement when they touched upon Kristin Loring.

Well, who could blame her, Kristy wryly conceded. In this rumpled gray suit, with the incongruous gaiety of a pink ginger lei bobbing about her neck, she must look a comical sight. Probably still green around the gills. Retrieving the remnants of her ticket, she stuck it in her shoulder bag and patiently shifted the cumbersome camera case that weighed down her other arm. Just another half hour, she implored the headache threatening her temples.

Inch-by-inch, the line crept down the crowded plane aisle as passengers stowed away hand luggage and then themselves. Kristy crept along with it. Preoccupied with finding her seat number, she did not see the tall young man who suddenly stepped out to remove his jacket. Kristy walked into him as if he was clear air.

The camera case swung out and clipped him smartly

7

in the ribs as she stumbled into a hard male chest. In agonizing slow motion, Kristy grabbed at something which turned out to be his arm. Her face rested snugly against crisp linen, and for a dizzying second, she was acutely conscious of his warmth, of the heady male scent filling her nostrils, the swift intake of breath that echoed her own shocked gasp.

Dismayed green eyes lifted to his, swiftly followed by a loud, accusing, "Ouch!" from Kristy. Strands of her hair had gotten entangled with his tie clip, and her sudden jerk of head provoked a wince of pain. Another quick movement coincided with her angered gasp. She could hear mutters behind them, a coarse, masculine query as to what was holding up progress. Thoroughly provoked, she twisted wildly and to no avail. A slide of red-gold hair spilled across his dark blue sleeve, but the clip-snarled strands held firm.

"Will you hold still!" he rasped. That deep, resonant voice was sharp with vexation. Kristy held still. She glanced up at him but his face registered only as peripheral awareness of deeply tanned skin, the flash of intensely blue eyes. Slim, tanned fingers freed her hair. Distractedly Kristy raised a hand to smooth it, and the camera case clipped him again.

The man swore softly, colorfully. Hugely embarrassed, Kristy thought she murmured something. Afterwards, she was not sure. Her heavy shoulder bag chose that instant to slide down her arm and into his flat stomach.

"*Lord,* woman!" he exclaimed, his voice cracking with disbelief.

"Well, I'm sorry!" Kristy hissingly returned. Disinclined to look at him again, she edged around his tall

8

form and gratefully fell into a seat. "*Lord,* Kristy!" she mocked his fitting reaction. Her headache had become more fact than threat, and the scent of him still clung to her nostrils. Undoubtedly one aggravated the other, she thought, catching a glimpse of that arrogant dark head. He was four rows ahead of her, and she devoutly hoped he would not turn to seek her out.

Surprised she still had one, Kristy gave a smile to the stewardess who suddenly appeared at her side. She held out a small pearl earring. "This was caught on the gentleman's shirt button. He asked me to return it," she said.

She looked much amused. Flushing, Kristy said, "If you'll thank him for me, please—" She hesitated, then added, "And please tell him I hope he wasn't mangled too badly in our encounter?"

"But of course," said the stewardess.

Watching her pause beside the man, Kristy heard his deep, melodious laugh. *Thank goodness he had a sense of humor,* she thought dryly. She stowed the malicious camera case under her seat, then dug out the novel she had started on the Pan Am flight. Pure fantasy, of course; girl meets boy, girl loves boy, girl gets boy and happy ever after. If one believed that, one had to believe in fairytales. Or unicorns.

Idly her gaze drifted back to that cap of curly black hair. The stewardess was still beside him. *Must be someone important to command that much attention,* Kristy mused. Or perhaps just terribly good-looking. Losing interest, she sat back and closed her eyes. Maybe she could sleep on *this* flight—the throb of the jet engines failed to arouse more than a flicker of anxiety. *None of that white-knuckled gripping of armrests that*

9

had greeted her first takeoff, Kristy thought, amused at her initial reaction to flying.

After what seemed an interminable delay, the plane taxied down the runway and pointed its nose towards an iridescent drift of clouds. Kristy pressed close to the window, watching entranced as Diamond Head faded into the dark blue haze that blended sky and sea. How extraordinary that she could be here! And how flatly disappointing her reaction. Where was the joy, the lovely excitement of a dream come true?

Steve spoiled this too, she thought bitterly, and with predictable results. Keeping her face averted, Kristy furtively wiped at tears. Dwelling on Steve Brady was courting disaster. Thank heavens she had no seatmate! She found some aspirin and rang for a glass of water, regarding her trembling hand with a rueful sigh. Another stupidity to be added to a wearyingly long list, ignoring what would have been a simple case of flu until she collapsed. However, this was one idiocy that could be excused somewhat. Cutting Steve Brady from her life had been a shattering experience. The only way to bear her misery with any dignity at all had been to keep too busy to think, and she had rationalized her worsening symptoms as a probable part of that misery.

Disgustedly, Kristy lowered her head and began mopping up the flood of tears. God, she did so hate this galling new weakness! She had always possessed a resilient young strength that could, seemingly, cope with anything; the loss of her mother, the brutal blow of her father's inoperable cancer, the agony of watching him die week by agonizing week. Having weathered these very real ordeals, she certainly was not giving in to a foolish bit of heartache.

However, lumbar pneumonia was not subject to will-power, and retribution for her stubborn disregard had been swift and merciless. And lingering. Three weeks after her unceremonious collapse, she was still prone to fatigue, and these despised tears. *Brave little Kristy,* she thought caustically, *who could absolutely be counted on to pick herself up, shake herself off, and start all over again!*

Digging through her purse for another tissue, Kristy resolutely turned her mind to another, equally confusing matter, the man who awaited her in Kauai. Alex Loring was a widower, and something of an enigma to Kristy. The last time she had seen him was at her father's funeral four years ago. Certainly not what one would term a close relationship; and yet, she loved him deeply. What he felt for her was anybody's guess. Duty, of course, a certain natural fondness. But enough to tolerate her presence for an entire month? Perhaps he would find her a nuisance and send her packing within a week. Or perhaps just a nuisance to be endured with grace.

Drat, she was out of Kleenex. But a thorough search of her purse turned up an intriguing piece of paper. A prescription, as it were. The friend who drove her to the airport, a third year med student and, to Kristy's mind, a rather awesome example of liberated woman, had used the time to unleash a torrent of advice, concluding with a "prescription" not to be opened until Kristy reached Kauai.

Close enough, Kristy thought, and opened the precisely folded paper. Her laughter burst free with a naturalness she hadn't felt in months!

"Kristy, my friend, using my credentials as your future family physician, I hereby prescribe for you the following, to be taken without the slightest twitch of guilt. I want you to pamper yourself—which translates to sleep till noon, dance till dawn, drench your liver in champagne, find a relatively harmless man who's simply looking for some fun and have yourself a delicious little fling. It is my professional opinion that your toes will not curl up and fall off; however, should this occur, I will transplant free of charge just as soon as I am licensed for such charitable work. A serious note, Kristy. All work and no play is fine for computers, but you're a woman, not a machine. The key word is fun."

"Oh Doc!" Kristy softly exclaimed. Replacing the whimsical little note, she studied her reflection in the plane window. Finding herself a man might be a bit difficult right now, the way she looked! Green eyes too big for her pinched white face, clothes that hung on a too slender frame, hair that had lost its healthy sheen. She drew a settling breath and fastened her seatbelt. Hardly a machine. But less than a woman?

Kristy's gaze flew to the black haired man who had just stood up to retrieve his briefcase. Tall, broad-shouldered, infinitely masculine. She would have liked a look at his face, but no such luck. *Probably just as well,* she decided, *one encounter with a green-eyed witch was enough for any man!*

* * *

Nothing in her experience could have prepared

Kristy for the deliciously wicked pleasure of doing absolutely nothing in a place seemingly created solely for that purpose. As predicted, to continue this delightful self-indulgence day after day severely tested a mind accustomed to inflexible routine. She awoke in the morning surrounded by the fragrance of ginger lilies and *piake,* a jasmine so lusciously, drenchingly sweet, a person could drown in it. She drifted through days that encapsuled the meaning of balmy.

Sunlight as warm as a lover's caress, perfect blue evenings that flowed into dusky moonlit nights, a riot of flowers that ranged from the incredible intensity of purple bougainvillea to the softest, palest blush-pink roses. To a young woman who had grown up on the monotone plains of West Texas, Kauai's lush, tropical beauty was overwhelming, and six days but a breath of time.

She slept until noon, danced till dawn, spent lazy afternoons lounging by the pool or trekking to her private waterfall for hours of intensely sensual pleasure. She had even tried drenching her liver in champagne, but the rest of "Doc's" advice was still tucked away at the back of Kristy's mind, too deeply embedded in the hard knot of pain and distrust to dare risk trying. Besides, there was still the matter of personal beliefs to resolve before she could fling herself into a stranger's bed. And despite all the socializing she had forced upon herself, Kristy had yet to meet a man who could raise so much as a flicker of interest.

As for being a nuisance to her uncle, Kristy's fears were proven groundless, simply because she rarely saw him. When she arrived in Kauai, Alex, surprisingly sensitive to her unspoken wishes, had alloted her this very special cottage rather than a bedroom in his home, and commanded her to relax and enjoy. Then he took himself back to the task of running a hotel.

Evidently a most arduous task, Kristy reflected as she stepped into the shower. Except for an occasional shared lunch, and an even rarer dinner together, she caught only glimpses of this harried, preoccupied man. Knowing she was welcome eased her mind, yet she still felt shy and awkward with Alex. He was her father's oldest brother, and so similiar in appearance, just looking at him hurt her heart, but his emotional reserve was as effective as a barbed-wire fence between them.

Given this bland indifference, Kristy had to admit that her hopes of bonding a closer relationship were without substance. *Or more likely, indicative of a distressingly simple nature,* she thought wryly. Alex was perfectly satisfied with a life uncomplicated by scatter-brained little nieces.

Wrapping up in a thick white towel, she pulled a face at her glowing image. It was after eleven and she was just getting up, a purely hedonistic pleasure. She felt wonderful and knew she looked it. She had a small, heartshaped face, wildflower pretty, nothing to rate a second glance, but this hair—!

Kristy caught it up and tumbled the shining mass. If she had one vanity, it was her hair, a thick, softly curling mane the color of a sunset, red and gold, peach tints and pale honeyed beige, reaching to the nipples of her breasts. *Not merely vanity,* she thought. She was shrewd enough to realize that this voluptuous red-gold cloud was the only thing that lifted her above the norm.

She flung down the towel and critically scanned her figure. Still too slim, but the way she was eating, that ten pounds would soon return and likely be doubled! She pulled on a sleek white maillot suit cut scandalously high on the hips and low in the bosom, then added a lacey white jacket. *The latter was nothing more than a tanalizing invitation to peek,* she thought with a satisfied grin.

She had already filled her beach bag and was opening the door when Steve's image popped to mind. Kristy paused for another look in the mirror. Soft curls feathering about her face, a fine, creamy complexion, huge green eyes luminous with delight. Not half bad, yet not enough for the man she wanted to marry.

Caught without defenses, hurt stabbed deep at the bleak admission. Angrily she denied it. Self-pity was foreign to her nature, and self-doubt becoming an all too prevalent force of late. "Not half bad," she retorted defiantly and hurried out the door.

Alex having tentatively agreed to a poolside lunch, she lingered in this lively area for several minutes before deciding to seek him out. Such a distracted man could easily have forgotten he had a niece. After all, another man had forgotten he had a girlfriend.

Kristy gave a brittle laugh at her twisted humor. Cutting through the lobby, she walked out a side door just as Alex emerged from the exterior gift shop.

He stopped short when he saw her. Momentarily distracted by her powerful surge of love, Kristy too paused. Then, not even noticing the man behind him, she impulsively stretched up and kissed her uncle's cheek. "You reckon there's the remotest change of holding you to lunch?" Kristy mischievously inquired.

"Sorry, I'll have to take a raincheck," came the all too familiar response. Looking embarrassed, Alex stepped aside to reveal the other man's presence. "Kristy, I'd like you to meet Jason Thorne; Jason, my niece Kristin Loring," he added somewhat tersely.

Sapphire blue eyes betrayed only the smallest flicker of surprise before Jason Thorne recovered, his mouth curving with amusement. "My pleasure, Miss Loring," a deep, resonant voice murmured.

Kristy's breath caught as she looked up into a face so pleasing, she felt a little flicker of protest. Instantly on guard, she coolly returned his greeting, but when he smiled, her own lips softened in helpless response.

He was tall and powerfully built, this Jason Thorne. Tousled jet black hair curled at the collar of his shirt, and his fitted cream slacks molded lean hips and the long, clean lines of his legs. He had a cleft in his chin, finger-tip deep. Kristy wondered how many women had been drawn to place a kiss there.

The heady scent of him seeped into her thoughts. Tantalizingly familiar, yet she was certain she had not met him before. He was incredibly good-looking, if one went for that sort of rugged male appeal.

Magnificent dark brows arched at her overlong perusal. Belatedly aware that he had extended his hand, she placed hers in it with an odd reluctance. His hard, warm clasp was disturbing; Kristy tried to snatch back her hand, but his held fast.

Green eyes flashed at this silly little tug of war with her own hand! Her uncle having turned aside to speak with an employee, Kristy tugged harder, but Jason was obstensibly studying the opal ring she wore.

"This is very attractive," he blandly remarked. Long, sooty lashes swept to unveil twinkling blue eyes.

"Thank you. It was my mother's," Kristy said with a

frosty rebuke in every word. That lazy smile still playing about his mouth, his gaze moved down her, lingering until she felt it like caressing fingers. Kristy's blush seemed to reach all the way to her toes.

She shot another look at Alex, but he was still engaged with business. At least he was not witness to this annoying little by-play. "Are you enjoying your stay at The Blue Pearl, Mr. Thorne?" she asked brightly, working in another tug at her hand while she spoke.

"Umm," said Jason, or some such thing. He glanced at the shapely legs which ended in small white sandals, before releasing her hand and letting her breathe freely again. *An obnoxious man*, Kristy thought. Little more than a minute had passed yet she was hotly flustered, and unable to gain the initiative in this subtle duel. Little drumbeats of excitement throbbed in her ears as their eyes collided again. She was suddenly intensely aware that she was a woman, something that had been in doubt for so long, she'd forgotten how it felt.

Angered at her reaction, Kristy stepped back with some inane comment on the weather. His reply was most courteous, but the suppressed amusement in those blue eyes was a challenge she could not afford to refuse. She tipped her chin with chilling hauteur, her ice-green gaze flat enough to freeze any man.

Jason grinned. "Going swimming?" he murmured.

Kristy eyed him with extreme displeasure. That wicked glint of humor in his eyes—what did he find so blasted amusing? Did she have a smudge on her nose or something? Noting Alex's now impatient attention, Kristy shifted her beach bag, repositioning the strap that sharply defined one breast. She started to close her jacket too, but Jason's widening grin checked that feminine gesture. Drat the blush that crept up her creamy throat—he hadn't missed that either!

She'd forgotten what he asked her. Oh yes—swimming. "Perhaps later. Nice to have met you, Mr. Thorne," she said, indifferently.

"As I said, my pleasure, Miss Loring. Perhaps we could have dinner some night soon."

"Perhaps," she said with polite disinterest. Taking it for granted that he was a hotel guest, she added a vague smile, then turned to Alex with considerably more warmth. "One of these days I'm going to call in all those rain-checks, Uncle," she impishly warned. "Now if you gentlemen will excuse me—"

"With reluctance," Jason murmured.

Couldn't he speak above that seductive murmur? Kristy's slanting glance got caught in the two long, slashing dimples that softened his arrogant mien. *Deceptively so*, she thought, *there was nothing remotely boyish about this man*. Her smile was the equivalent of a dismissing shrug, but Jason was still laughing as she left.

Apparently nothing fazed that colossal ego, Kristy nastily concluded. Thrusting him from mind, she headed for the kitchen and requested a picnic. "Nothing fancy, just a sandwich and some fruit and a thermos of iced tea," she coaxed. The request was promptly granted. Alex's niece was a great favorite with the staff, invariably referred to as *keiki*, child, and cosetted like one.

Since most of his staff were inordinately massive people, Kristy guessed her petite stature influenced their thinking. At any rate, her simple sandwich multiplied to three hefty rolls crammed with roast beef, ham, and four varieties of cheese before the chef was satisfied.

"Too skinny," he scolded.

"Not after this," she dryly assured. Adding the items to her beach bag, Kristy made her way to one of her favorite spots, the ancient banyan tree that shaded half the parking lot.

Thick, ground-hugging limbs created a tempting trap for a child. Settling within its shade, Kristy ate two of the monstrous sandwiches while she watched a lively four-year-old swarm up a limb despite stern parental disapproval. As agile as a tiny monkey, he leaped from limb to limb, crowing his delight. Kristy couldn't blame the boy. Had she an ounce less dignity, she would have climbed the tree herself.

When the child was eventually captured and borne away on loud squalls of protest, she lay down on her stomach and opened a textbook. There were three of these thick tomes, all suggested reading by a stern-minded professor who saw no sense in laying about for a month doing nothing. Since Kristy's conscience slyly concurred with this, there was nothing for it but to devote at least two hours a day to this soothing task.

Soon deeply absorbed, she did not notice the tall, black haired man who paused beside a small Cadillac Seville, his eyes crinkling as he watched her. One slender leg arched above her impudently rounded bottom, idly waving to and fro. A sandal slipped off. Kristy kicked off the other one and wriggled deeper into her towel.

Jason Thorne laughed to himself as the burnished head dropped to folded arms, and her soft, drooping mouth relaxed into a pout of a smile. Like a wind rippling through silken grasses, sleep flowed down the supple body with visible softening. Kristy yawned as openly as a child.

Jason laughed again, a soft, gentle sound, yet sufficient to arouse her to awareness. When Kristy's eyes popped open to meet the intense blue gaze invading her privacy, she came up off her towel with a gasp of anger.

"Please, Miss Loring, one assault was quite enough—I'm not sure I could take another one!" he beseeched before she could hurl her thunderbolt.

One assault? What was he talking about? Kristy sank back on her haunches, green eyes rounding with comprehension. That curly black hair, those wide shoulders—oh no, she inwardly groaned, not the man on the plane! They had not met again, either on the flight or in the airport, and she had completely forgotten the incident.

"I—you—my hair," Kristy said most lucidly.

What had to be the orneriest, wickedest, most infuriating grin in existence spread over his handsome mouth. "Um hum, your hair. I still have several strands attached to my tie clip. Shall I return them, or may I keep them as souvenirs? My bruises are healing nicely, and soon I'll have nothing to mark our memorable encounter," he sighed.

She was pink over ivory from head to toe, and quite a lot of it showing. Kristy located the edges of her jacket and brought them together, unevenly. Luckily Jason didn't insist on a reply to his impudence. She hadn't any that she could find. Glancing up at him through lush brown lashes, she worked up a frown.

"I wouldn't think you'd bruise that easily," she half muttered.

Laughing, his long frame arrogantly propped against the car, Jason let his gaze slide languidly down to her bare pink toes. She waited for some response to her remark, but he outwaited her. A *most aggravating man*, thought Kristy. "If you'll excuse me," she firmly suggested, "I'd like to get back to my reading."

He straightened. "Oh, I'm sorry. I certainly didn't mean to interrupt such diligent reading," he said, drolly grave, and got into the car. It came to life with a soft, savage purr. Inexplicably, Kristy shivered, a ripple that raced the satiny length of her. He made her uncomfortable and she irritably wished he'd get on. Instead, he leaned lazily out the window, his gaze meandering over one bent leg, traveling upwards as if following a roadmap.

He murmured something then, but it was lost in the soft roar of the car. Taking it as a farewell, Kristy gave a flippant wave, then stretched out on her towel again. She glanced over one shoulder as he drove away. He had all of Kauai to choose from, and he chose *this* hotel. Just one of life's little ironies, she supposed. At any rate, she now knew what had caused his amusement. Odd though, that she hadn't recognized him right off. Why hadn't he reminded her that they'd met on the plane? Any normal person would.

She was supposed to be studying, she reminded herself. Propping open her book, she tried to concentrate on the author's concept of design and beauty. "Jason Thorne," she murmured, tasting the name. "Steve Brady."

Unconsciously, Kristy rubbed at tensing shoulder muscles. Until now, she had refused to face all the ramifications resulting from her shattered love affair, but Jason Thorne had, somehow, forced the issue. Granted, the pain of betrayal had been a devastating new experience, yet given time, she could have handled it in her usual straightforward way. But Steve had done more than destroy her illusions. He had destroyed her surety of self, and replaced it with a confusion of doubt.

Sorting through this murkey haze required unobstructed, completely objective judgment. She still felt woefully inadequate to the task, but painful memories lay at the back of her mind like little ticking timebombs, and she was sick to death of evasive tactics!

Cautiously, Kristy closed her eyes and let him come in, her mouth tightening with the familiar, bitter pain. Steve Brady, quick, impatient, gray eyes intense, his thin, sensual mouth curling in that sardonic smile she knew so well. It had been so easy to fall in love with him. They had met at a barbecue given by a mutual friend, and Kristy had immediately noticed the sophisticated, well-dressed man cluttered up with several simpering women. But she was predictably surprised when he quickly singled her out. Later, he had told her that she possessed an air of haughty independence that challenged a man. She found that secretly amusing, considering the precarious condition of her knees as he approached her.

He had monopolized her evening with that eager outpouring of information so vital to building a relationship. He was thirty, owner of an advertising agency, a little too cyncial, far too desirable, possessed of a driving need for success. She was bright and idealistic and achingly vulnerable to his practiced charm.

She had never been seriously involved with a man; he had been married and divorced. He was totally serious about himself and devoid of humor; she saw humor as a saving grace and laughed at herself more often than not. Total opposites and cause for concern in the small town atmosphere in which she lived. But Kristy was in love, and if she had doubts, she shoved them down. She was too enthralled with the prospect of being Mrs. Stephen Brady to listen to friends. Implicit trust, because she knew no other way to love a man.

He bought her a lovely pearl and diamond ring that she treasured as the forerunner of the one to come. They had time. She derided her anxiety as months passed without a change in their relationship. They discussed marriage, in an abstract manner, to be sure, but the commitment was there, unvoiced but *there*. Or so Kristy thought. She had balanced his high-flying goals with her own rather common dreams of children and pets and sunny afternoon in the park, and laughed with him at her baby-carriage mentality.

Handsome, clever, ambitious Steve. She had not realized just how ambitious until that chill night when she had gone to his apartment to surprise him after a weeklong business trip. It was something she had not done before, despite the key he had given her, and something she would certainly never do again.

Her mind had recorded that scene with a camera's clarity. Letting herself in, then standing frozen with shock, her heartbeat slowing to a sickening thud as she saw Steve and the woman on the couch, disheveled, lovely, clad in a satin chemise, one hand holding a glass of wine and the other caressing the platinum head laying on her lap. Steve too held a glass of wine. It shattered on the parquet floor, Kristy remembered, a garish red puddle spreading over shards of glistening crystal.

It was only seven oclock. He wasn't even due in until nine. And this woman. . . . Kristy had stood rooted to the spot as tiny bits of comprehension crashed endlessly around her dazed brain. Even now she could feel that hideous sensation of paralyzed limbs that would not move, a mouth too dry to form words. After an eternity compressed into a single shocked gasp, Steve's hoarse exclamation shattered her paralysis. The only thing she recalled from that point was dropping his ring on a table, and arriving at her own home some twenty-five miles from the city where he lived.

Steve's subsequent explanation was another, equally incredible, shock. The woman was his new fiancee. He did not love her, but she had money, class, influential family connections. He loved Kristy, but she had none of these vital assets, and a man had to keep his priorities in order. Steve saw no reason he could not have it all; most successful men kept separate residences, he assured her, with a woman in each—one a wife, one a mistress. A common enough arrangement, and she would never regret it, he would see to that.

Kristy's blazing denials had ignited a raging bonfire. She had her own fiery temper, but it was no match for his black, defensive rage. He had crushed her proud spirit as easily as he shredded her righteous convictions.

Kristy's nails cut deep as she relived that ugly scene. He *loved* her? She did not understand that kind of love. In truth, she didn't understand much of anything. Steve's vicious attack on her most basic beliefs had badly damaged her inherent sense of self. Nor had she ever before been compelled to consider what sort of person she was. She had thought herself a modern

24

woman, of course, but Steve had flatly destroyed this pretty little illusion too. An anachronism, she thought with hurting honesty. Naive, simplistic, gullible; commitment as solemn a vow as the gold band that would complete it, marriage solidly based on mutual trust, sex synonymous with love. Steve did have a point, she reflected, it really was incredible that she still believed in unicorns. But she had, and it filled her with shamed confusion, a humiliation too nebulous to get a grip on.

Her friends had rallied round, of course, which made it ten times worse. *Knowing you had been a fool was bad enough*, she thought bitterly, *having it confirmed on every hand was salt on the wound.*

Kristy drew a deep breath of release. The blame for most of her heartache rested squarely on her own shoulders. For a supposedly intelligent woman, she had acted with inordinate lack of judgment. Now, lying here in the warm afternoon sunlight, she could begin adjusting to it. If one could call this empty ache *adjusting.* She felt bruised all over! As for what she was. . . .

Bright enough to learn from experience, if nothing else. As Jason Thorne's pleasing laugh sounded deep within her mind, Kristy coldly acknowledged the imaginary taunt. Bitterness served a useful purpose—she would never be so gullible again. Believing in the unicorns of pure love and implicit trust was a fool's pipe-dream.

She cushioned her head on folded arms. She really ought to get back to studying. But her lashes were so heavy. . . .

Chapter Two

The afternoon hours had slipped away by the time Kristy awoke. Annoyed at this new habit of falling asleep without half trying, she gathered book and towel, stuffing them into the beach bag while she scanned the parking lot for a white Cadillac Seville. No sign of it. An odd sort of rental car, she reflected, but strangely appropriate with her image of Jason Thorne. Picking up her bag, she set off down a winding brick path with visions of a reviving shower in mind.

Ribbons of flaming red anthuriums edged the path, flowing into great drifts of cream satin begonias, and some luminous pink flowers shaped like tiny ladyslippers, nodding and dancing in the wind. Kristy knelt and picked one. It smelled of vanilla and dusted her nose with saffron. Curious, she tasted a petal. Like green-apple ice, she decided.

She walked on, swinging the heavy beach bag in cadence to her thoughts. Why had Jason chosen this particular hotel? Jointly owned by Alex and his late wife's family, it was small in comparison to the lavish resorts beyond Lihue. *But then, The Blue Pearl was more a unique experience than a mere hotel,* she thought possessively. The long, four story building that comprised the hotel proper was located nearly a block distant from the graceful arc of one-story suites called the east complex. Behind this was a semi circle of twelve utterly charming cottages, the whole of it rambling over some ten acres of enchantingly lovely gardens.

Connected by paths of old, faded rose brick, the hotel offered the usual amenities of pool, tennis courts, chic boutiques and a fashionable nightspot, but in Kristy's opinion, its greatest asset was an indefinable feeling of pleasure that it simply existed. Granted, she might be a trifle prejudiced. Nonetheless, The Blue Pearl was much like a beautiful, highborn lady, one whose spacious, high-ceilinged rooms possessed a timeless elegance no modern hotel could possibly match. She loved it nearly as much as she loved the man who built it some thirty years ago.

The lady did have her faults, Kristy admitted. Alex's staff was wholly inadequate, and the service, particularly in the cottages, left much to be desired. Her bed was still unmade, and there wasn't a clean towel to be found. But a drift of blue jacaranda blossoms had gathered along the ledge of her bedroom window. Ample

27

compensation, Kristy decided. Humming to herself, she swabbed out the tub before filling it with scented water, then slipped into the silken depths with an audible sigh.

Deliciously relaxed, she gave thought to the evening. Since Alex had flown to Honolulu and would not be in until late tonight, she decided to have dinner in her cottage and devote her energies to something constructive for a change. Like addressing postcards—one a day to Cousin Flora, the beloved companion who shared Kristy's Texas home. Or perhaps applying herself to those textbooks; she was three quizzes behind.

A strange way to spend a beautiful, romantic evening, Kristy admitted, but if she was to be a career woman, then she would be a fine one. The devil of it was that she really didn't want a career all that much. However, since the choice had been forced upon her, she would strive for excellence. Maybe she'd become rich and famous—

"Beautiful designer Kristin Loring, who is decorating his new swankienda in Houston and his gorgeous new condo in Palm Springs, attended the gala affair with Reggie Rich—"

Maybe she ought to get out of this tub and find something to dry off with. And then again, maybe not. Kristy gave a sensuous wiggle. So relaxed, she thought dreamily. Floating in mindless enjoyment, she slipped deeper into the water. Her breasts poked up through the bubbling froth like two miniature islands, each crowned with a perfect bud. She touched, her palms passing seductively over these piquant mounds, each rosy bud taut and raised in quickening excitement. The long, slim fingers mentally replacing her own belonged to Jason Thorne. . . .

Kristy sat up with a shocked gasp. "Time to get out of this tub, Kristin!" she muttered. Which she did, and dried herself *au naturel*; with sunshine and balmy breeze. That lapse of mental discipline still pricked. To have actually become aroused!

"And by your own galloping imagination, no less!" she accused the hazy green eyes in her mirror. Twisting her hair into a no-nonsense bun, Kristy wandered into the bedroom. She fully intended to bury herself in a book tonight, and even went so far as to don a gown and robe, but thoughts of Jason Thorne kept flickering across her mind like summer lightning. And Steve Brady. The two men wove a daisychain of disturbance.

Restless, jumpy, unable to enjoy her simple meal, Kristy drifted out to the *lanai*. Flowers massed round it, and jasmine climbed to the latticed roof, drenching the night with perfume. The Blue Pearl was made for lovers, as was this fragrant, moon-dusted night. Stirred with poignant longing, she stalked back inside.

Jason. What was he but another ego-oriented male who knew how to use those dark good looks to his own advantage? And would have no qualms about doing so, if a woman crossed him. Strong, ruthless, dangerous even. Steve and Jason. The two images superimposed until there was only one, dark and featureless, like a photograph negative.

This was unfair, and she was an immensely fair person. She did not even know one of those images, not well enough to make a judgment. In this mood, she wasn't qualified to judge a goat, her mind bitterly jibed. Kristy wiped her eyes, despising this necessity. How did a man's values get so distorted, she wondered sadly. Steve was, potentially, such a fine person, so desirable and handsome. But twisted in some way, by forces beyond her powers of perception, devoid of the most basic human decencies.

She picked up her book, laid it down again. Memories were beginning to crowd her mind. Suddenly raw with frustration, Kristy strolled aimlessly through the quiet cottage. If she persisted in this mood, gave into depression and loneliness—but she would not. She had come too far to permit regression. Back to nights of gritty tears? Never!

Easier said than done, Kristy tiredly conceded. Oh God, how could she go on wanting a man who had made mock of everything she believed in. What kind of a weak-spined creature was she that she could not snap it off like a strangling cord!

Sometimes she could stand apart and laugh at her sniveling self, but this was not one of those times. She shed her nightclothes and took out a sexy new dress. The blue and white fabric was soft and clingy and felt like satin on her sun-warmed skin. A sense of pleasure began to blunt her urge to cry, enough to squelch it, anyway.

A seductive musk of perfume replaced her usual light fragrance. She brushed out her hair and left it loose around her shoulders, added the softest touch of eyeshadow to her lids, a burnished peach lipgloss for the final, sultry touch. Kristy ran her tongue over her lips to moisten them, a wet, shiny mouth that suddenly broke into giggles as she tried a vamping pose too absurd to maintain.

Tear-sheened green eyes sought the ones in her mirror. "You're okay," she whispered, "it's okay." Oh, this ambivalent mood! Making a face at her big-eyed image, she retired the halter straps behind her neck and slipped on dainty, heeled sandals.

A short time later, she was standing inside the hotel's nightclub, glaringly aware of her solo status and fighting an urge to fade into the background. Reminding herself that this was Alex's club helped a bit. When the hostess approached with a welcoming smile, Kristy requested a corner table and ordered pineapple juice, then sat back to observe.

It was a lovely scene and as usual, she recorded rather than saw, framing a series of stylized impressions. Tawny velvet upholstery, crystal vases, tiny white sparklers in lush plantings, multilevel seating, candlelight from wall sconces and tables gleaming on naked shoulders and arms. Flowers in long black hair, the seductive allure of filmy dresses and the most frivolous of shoes, expensive perfumes blended into the essence of a single exotic flower.

Ties were optional, but men in dressy shirts and tailored slacks complemented their women. It had the hauntingly beautiful ambiance of an old-fashioned garden party, thought Kristy.

She saw him as soon as he came in. Casual elegance in a white silk shirt and black trousers, Jason Thorne paused just inside the wide arched entrance to look around. Even though she was shielded by palms, Kristy shrank back to escape that sea-hued gaze. He too was alone, his easy assurance a decided contrast to her shy, creeping entrance. *It must be lovely to be so sure of oneself,* she thought wistfully, *to possess such absolute certainty.*

Curiously, she watched him as his gaze wandered over the room. A willowy blond in a stunningly skimpy dress held his attention for a moment. Noting the smile that curved his full mouth, Kristy felt a distinct shock. The beautiful woman was surely a delight for any man, yet his moody blue eyes held a faint touch of boredom as he glanced at her again, then idly continued his scrutiny of the room.

As if, Kristy thought, *something once lovely and pleasurable had become too common to arouse his interest.* Realizing she was thinking specifically of lovemaking, a blush swept through her body, uncomfortable, obscurely aggravating to her sense of womanhood. As if *she* had just been passed over. Kristy set down her glass with a sharp click. She was of half a mind to call out to him, just to refute the ridiculous warmth shining through her eyes.

Eyes which were irresistibly drawn back to the tall imperious man who sauntered on into the room and paused to request a drink. Leaning against the teakwood bar with indolent grace, his teeth flashed whitely in response to the pretty barmaid's sally. It was obvious that she, and every other woman in the room, for that matter, were attracted by his rugged good looks.

The rich fabric of his shirt clung to powerful shoulders, playing up his golden skin and glossy black hair. Tall, broadshouldered, devastatingly attractive, all of him radiating a potent maleness so tangible Kristy could touch it, and yet he was alone. Why? she mused. It must be by choice. There certainly had been no shortage of women in this man's life.

Her mouth twisting at her wry thought, Kristy stood up and strolled in the opposite direction, only to be brought up short by the glad greetings of the young man she had met on the Pam Am flight. They had spent two evenings together; she supposed he was entitled to that possessive smile. Oh ye gods, she inwardly groaned as he swept her up, had she promised this evening to him? Since their last date was the one she chose to drench her liver in champagne, she could not recall exactly what she might have said. Thinking back, there was some mention of meeting again, a casual one, but she ought to honor it now that he'd showed up and was practically lifting her off the floor.

But something cold and bitter moved inside her. She refused to consider another evening being bored witless just because he took her polite forebearance for something else.

Coolly she freed herself, and just as coolly declined his invitation to share a drink and a dance. One look at his crestfallen face, and she felt compelled to tone down her denial with a teasing laugh. After all, he was a nice young man, attractive in a gangly way. *And she was apparently incapable of cruelty*, she thought crossly.

She removed the arm around her waist. "No, Mark, I don't want to dance. Nor do I want company tonight," she said, tight with annoyance. She glanced up at him through her lashes. "It's nothing personal, you understand, I simply don't like men tonight. Not too many other nights either, for that matter," she added with a puckish grin.

A deep laugh sounded behind her. "Now how many men could resist such a challenge," Jason Thorne drawled.

She had known he would come, had been waiting, in fact, yet Kristy's heart jumped at the soft, husky voice. Half turning, she looked over her shoulder, amused disdain icing her half-veiled gaze.

"Well, do try to resist, Mr. Thorne, I don't like you either," she drawled in creditable imitation of his tone. She smiled at the man named Mark somebody. Practically two entire nights spent with him and she still could not recall his last name! She certainly had no such difficulty with Jason Thorne.

"Perhaps another night, Mark," she said vaguely. She was relieved—and piqued—when he promptly strode off to a lively group which boasted two unattached ladies.

"Friend of yours?" asked Jason. Kristy's indifferent gaze passed over him.

"An acquaintance. Excuse me, please," she said shortly, and walked off.

She had managed all of four steps before a strong brown hand caught her arm and spun her around to confront him. "I didn't excuse you, Miss Loring," Jason explained. "A lovely tune. Shall we dance?" he went on, blithely ignoring her displeasure.

"I really do *not* care to dance," Kristy replied, but she was, somehow already doing so. Jason simply tucked her hand in his and moved her to the space reserved for this purpose.

She was annoyed by his assertiveness, annoyed by him. However, this was not the time nor place to contest it, Kristy acknowledged, marking the eyes which followed them. Resigned to making the best of it, she placed a hand on his shoulder. She was ordinarily a very good dancer, light and graceful on her feet, but at the moment, one of those feet seemed determined to challenge his.

Beneath his thin shirt, she felt the warmth and smoothness of his skin, the sense of taut power made visible by rippling muscles. She misstepped again.

Jason gave a husky laugh and pulled her more firmly into his embrace. "Relax, Miss Loring," he commanded.

"What I do not need at the moment is a dominating male telling me to relax," Kristy muttered, marveling at her two left feet.

An eyebrow lifted. "You don't, hmm. What do you need at the moment, Miss Kristin Loring?" Jason murmured.

"Whatever it is, you can't provide it, Mr. Thorne," she tartly assured.

His seductive whisper vibrated against her earlobe. "Can't I?"

Kristy, perhaps deliberately, planted a heel in the

middle of his soft leather shoe. "You can't," she said firmly. *Such confidence needed taking down a notch or two,* she thought, stiffening against his low chuckle. However, she was grateful that he did not pursue her taunt. At the moment what she needed was a dash of cold air. He was a skillful dancer and there was nothing at which she could take offense; he held her firmly but correctly, his thighs lightly brushing hers, his fingers a warm, light touch on her back. And yet Kristy felt dizzied by the strong sexuality pulsing between them. She had never encountered anything like it before, had never been so intensely aware of a man's smell or the warmth of a masculine body. She did not know how to deal with this totally new experience, and her dancing reflected it.

The couple behind Kristy turned too sharply and pushed her into Jason. Her reflexive movement was instantly countered, his arm holding her to his male hardness for a startling instant before he pulled away.

Jason smiled at her soft gasp, obviously enjoying what had become more a contest than a simple dance. A burning anger welled up in direct proportion to that knowing male smile. *Not this woman, Jason Thorne,* she thought with flaring resentment. The second their dance ended, Kristy pulled free of him and walked stiffly back to her table.

Jason sauntered along behind her and pulled out her chair, then one for himself. Kristy flung down her evening bag. "Do join me, Mr. Thorne," she acidly invited.

"Why thank you, I think I will," Jason smoothly accepted. Not at all perturbed by her cold look, he sank into the chair and beckoned a waiter. "How long are you staying on Kauai?" he asked with idle curiosity.

"Three weeks or so," Kristy said shortly. She shook her head at his questioning hand gesture, her eyes moodily upon him as he ordered a cognac. Worldly, sophisticated, supremely certain of getting what he wanted. Stephen L. Brady all over again. Jason leaned to her and smiled, dark where Steve was silver and gold, but that smile held the same practiced surety. *Danger.* The warning crossed her mind like winter smoke, barely perceived, yet unmistakably there. Kristy reacted instinctively. She was already on her feet when Jason realized her intent.

He moved with stunning swiftness, catching her arm before she had completed a step. "Now surely you're not thinking of leaving me here alone?" he drawled, an eyebrow quirking in surprise.

He could have his choice of women—what did he want with her! Kristy looked up at him, thickly fringed green eyes hot with anger. Oh this man, this smug, cocky man! Shaking free of his clasp, she laughed her sweetest. "Surely I am, Mr. Thorne," she mocked."Naturally I assumed you were alone for the same reason I am—because you wanted to be. While the dance was lovely and I do appreciate your kind attentions, I must confess to being bored and sleepy. So thank you and goodnight, Mr. Thorne," she intoned.

Jason's eyes narrowed. "Impudent little thing, aren't you, Kristy Loring," he said softly. Just then someone clapped a hand on his shoulder, and during the round of greetings, Kristy made her escape. And it was an escape, she wryly admitted. She felt like she'd just fled a tiger's lair. She shrugged, foolish perhaps, but undeniably true.

She hurried on, her slim legs flashing down the steps which led to a flagstone terrace. Suddenly struck by the nature of her ignominious haste, she paused on the flower-filled landing to catch her breath. Irritably she shoved at her hair. If she had any gumption, she'd go right back inside and enjoy the evening, Jason or no Jason.

What was it about him that disturbed her so? That undercurrent of sexuality she had so vividly sensed between them? Oh, yes! Irrational fear strengthened by rational fact; he radiated a raw male virility that aroused her most basic instincts, and she was, as yet, appallingly ill equipped to deal with her confused emotions. Kristy captured a curl dislodged by the wind, a small sigh escaping. Yes, something deep within her had realized how very easy it would be to reach out blindly and take the reassurance she needed after Steve's devastating betrayal. But Jason Thorne would demand from her far more than he would give.

Her heart jumped at a low, familiar laugh. Jason and his burly friend had come out behind her. Marveling that she did not trip over her own feet and knock into the balustrade, Kristy gained the terrace. She paused at the edge of it and glanced over her shoulder. In the quickening moonlight, gleaming blue eyes entangled, held, then casually turned aside.

Kristy slipped into the shadowed path as silently as a night creature, her face set against the loneliness that suddenly walked with her. Rivulets of moonlight spilled through darkly etched foliage, and somewhere a nightbird called lonely in the darkness. Kristy shivered. She would give anything to be with someone, to be held close and warm and secure in masculine arms.

Kristy had trouble getting to sleep that night. After several hours of tossing and turning, she snapped on a light and read herself into a stupor; thus once again it was after eleven before she awoke next morning. She lay still for a time, enjoying the sweetly cool air flowing in through her window, thinking, lazily, of Jason Thorne. Last night's confusion had inexplicably vanished in the bright morning sunlight. Birds sang with a lusty sweetness that made mock of nebulous fears and doubts, and she stretched with catlike languor.

Was Jason around the hotel this morning? Probably long up and about, she mused, he didn't look like a man who enjoyed sleeping until noon. What did he enjoy? Idle speculation concerning this, as well as his occupation, prolonged her time in bed. He dressed extremely well, and the big gold Rolex on his wrist underscored that subtle suggestion of wealth. Recalling his aura of vibrant, almost electric energy, she couldn't feature him enjoying a long vacation. Still, even an executive must relax now and then—

Why this swift conclusion as to his position in life? She had deliberately refrained from learning a single fact about Jason Thorne, yet she sensed two things with absolute certainty; he was an authority in his own right, and he was not married.

The latter was easily divined, thought Kristy with satisfying scorn. A married man did not possess that untamed charisma that hovered around Jason Thorne. And too, she could so easily interpret his insolent reasoning. Why limit himself to one woman when there were hundreds—heavens, *thousands* for the taking? Kristy made a rude noise and headed for the shower.

Ravaged by hunger, she kept it short, and was soon snugged into a silvery bikini that would have made Steve's eyes pop out. The new wardrobe she had purchased for this trip contained several such daring items, which she loved, and which unnerved her each time she glimpsed her startling self.

"Hopelessly provincial," she muttered accusingly. Pulling a gauzy white shift over her bikini, she floated its soft folds around her thighs. The gentle swell of bosom tantalized above the low, elasticized neckline, its tiny, self-ruffled edges setting just off her shoulders. Definitely attractive, Kristy let herself admit. She felt a little strange with the image that faced her. Sometimes this Kristy in her mirror was surprisingly unfamiliar and she wasn't sure the change was for the better. She had rather liked that Kristy who still believed in unicorns.

Her mood dampening, Kristy hastily piled her hair atop her head, then took time to address another postcard to Flora. Olu Pau Gardens was the card she addressed this time, a horticultural fairyland, so described. *With her love of flowers, Flora would adore seeing it,* Kristy thought wistfully. So would she, for that matter.

Cramming a pink velour towel into her beach bag,

she called the office in quest of her uncle, per chance to lunch. A laughable notion. He was in conference and could not be disturbed, said his secretary.

Kristy thanked her and hurried to the sunny restaurant. An enormous brunch dispersed her hollow feeling, but as she emerged from the hotel, Jason Thorne's husky voice arrested her breathing, and that pesky sinking feeling was more pronounced than ever.

He was accompanied by her uncle and Kristy wondered about that, but she had no time to pursue it. Jason glanced down the shapely legs which ended in small white sneakers this day and smiled enchantingly. "Hello, Miss Loring," he said as they approached. He was dressed in a dark green shirt of fine lawn and casual gabardine slacks, exuding, as usual, a veritable cloud of sex appeal, Kristy noted sourly.

"Hello, Mr. Thorne—and good morning, Uncle Alex!" she said with much more warmth. A mischievous grin curled her lips as she eyed her beloved relative. How like her father he looked with his fine gold hair and handsomely weathered face! Kristy danced towards him, and like it or not, he received a warm kiss on the cheek before she released him.

Alex was very tall, as was Jason. For an instant, she felt like the filling of an all-male sandwich as the two men surrounded her with their powerful presences. At least she did not have a camera poking her in the back this time! Laughing at her whimsy, she looked boldly at Jason. No more fleeing this man. She felt as strong and invincible as he looked.

"Going swimming again?" Jason inquired. His gaze

sharpened at her response.

"Yes, again! I'll be at the waterfall most of the afternoon, Uncle Alex. Oh, would dinner tonight be within the realm of possibility?" she asked liltingly. When Alex admitted that it was, Kristy accepted his qualified agreement as lightly as he gave it, and bid him a gay farewell until then. Jason was still watching her with that peculiar intensity, his head cocked, a thin, humorless smile playing about his handsome mouth. A little piqued about last night, she guessed.

She looked into narrowed blue eyes, her vivid little face flushed with enjoyment. "Bye, Mr. Thorne," she said carelessly.

He tipped an imaginary hat. "Bye, Miss Loring," he returned in like manner.

Sensing the faintly mocking gaze on her back, Kristy forced herself to a slow saunter instead of the wild dash her fast-beating heart suggested. Where was the firm resolve of just minutes ago? Oh well, it was lovely while it lasted.

Fortunately her feet knew the way, her attention was entirely absorbed by the two men she'd just left. Who was Jason Thorne, anyway? And what business did he have with her uncle? Come to think of it, why hadn't she met him prior to yesterday if he was a guest at the hotel? Was he a guest? It would be next to impossible to overlook a man like Jason Thorne.

"Dummy, all you have to do is check the hotel register," she muttered. But she was not that interested. Just a little curious, that's all.

Having paid scant attention to her surroundings, she

42

was mildly pleased to find herself already far beyond the hotel grounds. Alex owned this land outright, and although he discouraged trespassing by guests, she had complete freedom to roam at will. She kept to the path for a few more yards, then plunged into the beautifully wild terrain, following a laborious course that led steadily upwards. It was marvelously rough going, and her panting breaths were audible by the time she reached a small rushing stream, and very shortly, the ledge of a miniature waterfall.

Kristy sat down and dangled her legs over the edge. Her waterfall might be small, but it was enchantingly lovely. Down below the lacy fall of water lay a dark green pool, rimmed with great black boulders glistening wetly in the sunlight, attended by clouds of yellow butterflies fluttering around them like lemon snow. The water was cold and sweet tasting. She drank deeply, then walked the ledge to a wall of rough black stone.

Here the enchanting sense of diminutiveness ended with soaring cliffs of massive rock, and the greenish twilight of sun and shadow. She leaned back against the stone with a dreamy smile, her eyes soft and green as a vixen's as she surveyed her realm. A realm that would, by all rights, someday be hers. A dusky, secretive, utterly sensual realm which she loved with a passion. Enormous cibotium ferns spread their fronds over delicate pink fuchsias and myriad tiny, shade-loving plants. Up through this vigorous canopy thrust ancient trees with mossy limbs dripping parasitical growth and the shyest of ghost-white orchids. And over it all hung a haunting sense of timelessness, that touched deep, primitive chords.

Down one side of the moisture-sheened wall draped a sheet of deep green moss. Kristy rubbed a naked thigh against it, reveling in its velvety texture. Soft, sensuous, seductive. Tilting her face to the wind, it seemed oddly fitting that Jason's dark features danced through her mind. *Like Adam*, she thought, flicking him away and frowning as he came right back again, *he belonged in this primordial Eden.*

A low, throaty chuckle welled through her lips. Playing Eve to the untamed savage lurking behind those celestial blue eyes would certainly be easy. She laughed again, harshly this time. "Best watch out, Kristy, this place is starting to get to you," she mocked.

Somewhat reluctantly, she deserted her lofty perch for the pool below, a good ten minutes of precarious descent. Arriving rumpled and flushed, she skinned out of her shift, then got a bathing cap from her bag. Moodily she let her gaze drift along the banks. In sunny spots, tiny meadows were dotted with flowers, and what looked to be a golden sea of dandelions massed at the base of a huge gray boulder. Across the pool lay the loveliness of pale green slipper orchids fringing a stretch of shaded bank. *God, it was so beautiful!* Profoundly moved, she stretched out her arms to the sky, feeling the powerful *mana* of this land as deeply as any ancient.

A prickling sensation raced up her spine as a twig snapped sharply very near at hand. Kristy stilled, not really alarmed, just curious as to who might be joining her. No one had ever invaded her privacy, but of course the hotel staff had access to the pool.

The silence was absolute. Kristy relaxed and put on

her cap. Nothing, she decided; a small animal perhaps.

She swam for awhile, up to the merry little whirl-pool of frothing water, back to the point where the stream left the pool in a series of shallow falls. After several more laps from end to end, she climbed atop the smooth black rock and stretched out like a lovely cat in the sound. Not an alien sound, just wind and water and bird song, and a soft, contented sigh. She lay there long enough for the butterflies to settle down again.

Pangs of hunger eventually drove her back to shore. Suddenly positive that she was famished, Kristy took off the bathing cap with less care than usual, a dismal mistake. Her hair rained down in a shower of shot-gold silk, hairpins scattering in the grass before she could retrieve a single one. Oh, brother! This hot, heavy mane was going to look like a witch's nest before she reached the hotel, but there was no help for that. Maybe she could get back unobserved.

She stepped into the shoulder high ferns and re-moved her swim bra to find a tickling leaf. Naked except for the tiny bikini briefs, she stretched in the dappled sunlight. For a moment she tested the idea of nude sunbathing, but she wasn't that liberated yet. She recovered her breasts, wriggled the shift down over her wet body, and set out for the hotel.

The downhill course was much easier going, but when Kristy reached the ravine again, she saw that she was well below her crossing point. It was too wide to jump, yet a detour meant an uphill climb, and she was too darned tired for that. Musingly she eyed a fallen log spanning the gap. How reliable was that log? And how good was she at log-walking? She sat down to rest a minute, as well as study this possible means of passage.

The log looked sturdy enough, and even if she fell, it was a harmless six inch drop. The ravine was nothing more than a ditch at this point, floored with water just barely glimpsed through the mat of aquatic weeds. The log was fat and fairly free of limbs. Nothing to it, really. Telling her dubious self all this, she got up to try it.

Halfway across, Kristy glanced down with a shudder. She had never been too keen on slimy things that lived underwater. Why hadn't she remembered that? Holding her breath until she gained the other side, she gathered herself and jumped sideways, landing securely on solid ground. She gave a pleased laugh at her accomplishment. "Safe!" she whooped, and took a step up the low, grassy mound that barred her path.

What happened next did so with stunning speed. Her bag snagged on a limb, she jerked at it, lost her balance, and landed on her bottom smack in the middle of the ditch she had just traversed.

Kristy's furious outcry strangled in a burst of masculine laughter. Jason Thorne stood on the opposite bank, hands on hips and head thrown back, his powerful frame seeming to reach to the sky. That odious laughter rolled on and on while she sat staring at him in dumbfounded confusion. Kristy could not have been more amazed had King Kong suddenly confronted her.

Chapter Three

Kristy raised her hands from the water, but then she could not think what she meant to do with them. Jason stood naked to the waist and she was mesmerized by all the muscular flesh. His skin gleamed with the richness of newly minted coins, furred with silky dark hair, moist with sweat and somehow dreadfully intimate. Her hands fluttered down like indecisive butterflies. Kristy made a tiny moaning sound.

He was still laughing. And she was just sitting there in this ghastly ditch! Coming alive with a shocked gasp, Kristy tried to gain her feet, but she had not reckoned with the forces of entangling weeds and a slippery clay bottom. She plopped back down with another inglorious splash. Several more of these frantic, disorganized attempts at rising provided her audience with a marvelous source of amusement. Kristy's outraged shriek sliced through his laughter and echoed round the hills.

Jason's reaction was immediate, if not laudable. He stopped laughing for at least ten seconds. When she made a violent lunge upwards and hit the water on a squall of pure aggravation, he clutched his belly and howled like a maniac. Kristy lurched to her knees. When and if she got out of here she would kill him. But meantime—her second shriek quivered every leaf within a two mile radius!

It also silenced Jason's joyous sounds. Moving as lightly as a cat, he stepped into the water. "Come on, Mermaid, let's get you out of there," he chortled.

Raging green eyes slashed at his face. "Don't you dare lay a finger on me!" Kristy spat. She would sit here until Christmas before she'd accept his help!

Jason cocked a wondering brow. "Why green eyes, I only meant to help," he chided. "Have you grown so fond of your ditch, then?"

Green eyes. Mermaid. Kristy hissed again. "Don't you dare—" but he had already dared. Slipping his hands under her arms, he pulled her erect, then stepped back up the bank and swiftly, effortlessly, lifted her up beside him.

Despite her chaotic fury, Kristy was keenly aware of the gentleness in those big, powerful hands. They held her as though she were a fragile piece of china. Dripping water and assorted bits of greenery, she snatched at her scattered wits. That darkly furred chest completely filled her vision. And then her face was suddenly flat against it as her feet slipped on the grassy incline.

Gentleman that he was, Jason wrapped his arms around her and solicitously inquired, "Are you hurt?"

Kristy removed her nose from his chest. He smelled sweaty, spicy, musky, a combination any cosmetic firm would pay a fortune for. "What are you doing up here?" she snapped.

He brushed at the curls entangling her lashes, chuckling as her scowl grew fiercer. "Oh, just enjoying a stroll. Lucky I was, hmm? No telling how long you'd be sitting in that ditch."

When Kristy jerked back to answer his bedeviling taunt, her mud-soled shoes took off in opposite directions. "Oh!" she gasped, and clutched wildly at whatever was available. Which was him. Jason stumbled, she fell heavily against his chest, and they went tumbling down on the grass in a mad tangle of limbs.

When the dust cleared from Kristy's brain, she found herself laying full atop Jason Thorne, wrapped tightly in his arms, her face now driven three inches into his naked chest. The potent smell of him took what little breath she had left. Feeling utterly bemused, she lay limply for a moment. Her open lips registered his spicy taste, and the beat of his heart was an intimacy more shocking then the lean hard body she was welded into.

When she raised her head, the sky spun in a giddy swirl of blue and green. She felt—she didn't know how she felt. Insane perhaps. She managed a weak, protesting wiggle, but their legs were madly entangled, and his arms pinned her flat to his chest. Kristy heaved a despairing sigh. For a girl who valued dignity at all costs, she was in one devil of a position!

Her eyes flew wide at the tremor shuddering through his chest. *Why, he must be as embarrassed as I am!* she thought with hot chagrin. Although he certainly got a kick out of her predicament, doubtless he was horrified by this one. What on earth could she say to ease their mutual plight?

Another shudder rippled through him, another and another. He was laughing! The joyous, irrepressible laughter of a small boy who has found himself a delightful mischief and intends to enjoy it no matter what the consequences! It burst forth in an awesome roar.

"Mermaid, do you make a habit of this, or am I just . . . singled out!" he gasped.

Mad, humiliated, stingingly aware of the steely strength pressing into every soft curve and hollow of her body, Kristy raised her head and gritted, "If you do not stop that hideous sound, I will perform a tracheotomy on your throat. With my fingernails!"

Jason instantly sobered, although his mouth continued to twitch as he cleared his endangered throat. "I'm so sorry. Are you hurt, Miss Loring?" he asked.

"Of course I'm hurt, you idiot!" Kristy flared. "By tomorrow morning I'll have bruises all over my . . . my . . . I'll be black and blue from the waist down!"

Blue eyes danced with devilment. "I do hope not. The thought of bruises on such a lovely little . . . lady distresses a man," he gravely assured.

"Oh you—*you*!" Her mouth a wrathful pout, Kristy wrenched against his clasp, but the arms around her yielded not an inch. Her hair tumbled around her face and spilled over his shoulders in rivulets of tangled gold, half blinding her, covering his laughing mouth as she wildly shook her head. This was becoming downright ridiculous!

"Let me go!" she commanded, but his arms only tightened. As yet he had posed no threat, but, suddenly made aware of just how defenseless she was against this powerful man, Kristy's eyes widened in an almost fearful look. They were completely alone up here. Wedged between his thighs, her arms pinned flat by his grip, she was caught fast, helpless to move unless he willed it, powerless to stop him if he—

As if perceiving the drift her thoughts were taking, Jason gave her a smile that both eased and infuriated. *Nothing so sinister as rape,* Kristy thought wildly, *just a bit of sport at her expense!* She would *not* struggle. Where his body touched, hers flamed, but she would choke before she'd let him know it.

"Will you kindly let me go?" she asked as calmly as she could.

"Do I have to?" came his plaintive sigh.

"Of course you have—" Looking into glowing sapphire eyes, Kristy's fierce retort died in a gasp of sound. His arms had loosened, but now his hands seemed to cover an astonishing amount of her back. Acutely conscious of his tensing body, she would move from him and obey the strident commands of her mind, but he was staring at her, no longer laughing as his fingers pressed deep into her skin.

Kristy's heart began a slow, langorous beat as it began again, that throbbing sensuality she had sensed last night. The invasive warmth of him flowed through her body like wildfire, and she could not breathe, nor unlock her gaze from his. Warm, caressing hands slid deep into her hair.

"Do you really want me to let you go, Mermaid?" Jason murmured huskily.

Her mind screamed *yes*! but her body softened until her breasts were crushed into his unyielding chest. The sound which escaped with her breath was a choked, "Please?"

He drew back, his eyes so intense, Kristy had a sensation of falling endlessly, down and down into those gleaming blue depths. Her lashes fluttered down in weak defense against something so persuasive she trembled. That undercurrent of sexuality which she must evade, ignore—deny! Her involuntary movement caught in the contours of his body. Nothing obeyed, her urgent, instinctive messages simply got lost in the warmth flooding through her body.

Jason was kissing her hair as though savoring its texture. "You smell like April flowers, Mermaid," came his husky whisper.

Kristy shivered. She felt his breath on her face, the slow, burning touch of his mouth on her cheek, caressing down to the corner of her lips. He stilled there, and the tip of his tongue licked her skin like rough warm velvet.

She shivered again, and his body intimately knew it. A throb of desire beat in her blood as she waited, caught in electric suspense. She thought, *He's going to kiss me,* and that was shocking enough, but what shocked her more was knowing she wanted him to. And yet, when he did, she was genuinely outraged. The sweet, fiery touch of his mouth coming to hers was only a brief flash of excitement before she jerked away.

The desire he had aroused underwent instant transformation. Hot green eyes flashed to his. "What on earth do you think you're doing?" she asked so incredulously, his mouth quirked with amusement.

"Now, Mermaid," he said warningly.

Kristy wrenched free of him, the lower half of her body striking ground with jarring impact. Another bruise! "I asked you what you thought you were doing!" she furiously reminded.

Jason sat up and peered at her with wounded innocence. "Well, I did save you from drowning, Mermaid, surely I deserve a kiss for such a meritorious act?"

Realizing she was still half laying on his lap, Kristy surged to her feet. "You are insane if you think that's— I happen to value my kisses. I don't pass them out like popcorn or . . . or as rewards for good behavior!" she sputtered.

"But mine was *exemplary* behavior," Jason explained. "Drowning can be very unpleasant, I hear!"

"Oh will you shut up about drowning! That water wasn't even knee deep! And since it has apparently escaped your attention, may I remind you that it wasn't my head that was in that ditch?"

"Oh. Well, with all that flopping around, who could tell what you were going to do next? For all I knew, you could go under at any minute," Jason sighed.

Kristy burst out with a spontaneous laugh, her green

eyes lighting despite herself. He was so different from the debonair man she had met last night, a vibrantly rumpled, sweaty, sensually attractive male who set her pulses sky-rocketing. But fire had an unforgettable way of impressing its power upon a person once burned, she reminded, and there was fire here, indisputably.

Setting her chin, she sought to reclaim a measure of dignity, which was promptly strangled by his next words. "You could use a few lessons in crossing ditches," he remarked. An eyebrow tilted. "Also kissing. Evidently you don't get too much practice at that either."

"And you, of course, are an expert on both?"

"Well, not so much at crossing ditches. But then, I don't enjoy that. You just hang in there, Mermaid, sooner or later you're bound to get good at one or the other," he cheerfully assured.

"I happen to be very good at crossing ditches. And that certainly couldn't be called a kiss, not by anyone's standards," she snapped.

"Not my fault. You started thrashing around like a scalded cat the minute I tried," Jason pointed out.

True, but who wanted to admit it? Kristy set her hands on her hips and glared at him. Marvelously unaffected by this, Jason stretched himself out lazily and leaned back on his elbows, grinning as his eyes wandered over her.

Kristy startled as she realized what held his interest. The wet white shift clinging to her body was far more erotic than nudity. Her small breasts were pointedly displayed, and the supple fabric was particularly loathe to disengage from her hips and thighs. Each time she pulled it loose, it simply snuggled down in another spot.

"Would you like my shirt?" Jason kindly offered.

Just then Kristy became aware of something soft and slimy on her thigh. A leaf, so sticky and rotted, it resisted her fingers and must be picked off in pieces. Angrily she glared at his strangled sound. "No, I would not. There's a towel in that bag over there. If you're not too weak to fetch it after all the energy you expended saving me from drowning?"

A pulse throbbed in her ears and she still felt lightheaded, though whether from his kiss or her fall, she would just rather not know. Kristy stepped back as he eeled to his feet in a lithe, uncoiling motion that took her by surprise.

He grinned. "Why, certainly, especially since you asked me so nicely."

Why bother replying? She attacked the leaf again. Ridiculous thoughts swarmed through her mind as she watched the tall, slim figure striding towards her beach bag. She would like to touch that golden back, trace the slim lines of his waist. He retraced his steps, moving with the grace of a sleek, sensuous animal. A magnificent animal—what a perfect description! Smiling a little, she tilted her head and watched him through her lashes. A shiver tingled her spine as his eyes lazily engaged hers. Limned by sunlight, there was a subtle hardness in his face, a daunting arrogance in the way he came towards her with long, powerful strides.

Refusing to be daunted, Kristy frowned as he

stopped in front of her and held out the bag on the tips of two fingers. But when she looked up at him, the full impact of his height and size and the sheer animal strength of him registered as a gasp she quickly swallowed.

"Must you tower over me so?" she asked, taking the bag with a jerk.

"Sorry. You might thank me, Mermaid. Did your mother never teach you manners?" he asked wryly.

"Of course she did. And stop calling me by that ridiculous name," she ordered. "I'm called Kristy."

"Lovely name," he nodded. "But I prefer Mermaid. Did I not fish you from the water?"

"Did I ask you to?"

"Well no, but the situation didn't seem to require permission," he said.

Kristy deigned not to answer. Unzipping her bag, she extracted a towel and dried her legs, while Jason leaned against a tree and idly watched. Her shoes squelched with every move she made. She sat down and took them off, then began cleaning mud off the soles with a sharp stick. The black smelly stuff was deeply embedded. Her mouth screwed up in disgust, she dug harder. The stick broke and stabbed her palm. Kristy gasped.

"Oh here, let me do that," Jason growled.

Obstinately she shook her head. "I really do not require your help all the time, Mr. Thorne," she irritably informed him. "Why don't you go on now. I'll be fine." Jason settled comfortably against his tree. Picking up another stick, she scraped more mud. "What are

56

you doing roaming around up here, anyway? This land is posted against trespassers."

"Perhaps you're the one who's trespassing," Jason murmured with an enigmatic smile.

"Oh nonsense! My uncle owns this land. And it isn't part of the hotel, either, it's privately owned, thus not public domain," she smartly rebuked.

Jason tipped his head and regarded her through sooty lashes. "I assure you, I had permission."

"From my uncle?" Kristy looked up, her eyes narrowing. "You are staying at the hotel, then?"

"No. I own a condo above the Kauai Surf," he said matter of factly.

Kristy stopped scraping. The plush condominiums he referred to clung like limpets to the cliffs above the Kauai Surf Hotel, not precisely your average domicile, to say the least, she thought, impressed in spite of her indifferent glance. "You work on Kauai then?" she asked.

"No."

Like pulling teeth, she thought. So much for her dread of being flooded with confidences. "Where then? And with whom?"

"R.J. Thorne, Inc. We're an international firm, but home base is in Honolulu."

Kristy swallowed. "Who's this 'we' you speak of?"

"My father, my two brothers and myself," Jason patiently replied. "My grandfather retired from the firm some years ago."

She started to ask his occupation, then switched to a more urgent question. "Practically everytime I've seen you, you've been with my uncle. Are you two friends or something?''

''Or something,'' Jason smoothly agreed.

Kristy diligently attacked another layer of mud. ''Are you married?'' she asked, sparing him a glance. Jason shook his head, that infernal glint of humor crinkling his eyes. *A rich, handsome, madly eligible bachelor, every woman's fantasy,* she thought sourly. She wondered if he had ever been married, in love, engaged, currently involved—

Annoyed at her seething curiosity, she tossed aside the stick. It was like swallowing pebbles, but one did not display such inordinate interest unless one was interested. And he hadn't asked her a single question, had he?

Kristy's gaze wandered up the length of that arrogant male stance. If he thought she was at all intimidated by his vastly elevated status, he had another think coming. She put on her shoes and started to get to her feet. Jason was at her side so swiftly, she blinked. Thinking he meant to give her a gentlemanly hand, she held up one of hers, then gasped with surprise as he bent to her and spanned her waist with two strong hands, lifting her as effortlessly as breathing.

''Now, Kristin, that treacherous bank is less than a foot in front of you,'' he quickly explained to the spark of green eyes.

Malice or genuine concern? Who knew with this man. Aware of the fingers pressing warmly into her skin, she gently pulled free of him. ''I think I could have managed without tumbling into the ditch again,'' she said with fine irony. Jason folded his arms across his chest and rocked back on his heels. So close was he, the muskiness of man and cologne flared in her nostrils. She walked to her bag and replaced the towel.

"You certainly don't fit the usual corporate image," she remarked.

"I don't, hmm?" Jason lazily responded.

She shook her head. "I thought corporate types were harried, ulcer-ridden people who didn't have time to smell the roses!" she quipped. Her nose wrinkled. "You sure you are one?"

Jason shrugged. "The last time I checked, my name was still on the roster."

"When was the last time you checked? Seems like everytime I turn around, I'm running into you on a plane or at the hotel or in a ditch," she said dryly.

"I was in my office all day yesterday. Does that satisfy?" he asked, looking amused. A thread of seductiveness laced through his voice. "But I learned long ago that there's more to life than profit and loss statements, Mermaid, much, much more. My father has a working pilosophy. You run the business, it doesn't run you."

He laughed, blue eyes gone devilish. "He's sixty-four and in the prime of life. Apparently very much so—I've just recently learned I'm to have a new brother or sister. Sister preferably. Mother absolutely refuses to raise another rascally boy. She still has vivid memories of raising *me*!"

Those devilish, dancing, delightful blue eyes! Kristy's laugh chimed out, a wholly involuntary response. "How old's your mother?"

"Forty-four. She's my stepmother. They were married on her twentieth birthday, and this pregnancy is really a bit of luck for her. Dad says he was about ready to trade her in for two twenty-year olds," he said with droll relief.

"Oh, Jason!" Nonplussed by her joyous response, as well as this sudden introduction of a too personal subject, Kristy turned in profile and shook back her hair, trailing her fingers through the tousled mass of curls with provocative pleasure. The air was warm and utterly still, and the sun beat down on her face. Some deep, primitive, sensuously erotic force stirred within her. Moving with the same deliberation, she smoothed the shift over her hips, laughing as a quickening breeze danced the skirt around her slender thighs. Kristy sensed his gaze like a physical caress.

When she glanced at him again, Jason was gazing raptly off down the hill. His eyes lit on her with about the same interest as he gave the *bauhinia* tree just beyond her shoulder. He smiled, an insufferable smile that was purely a masculine taunt. Feeling utterly foolish, Kristy picked up her bag and walked off.

"Kristin, you are the most ungracious young lady I've ever had the displeasure to meet," Jason drawled, stopping her in her tracks.

Flushing, Kristy turned back to face him. The truth of his words were smartingly evident. His trousers were blotched with water, and the expensive suede boots none the better for having gone wading. *I wish he'd put on his shirt,* she thought, looking away from that disturbing nudity. The hair on his chest formed a masculine T, the thin dark line tracing down his flat stomach disappearing into the waistband that set low on his hips.

Displeased at her response to that magnetic male attraction, she placed her bag on the ground and slowly met his gaze. What did he expect from her? Gushing gratitude for having lifted her out of a ditch? Even wind-mussed and water-stained, he exuded an indefinable elegance. She was splotched with mud, her hair doubtless a tangled mess, her fiery pride in tatters, and there he stood looking every inch the lordly male!

However, that did not excuse her rudeness, and she supposed an apology was due, much as she hated to give it. She looked at him, her expressive green eyes revealing her conflict. "You're right, I was ungracious. I apologize, Mr. Thorne."

"That's better," he blandly approved, as if speaking to a precocious child. "But just the same, I'll walk you there. Just in case you have to cross another ditch."

It was all she could do to restrain her fiery temper against the twinkle in his eyes. "That won't be necessary. I shall be quite alright, I've come this way many times before," she said with cold dignity—what she could find of it.

He stared at her for a discomfiting moment, then shrugged. "As you wish. This is one of your favorite places, is it?"

"Yes, I—well, not exactly here. I come up here to swim in the pool, you see. It's quite a climb, but it's so lovely . . . well, alright then. And thank you for—for whatever," she said primly.

Soft amusement spread over his mouth. "You're most welcome, Miss Loring," Jason said with beautiful formality. He leaned down and picked up his shirt, straightened and tossed it over his shoulder, all in one smooth flow of oiled muscles. Kristy suddenly flinched back. Without taking a step or making a move other than the fluid sway of body, his mouth was hovering far too close to hers. Her eyes widened with her quick breath.

Jason laughed softly. "Ah, Mermaid," he said, low and husky. A finger tip touched the flickering dimple at the corner of her mouth. "Aloha, *keiki*," he murmured.

Kristy drew back even further. "Goodbye, Mr. Thorne," she said, and half turned away, listening to his footfalls fade into silence.

Alone again, she touched the slick gray trunk of a tree, feeling the need for contact with something solid as a curious sense of desolation washed over her. A brief glimpse of that proud dark head evoked an urge to call him back. Nervously she fingered the beach bag that had somehow gotten into her hands. Why had he kissed her? An impulse of the moment? Yes, just that. Hardly anything to cause this quivering in her stomach at the memory of a fleeting touch of lips. Warm, firm lips, opening to claim hers just as she jerked away . . . .

Startled to find she'd come so far, Kristy veered right and hurried down the now gentle incline. She was thinking on two levels as she walked. Of Jason, of course, but more actively, that she had seen so little of this lovely area, outside Lihue. Alex kept far too busy to indulge her yearning to explore. Perhaps tomorrow she would borrow his car and venture out on her own.

Moving too swiftly and with rash inattention, the inevitable happened. Kristy slipped and went down on one knee. Catching hold of a limb, she pulled herself erect and cautiously tested her ankle. A bit painful, but nothing drastic. She released her full weight with a wince.

"Clumsy Kristy," she chided on a gallant laugh. Her talent for taking tumbles without major damage to herself had always been subject to good-natured teasing. Kristy saw no sense in whining about the fact that she had a congenitally weak ankle which could, given a precise set of circumstances, turn inward and throw her off balance. She was too long accustomed to this minor defect to take it seriously. Falling down was simply something she did inordinately well, and with a grin-and-bear-it attitude.

Waiting for the pain to subside, she cast a surreptitious glance around. The absence of incredulous blue eyes witnessing her tumble was sweet relief. Thus far she had exhibited as much grace as a newborn colt when with Jason Thorne, she unhappily reflected. He must think her an extraordinarily clumsy person, and yet she was not, except for this one defect.

Limping slightly, she walked at a much slower pace along the back paths to the cottages. Although similar in design and decor, the one she entered was very special to Kristy. Her parents had spent their second anniversary here, and approximately nine months later, Kristin Ann Loring was born.

Smiling softly on that thought, she stepped inside,

her eyes flying around the large, oblong room in an effort to see it as they had seen it so very long ago. *It must have been lovely then,* she thought wistfully, but unlike the elegant rooms of the hotel proper, the cottages offered little more than utilitarian comfort, and that a little shabby.

What fun it would be to be turned loose on this essentially pretty room—with lots of money, of course, and free rein for the marvelous ideas which continually seethed in her artistic mind. "Oh, stop it, Kristy," she tiredly advised. "If Alex wanted your advice, he'd have asked for it. And stop that too," she ordered as images of a more sensual nature flickered across her mind. Jason Thorne. Vividly he swam to mind, the tall, powerful force of him, his dark face alight with humor while his piercing gaze stripped her naked. *Obviously an old hand when it came to women,* she thought contemptuously.

Kristy flung down the beach bag with unnecessary force, then shook her head in wry disgust. Imagine letting a man affect her so—and a perfect stranger at that! He certainly is perfect, a tiny part of her mind purringly agreed. Those eyes . . . the sea just off Waikiki was the same, iridescent shade of blue. What would it be like to kiss him when she wasn't practically unconscious?

The intensity of that thought annoyed her even more. "Ridiculous," she said aloud. And since it was, she set him and his kiss and the sublime feeling of his arms around her and his deep husky voice and those blue, blue, *blue* eyes, firmly, positively, from mind.

Kristy took off her wet clothes and slung them over

the shower rod. Hand laundry tonight, she reminded. *Keiki*, he had called her—child. Why? There was nothing childish about the curvaceous woman's body in her mirror.

Reflectively, she sat down on the edge of the tub to wait for it to fill. Perhaps she was immature in many respects, especially in the sensitive area of man–woman relationships. She had never been too good at them, disinterested in shallow ones, shy of deeper involvement. Even with Steve, there had been a barely discernible, yet always present sense of unease. Kristy dabbled a toe in the water and hastily adjusted the temperature. Just how the devil did one grow up, by playing musical beds? Were indiscriminate sexual romps a requisite of maturity?

"Good grief," Kristy muttered at this sudden avalanche of doubt. She was too level headed to believe that. Steve's ethics were firmly rejected, but her doubts were nonetheless solidly based. Jason Thorne might be many things, many of them undesirable, she quickly added, but he was a man who knew a woman when he saw one. And on the main, he had treated her as if she was still in pigtails.

Chapter Four

Kristy unwound the towel from her damp hair and gingerly sat down on the windowseat to brush it dry. After a luxuriously long bath and follow-up shampoo, she had begun reading, and completely lost track of time. Outside her window, twilight throbbed with the muted serenade of tree frogs, the air heavy with that sultry earthiness and the fragrance of a thousand flowers. Rhythmically she brushed, enjoying this purely feminine pleasure. Perhaps Alex would like to dine in town tonight, she mused, as her guest this time. Heaven knew she would like to repay his generosity, even in this small way.

She finished up with a hairdryer, then put on a strapless dress of fine rayon weave. Although tightly fitted to her breasts, the icy, very pale lavender blouson looked deliciously unreliable. Kristy chewed her lip as she wondered if it was. She wore nothing under it save for a pair of lacy briefs, and she felt utterly naked. Or would, the moment Jason Thorne set eyes on her.

Oh nonsense! The dress was fully lined. And it wasn't likely she would see Jason tonight. If she did succeed in dragging Alex away from his hotel for dinner, she darned sure would keep him away.

She coaxed her shining hair into a french twist, but applied no makeup, leaving her huge green eyes as the only color in her face. She needed nothing else, not with skin like soft, rose-flushed ivory. Besides, Alex, like her father, detested makeup on a woman, and she wanted very much to make him proud to be with her tonight.

Perhaps this would be an opportune time to reopen the subject of vacating this cottage for a bedroom in his house. She had a horror of imposing, and after a week of free lodging, Kristy felt obliged to surrender the pleasure of privacy. The cottage was, after all, a source of income to Alex. And in his own way, he had been so terribly kind, offering no comment on her blighted marriage plans, except a simple word of sympathy.

Absolutely no thoughts of Steve tonight. Or Jason Thorne either, she commanded. A frown marring her pretty face, she slipped on cream-colored pumps and changed her everyday purse for a slim leather envelope in the same meltingly soft shade. And now to see if she really did have a dinner companion tonight. Hopefully it would be so, she detested eating alone and the food here had begun to pall.

She crossed the terrace at the rear of the hotel and tapped on a door, then entered the handsome quarters which served as her uncle's office, as well as a temporary home at times. "Hello, Uncle Alex! Would you like to have dinner in town to—"

Kristy stopped in mid-sentence as Jason Thorne came lazily to his feet. The quick throb of excitement brought her chin up with a snap, and just what the devil, she wondered wildly, was *he* doing here!

Looking uneasy, Alex lay aside the papers he had been reading. "I'm sorry, Kristin, but I'd forgotten about dinner tonight. Oh, you remember Jason?" he added with a casual wave his way.

Oh yes, I remember Jason, thought Kristin. Should she mention this afternoon? Swiftly she decided against it; it would serve no purpose for Alex to learn of that embarrassing meeting, nor did she care to dwell on it. Feeling distinctly awkward, she extended her hand, saying pleasantly, "Mr. Thorne. How nice to see you again."

"My pleasure . . . Miss Loring," Jason murmured, and she knew he had nearly called her by that ridiculous name again. Giving him a coldly warning look, she turned to Alex. "I didn't realize you had company, Uncle Alex."

"Technically speaking, he's not company," Alex said with an oblique glance at his guest. "Jason's a hotel tycoon," he added teasingly, then his voice flattened. "He's here on business, Kristy."

Kristy tensed, already sensing what was coming.

"Business? What kind of business?" She aimed her tight question at Jason, but he looked to Alex in obvious deference.

"Jason's bought The Blue Pearl," said Alex.

Kristy's face visibly whitened as she looked from one man to the other, her eyes wide with dismay. *It hurts so much!* she thought, bewildered at the force tearing her heart. She shook her head as though to clear it, moistened her dry lips. Her hands fluttered up in a gesture of appeal.

"You're selling the hotel? But why?" The golden head shook again. "Uncle Alex, there isn't a lovelier hotel on this entire island. Why would you want to sell it? If it's not doing well, a few changes here and there . . . the cottages . . . that dull bar—" She gulped air as another, even more hurtful possibility occurred to her. "Alex, the waterfall—you didn't sell it too?" she cried, her impassioned voice rising like a flute in the silent room.

He had—she knew it instantly. And she knew why, she thought bitterly, Jason wasn't blind to the commercial prospects of that lovely vista! She looked at him with loathing before whirling back to Alex.

Before she could say anything, Alex roughly took command, his innate dislike of scenes sharpening his voice. "That's enough, Kristy! There's a more appropriate time and place to discuss this."

When her small face paled with hurt, Jason made a sharp, almost angry movement, but Kristy's attention was focused solely on Alex. That he had neglected to tell her—had not so much as dropped a hint about selling the hotel—made it crystal clear that he considered this his private business and not open to speculation or advice from anyone. *Most certainly not his niece,* she thought wretchedly. Her heart wrenching with pain, she dropped her hands. She was by nature a well-mannered girl, and courtesy decreed that she apologize for her disruptive outburst. But how could he sell The Blue Pearl!

Because it was his to sell. She took a deep breath, her hands coming tightly together as she sought control. "I'm sorry, Alex, I shouldn't have butted in—please forgive me. And excuse me, too. I'll let you get back to your business," she said tonelessly.

"I'm sorry too, Kristy, for snapping at you," Alex said. "I know how much the waterfall meant to you." He smiled, wryly. "But I didn't know you'd come to love this pile of wood and stone so much. I guess losing it is a real disappointment."

"A disappointment I'll get over, I'm sure," Kristy said, smiling back. She turned to go, but Alex touched her arm.

"It was all sort of special, wasn't it," he said gruffly, looking saddened at some private vision.

Kristy shrugged. "Sort of special," she lightly agreed. "Well, I'll let you get back to it then. And don't worry about dinner, I wasn't all that hungry anyway. Mr. Thorne . . ." She inclined her head to the man who stood quietly watching them, and walked swiftly from the room.

Holding herself in rigid check, Kristy went directly to her cottage. But her feelings wre inescapable once the door closed behind her. She slumped on the couch and softly, soundlessly wept. Bitterly she reproached herself for her unrestrained outburst—and with Jason as an audience at that! She hated him seeing her so vulnerable, despised her childish reaction!

She mopped at her eyes and the tears kept coming. The raw sense of grief she felt at the loss of a hotel struck her as foolish, yet The Blue Pearl was more than inanimate wood and stone. It had simply *always* been there, a shining constant in an ever shifting world. Something, she thought with sere desolation, that she could absolutely depend on.

And now Jason Thorne owned it, a man who alternately fascinated and repulsed her.

"Enough, Kristy," she fiercely commanded herself. She got up and began repairing her ravaged face. Stupid to get so upset over such a comparatively trivial matter! But that was Kristy for you, always one step behind. The knot in her throat induced a few more tears which she angrily brushed away. It suddenly dawned on her that Alex was probably a very wealthy man now. Surely his part of the hotel was substantial? And since she was his only heir, perhaps someday she would be rich too—

The attempt at cynicism collapsed of its own weight. She could support herself, she didn't need his money. The inheritance she had wanted was The Blue Pearl— even a tiny part of it.

A soft tap on her door interrupted her possibly melodramatic misery. Kristy hastily checked her face. "Who is it, please?" she called.

"Alex."

71

Slim shoulders straightened, Kristy hurried to the door and flung it open, a smile transforming her woebegotten mien. Alex stepped inside, his seamed face inexpressibly weary as he regarded her. Kristy's smile became genuine.

"I just wanted to make sure you're all right," he said lamely.

"I'm fine," came her soft assurance. "Uncle Alex, why didn't you tell me before tonight—about selling the hotel, I mean?"

"Kristy, this was in the works weeks ago, but I saw no reason to spoil your vacation, not until I had to."

"I see. Did you sell the house too?"

"No, that's mine and Lanie's house," he said heavily, referring to his late wife. "As to why I sold it, I've been barely breaking even for the past few years and it's my own fault. I just don't care anymore, Kristy. I'm tired of the hassle, tired of being staked like a goat to one spot of land! I was a seagoing man when I married Lanie, then I settled down. I'm going back to the sea again. It's been a dream for years, but I—" Alex sighed deeply. "Last year I had a mild stroke, Kristy—very mild, but it jarred me into realizing something. If I wanted to realize that dream, I'd better get around to it," he ended matter of factly.

Kristy startled. "You didn't tell me you'd had a stroke!"

"No reason to fret you. I'm fine now," came his laconic reply.

Kristy blazed with questions, but he patently did not want to pursue the subject. She swallowed hard.

"When does Jas—Mr. thorne take possession?"

"Soon. Listen, honey, I'm really beat and I've got a seven o'clock flight to Honolulu in the morning, more lawyer stuff. We'll talk some more, but right now, Jason's waiting for me—we need to iron out a few last minute details. And then—" he grinned, suddenly. "And then, with your permission, I'm going to bed!"

Kristy smiled. "Permission granted, sir."

"Well, thank you," he said, his gentle irony giving them both relief. "Kristin, I'm sorry about dinner tonight. I'd like to say for sure tomorrow night, but I'll likely be getting back late. But after this business is concluded, I'm going to make it up to you. And Kristy, this sale doesn't have to affect your vacation, you know. You're welcome to stay in my house as long as you want. Well, I just wanted to—to say I'm sorry about you gettin' upset."

With this gruff apology, Alex took his leave. Kristy sat on the *lanai* for a time trying to sort out her feelings. She was still shaken by the thought of her uncle's stroke; mild or not, she should have been notified. And done what? Kristy sighed and rubbed her gritty eyes. She was simply not that important to him. *As for this burdensome hotel,* she thought resolutely, *he had good reason for wanting to sell it, and she would not bring it up again.*

She leaned back with a long sigh as Jason's dark visage swam to mind. This afternoon, at the waterfall, she really had been the transgressor. Why hadn't he told her that he . . . but of course. Alex had asked him not to, and Jason had honored that request.

Too restive to sit, she paced the length of the terrace. Her feelings for Alex were unchanged, but thoughts of Jason produced a puzzling emotion. The hotel, the waterfall were his now; a simple business transaction, something for sale and someone to buy it. Intellectually she knew this. Yet what she felt for Jason was an icy black anger very near to hatred.

This illogical but decidedly strong feeling persisted through the following morning. Wanting to avoid Jason until she had simmered down a bit, Kristy took her uncle's car to Kalapaki Beach for a day of sun and sand. She did not spend the entire time loafing. Her father had gifted her with an expensive camera on her eighteenth birthday, and she had since become an excellent photographer. An exploratory walk about the area yielded several lovely shots, including the magnificent starburst of the *iliau* plant. Its silvery, swordlike leaves had a purity and strength which reminded her of Jason. She shot it from several angles, but the one she liked best, sharply silhoutted against a dazzling blue sky, would make an exquisite print for framing. She was quite certain she could sell it. Her better photographic prints had provided a profitable little hobby. Choice specimens, enlarged and beautifully framed, hung in several Texas homes and businesses.

All in all, a very good day, she assured herself that evening. She had succeeded in evading Jason, and gotten herself a tawny, sun-kissed look in the bargain.

Since lunch had been an outrageous wallow in calories, she decided to skip dinner. Curvaceous was going to become pleasantly plump if she wallowed too much. After a delicious soak in rose-scented water, she dressed in a camisole frock that left her back and shoulders beautifully bare. The sea-green fabric offset the voluptuous red-gold mane surging around her shoulders like some exotic tidal sea. Kristy added a gold serpentine chain sparkling at her throat, and a delicate touch of eyeshadow to deepen her eyes to jade.

Wispy scraps of sandals completed her ensemble. Assessing the results, Kristy's pleasure was tempered with dismay. With the darkness would come Jason, and this painstaking care to her appearance was motivated solely by that fact. Or hope?

She had tried, fairly successfully, to put things into perspective today. Having accepted the unalterable fact that she was losing something very precious to her, she framed it with the knowledge that it had not been hers to lose. *Childhood fantasies did not reality make,* she thought with poignant sorrow. But no rancor. She felt pleased at that, if nothing else. Jason was completely extraneous to the matter, and to her life.

Picking up a small evening clutch, she stood on the steps poised in indecision. The club did not appeal tonight, and at length she turned in the direction of the bar which sat under a canopy of tall, graceful palms. Kristy hopped up on a stool with a genuine smile for Ben Soames, the bartender. They were fast friends by now and she liked him immensely.

"Your usual, Madam?" Ben gravely inquired. "Yes, please," said Kristy.

Ben placed a tall glass on the counter, filled it with

fresh pineapple juice, added a succulent stick of pineapple, then ceremoniously topped it with a plum red cherry and a swizzle stick. Kristy loved the tangy nectar so relative to the islands. Did anyone ever think of pineapples without Hawaii tucked on like a comet's tail?

"Got the blues?" Ben asked.

Kristy looked at him with her usual curiosity. Ben was a big, rangy man in his early fifties, with clear gray eyes and dark auburn hair, an attractive man and yet he had never married. She wondered why. She wondered if he knew the hotel had been sold. She started to ask him, then thought better of it. Alex's business again.

"Yea, a touch of the blues," she sighed. He gave her a commiserating look and moved off down the bar. Ben respected a person's mood.

Kristy sat quietly, her mind taken up with last night's embarrassing scene. She didn't want Alex riddled with guilt, or feeling obligated towards her in any way. He had his own life and she had hers. The two had always run on separate tracks, she sadly admitted, why try to change at this late date? She had a job offer waiting, something to tide her over until school reopened.

"A Scotch and water, please?"

Kristy's head snapped up at the authoritative male voice. Jason settled on the stool beside her. "Good evening!" he said, dimples flashing. He was dressed all in black tonight, a devastating frame for his lean, handsome body and dangerously dark good looks. *Something of a pirate tonight*, Kristy thought. Striving to subdue her racing pulses with notable lack of success, she picked up her drink and eyed him over the rim, green eyes sparking to the challenge he posed.

"Ah, tis Mr. Thorne, in the tall, dark and breathtakingly handsome flesh," she drawled, highly pleased at the perfect touch of light sarcasm since he was precisely that.

"Ah, 'tis Miss Loring," he mocked, "hair combed and not a spot of mud to be found!" His voice deepening, he touched her chin with a fingertip. "Are you okay, Kristy?" he asked softly.

"Of course I'm okay," Kristy said, surprised at the tender note of concern. She cocked her head. "Shouldn't I be?"

"Yes, of course. I just thought . . . how are those bruises, hmm?" he asked, reverting to his teasing manner.

"They're there. But bearable," she said, shifting on the stool. They really were *there*.

Jason chuckled. "Well, if I can be of any assistance, don't hesitate to ask, Mermaid."

"Would you please stop calling me by that ridiculous name?" Kristy hissed in a whisper, noting Ben's startled look.

"Like it or not, it's my name for you from now to eternity," Jason said expansively.

"Since I'm leaving tomorrow, eternity is mercifully short," she retorted. Brushing at the curl annoying her eye, Kristy missed his start of surprise. She propped her chin in hand and musingly regarded him. "Alex said you were a hotel tycoon?"

"Um, actually that description is a trifle limiting. I have many interests to occupy my time." Jason gave her an engaging grin. "My talents are manifold and I use

77

every one of them to the fullest," he continued with such charming lack of modesty, she could not prevent her spontaneous laugh.

Feeling she was slyly being gotten around, Kristy recrossed her legs, a movement he followed with lusty interest. "Why did you buy The Blue Pearl?" she asked without preamble.

"For purely professional reasons," Jason said. Darkening blue eyes captured her wavering gaze. "I assure you, my intention was not to steal something from you, Kristy."

"It's Alex's hotel, his waterfall, not mine," she said flatly.

"And it didn't bother you at all, hmm?" he countered.

"I was shocked, yes. I had no idea that he was even thinking of selling, so naturally it took me by surprise," Kristy admitted.

Jason glanced at the proud tilt of chin, glanced away. "You may not think so, but Alex made a wise decision. When a man loses all interest, he also loses incentive and perspective, which doesn't leave him much to work with. I suppose he also didn't tell you that he was operating at a loss? Or close to it—marginal profits at best."

"He told me he was barely breaking even. But you won't, will you."

"Not if I can help it, no," Jason said dryly.

Kristy fished out a sliver of pineapple and popped it into her mouth. "So what are those purely professional reasons for this charitable act of yours?"

Jason shrugged. "Hardly charitable. More like simple economics; a substantial increase in affluent tourism, as yet underdeveloped facilities to accommodate that increase, a hotel for sale and my quest for a hotel. The Blue Pearl would be impossible to duplicate at today's construction costs, within reason, I mean." He glanced at her, his eyes hardening for an instant. "And then there's the waterfall—"

"Yes, there's that. I think it's worth a great deal in itself. At least it was to me," she said, impassive.

"A great deal. Not to mention the nice piece of land that goes with it," Jason gave sardonic agreement. "I've had my eye on that tract for years."

"And finally got what you wanted," Kristy said.

A rakish grin lit his face. "I usually do," Jason said. "But enough of this, I came here to relax and enjoy. Your glass is empty. Let me have the pleasure, Mermaid, what are you drinking?"

"My name is Kristy, and I'll buy my own drinks," she said shortly.

"Tsk, tsk, you do have a nasty temperament," he rebuked, ruffling her hair. "Give the lady her pleasure," he instructed Ben.

Kristy was finding it nearly impossible to resist that suddenly warm, teasing voice. When she looked at him, Jason laughed, and she could swear there were little devils dancing in his eyes. She felt her own anger dissolving like a lump of wet sugar. *How could you resent a man who made you want to laugh as joyously as a child,* she thought crossly.

"You're going to turn into a pineapple, Kristy," Ben said, taking out the pitcher again.

Jason arched an eyebrow. "Pineapple juice? You don't drink?"

"Very seldom. Never mind, Ben, I've had enough for

tonight," she asserted.

"Let's exchange these stools for a booth and you can tell me what other things you do very seldom," Jason suggested, half-rising.

"One of those things is picking up men in a bar. You're just wasting your time with me, I'm really not interested, Mr. Thorne," Kristy said indifferently.

He laughed. "Careful, Mermaid, I may decide to test that, and you wouldn't stand a chance," Jason softly challenged. His head dipped as if drawn to her lips, and Kristy's heart jumped so wildly, he could not miss her too-quick breath, or the swiftly blooming roses in her cheeks. Sensing his soft, knowing smile, she wiped her fingers one by one, a delaying tactic. *Nothing like making a liar out of yourself,* she thought with a certain bitter humor.

She managed an offhand shrug that mocked her inner turbulence. "Perhaps—perhaps not. At any rate, it isn't worth the bother of finding out," she said. Rummaging through her evening bag, she extracted a five dollar bill and laid it on the bar. "Well, as usual, it was lovely, Mr. Thorne, but I think I'll call it a night. Goodnight, Ben," she called.

She had reached the cottage path before Jason fell into step beside her. "Let's sit down over here," he said, indicating a secluded redwood bench. "Now this isn't a pick-up, Kristy, we need to talk."

"Right offhand, I can't think of a single thing we need to talk about." Kristy mildly resisted the pressure on her arm.

"I'll talk, you just listen. Sit," Jason said.

Intrigued, Kristy sat down and clasped her hands in her lap. A nearby lamp-post was completely engulfed in a cup-of-gold vine, its foot-long blossoms spilling an extravagance of perfume. She leaned back with a wistful sigh. How lovely it all was! And how very much she was going to miss it. Cold green eyes raised to Jason's. "So talk," she said.

She moved over to give him room, but the bench was too short to avoid contact. His thigh nestling warmly against hers, Jason stretched out an arm behind her and settled himself more comfortably.

"How old are you, Mermaid?"

"Twenty-two."

"That figures," he drawled. "Where in Texas are you from?"

"A little town outside Amarillo."

"And why are you returning to Amarillo?" he relentlessly persisted.

"I'm returning because it's my home, because I have a job and a house and Flora waiting for me," she said irritably.

"Flora?"

"Flora is—" Kristy's voice softened. "Sort of hard to explain," she ended with an indulgent chuckle. "She's a distant cousin on my mother's side. Mom died when I was seven and Flora moved in for a temporary caretaker's job, and just stayed on. She's forty-six and a spinister—"

"Ah," Jason interjected.

"Don't say *ah* like that," Kristy rebuked. "Being a spinister doesn't necessarily correspond to dried up old bag! I'm seriously considering it myself."

The amused gleam in his eyes deepened. "Not a chance!" Jason snorted. "You're marriage and babies, Mermaid, it's written all over you; a boy, a girl, a two-

81

story brick in Suburbia, one huge woolly dog and a cat that has kittens every six weeks. Right?"

Kristy's cheeks flamed at his uncanny assessment. Was she so blasted transparent? "Goodbye, Mr. Thorne," she tartly suggested.

"Call me Jason, please? After all, I feel like we've known each other for several very long years," Jason said wryly. "A boyfriend waiting too?"

"No," she said flatly.

"Ah, a tragic romance. That explains all," he sighed.

"That explains nothing!" Kristy flared at his expert strike on a very raw spot.

Jason snaked a finger into her hair, winding a curl round and round the exploring digit. "So what happened to this grand love affair, hmm? And is this going to be a one-handkerchief tale, or shall I fetch another?"

Stung at his cynicism, Kristy retreated behind her lashes. The fierce urge to confide in him was crushed by pride. What would he know of heartache! That humorous mockery stiffened her spine. When she looked up at him, her eyes were clear and cold. "No handkerchiefs. And it was not a grand love affair. Just something that went sour."

"And now you're soured on love forevermore," Jason mockingly sighed.

"It sounds to me that you're the one soured on love," she observed.

Jason found this profoundly amusing. "Now, Mermaid, how can I be soured on something that's only an unsettled state of mind, hmm? I have a very well-balanced mind, far too strong for fly me to the moon on gossamer wings . . . was it gossamer wings, hmm?"

"Oh, shut up!" Kristy sighed at the petulance in

82

her voice.

"And well you should sigh," Jason approved. "Here I am trying to console you in your hour of anguish—Are you still in love with the blackhearted knave who smashed your tender heart?"

Kristy shrugged. "Reckon women are just fools that way. But then, we have such a limited choice; it's either a blackhearted knave, or a natural-born Superman. Present company not excepted," she drawled, beginning to enjoy this.

"And you've had ample dealings with both, have you?"

"Would you believe he was my one and only? Or are you even familiar with the term?"

Jason began to laugh. "Vaguely. But a word of advice, Mermaid. Uncurl that delectable lip and remember that immortal maxim; practice is the best of all instructors!"

"There is moderation even in success," she dryly shot back.

Jason leaned his face very near hers, his soft chuckle warming her lips. "Ah but no pleasure endures unseasoned by variety," he crooned.

Kristy's annoyance simply vanished in that devilish grin. He had the knack of delighting a person merely by appearing so absolutely delighted himself at being with that person—and if that wasn't a convoluted thought! She flung back her head with a chiming laugh. He need not be so darned attractive, she mused, that utterly charming personality would suffice to enchant a woman. To be with Jason Thorne, she was beginning to suspect, was to enjoy oneself without really knowing why.

She looked up at him, her lips still spilling laughter. Was he always like this? Surely not. Yet on the surface, it seemed a completely natural attribute. One which pleased her far too much. Her preconceived image of Jason Thorne was beginning to disintegrate a little more with each meeting, and she didn't like that.

Jason lazily stretched his legs, a crisp authoritative note entering his voice. "I've got to be getting along, so I'll tell you my plans for the hotel—"

Kristy's mood abruptly reversed. "I'm no longer interested in the hotel, or your plans for it," she cut him short.

Jason got up and began pacing in front of her. "Do hush up and let me finish? I'm keeping a lovely young lady waiting," he mildly reproved. "And of course you're interested, or you'd better become interested. Because you're going to be a part of those plans. Since your uncle said you were an interior designer, I'm thinking of adding you to my staff. Just temporarily, of course—"

"Oh stop it!" Kristy exclaimed. *His teasing wasn't so funny this time,* she thought with gusting anger, he was exploiting a very tender subject! "And what on earth makes you think I'd even consider working for you? I'd sooner go down that waterfall as spend ten minutes in your presence!" she flared.

Jason sighed deeply. "Such ingratitude, but what can I expect? Look what I got when I saved your life at such terrible risk to my own. Did you know that in certain countries, saving a person's life makes that person indebted to her rescuer for however long she lives?" he thoughtfully added.

"Mr. Thorne, your refrain is becoming rather tedious,'' Kristy warned.

"Kristin, you're provoking me greatly," he warned. "I'm well aware that you can swim like a fish—a mermaid, even, but when you fell—"

"You're aware . . ." Kristy stopped in sudden suspicion. "How do you now I can swim like a . . . have you been spying on me in my pool?"

"Spying? A strong word—nasty, too. I was merely exploring the land around my latest acquisition, and naturally I noticed your frolicking in my pool." His voice deepened, seductive as he turned to face her. "You do frolic nicely, Mermaid."

Kristy gasped at such effrontry. "Of all the nerve! Sneaking around spying on me!"

"I said I wasn't spying."

"Well, I call it spying!"

"A minor difference of opinion," he conceded.

Kristy's eyes flew wide as another thought occurred. "Were you watching when I came out of the water and stepped into those ferns to . . . to dry off?"

Jason smiled. "Yes, I was."

"So now we add peeping tom to all your other faults!"

"Oh, nonsense. I just happened to be passing by and—what faults?"

"A shocking lack of respect for a person's privacy, for one!" Kristy hotly retorted. "And then we can go on from there with any number of choice descriptives—insensitive, arrogant, ill-mannered, domineering—"

"Are you about finished?" Jason asked curiously.

"And let's not forget that wonderful catch-all—chauvinistic!" Kristy wound up with a blast of sound.

"Oh come on, Kristy you know very well that no man in his right mind would turn the other way at such an intriguing sight," he chided, half exasperated, half amused. "Besides, those damn ferns were taller than you are. And as for the rest of your absurd charges, I refuse to dignify them with a rebuttal."

"I told you once and I'll tell you again—I do not like you," Kristy said severely. He grinned. She felt an urge to hit him, which was only logical. That she also felt an urge to hug him was not, but since either course of action was wildly impractical, she ignored both.

"And you're an unpracticed little liar, Kristin," Jason observed.

"Is lying such a virtue, then?" she asked bitterly. "If so, you must have it down pat by now!"

Jason tensed, the dark face suddenly masked. "I'm not a devious man, Kristy," he said with steely softness. "And I don't particularly enjoy being brushed with the tar of another man's guilt."

Kristy's head lowered. "You're right. I apologize for that remark," she said. She looked up at him, relieved to see his firm mouth relaxing into a half-smile. "However, I really don't think I like you," she said with a little more spirit.

"And I think you do. But time will tell. Now, can we return to the subject?" Jason growled.

"Whatever the subject is—I've forgotten by now," sighed Kristy.

"Fortunately, I don't distract so easily. And the subject pertained to who's going to be the boss. Which is me. I think. And I also think I should warn you before you go blazing up again that I've always been fascinated by fire. I have this uncontrollable urge to put them out.''

His good humor restored, Jason caught her hands and pulled her to her feet. ''Now listen—will you just close that pretty mouth and *listen*?'' he demanded. ''I'm aware that in hiring you, I'm behaving out of character, vastly so, hiring a pig-in-a-poke, so to speak. I have an excellent staff of professionals, I really do not need an unknown, unproven, and likely unstable little amateur on my payroll. But I can afford it, you see, and it might be an amusing diversion to see—''

''An amusing diversion?'' Kristy repeated dangerously.

''To see what you can do. Naturally you won't be given carte blanche to run wild through the tulips, but I will give you a chance to prove that there's more to you than this skinny little body and those big green eyes.''

''Skinny?''

''Well, certainly not plump. Rather small and insignificant—but appealing, in its own quaint way,'' he blandly amended.

Kristy was caught between anger and an explosive urge to burst out laughing. Her mouth opened in furious rebuttal.

Jason shut it with a kiss.

Chapter Five

Kristy stilled as his mouth touched hers, lightly, his hands cradling her face in an enveloping caress. Her first instinct was to lash out at him, but a deeper, more basic need took command. Expecting fire of an entirely different sort, Jason tensed as she came into him, winding her arms around his neck, her body softening to his. The lips he kissed were suddenly, sweetly responsive, a honeyed surprise to his experienced mouth. When she would draw back, his powerful arms wrapped around her until they cast one shadow on the moonlit ground.

To Kristy, what had begun as a form of curiosity swiftly got out of control. She had simply wanted to know how it would be to kiss him. And it was like this! What she had felt at the waterfall was nothing in comparison to *this*, a pulsing, throbbing warmth, a soaring excitement with stunning impact. Her hands plunged deep into his thick silky hair, each sensitive fingertip marveling at this sensual pleasure. Her lips opened and clung and welcomed the insistent thrust of his tongue, thrilling to a sensation as powerful as the emotions rousing within her, the sweet, hot delight of coming together, mouths and tongues and bodies hungrily searching.

Jason moved his mouth from hers long enough to whisper her name, then began brushing her lips with soft, electric kisses, his hands moving expertly down her back in erotic stimulation. *Those hands*, she thought, but she was conscious only of the glowing flame they lit within her. She pressed closer to the lean, hard form carrying her into a floodtime of passionate enjoyment. She kissed him hotly, wetly, her soft moan taken into his ragged breath. "Jason," she whispered, her hand locking in his hair.

Jason responded with a wild surge of passion, wrapping her tighter, holding her crushed into him, his mouth taking hers with fierce insistence. There was only molten fire and the burning, bruising hunger of his mouth. Kristy was utterly lost in delight.

When he slowly pulled free of her clinging lips, hazed green eyes opened in mindless resentment. "A spinister, Mermaid?" he laughed softly, and brushed her wet mouth as if licking up honey. "What are you going to do with all this fire, little Kristy?" he asked huskily.

Kristy hit reality with a jarring bump. She was literally trembling from his kisses, her breath coming in painful little gusts and her heart pounding wildly against her chest. And he was laughing, softly, tenderly, but *laughing!* It was outrageous and indefensible that he could be so unaffected! She lifted blazing green eyes to his, her hands slamming against his shoulders.

"You're despicable!" she spat.

Jason merely held her fast and smiled at her futile efforts to escape his arms. "Now, Mermaid, surely not despicable? Perhaps not even repulsive, hmm?" His teeth flashed whitely against his dark face. He was enjoying this! Kristy shoved with all the strength she possessed. He laughed and kissed her nose. "I do enjoy spirited women," he murmured.

"And is that the reason you want to hire me? Another spirited woman for your trophy case?" she flared.

His arms tightened. "My dear Kristy, my life is weighed down with spirited women. I find them in my pockets, scattered like rose petals in my path—I certainly don't need to hire a women for that purpose." He said it lightly, mockingly, the way a man will say such an outrageous thing, yet the wryness of his smile diffused that mockery. "You hardly fit into that category, anyway," he added as an afterthought.

The moonlight clearly illumed the expression on his face. Realizing that her efforts to escape him were only adding to his enjoyment, Kristy set her hands flat on his arms and studied him with contemptuous disdain. A smile still curved his fine mouth—the mouth she craved to taste again. She took a deep breath, greatly needed but oddly unhelpful; she still felt unsteady.

Her voice leveled. "I don't doubt your prowess with females, intelligent or otherwise. But while I grant you a certain physical attraction, I don't like being grabbed and kissed." Her lashes lowered against his widening smile. "I realize you might have thought differently, but that was because you caught me off guard and I— oh, will you stop smiling like that!" she hissed.

He threw back his head and laughed, and to her consternation, Kristy felt a tickling urge to laugh with him. *The sound was so infectious*, she thought despairingly. After another steadying breath, she calmly requested, "Will you please let me go?"

"Of course," Jason said, surprised that she wanted it.

Clenching her fists, Kristy stepped back as his arms fell away. His tall, black-clad form filled her vision. Moonlight glossed his hair and outlined those pleasingly rugged features. *An attractive man, but still, just a man, easily tucked into a well-defined slot.* It felt pathetically good to tell herself this.

Deliberately, insultingly, meant to disparage any ideas he might have to the contrary, Kristy gave an eloquent shrug and picked up her bag. As far as she was concerned it was over. Whatever *it* was. She turned from him and walked past the bench with quick, decisive steps.

His hand shot out and jerked her to a halt. "Kristy, so help me, if you walk out on me again, I'll—!" Jason said explosively.

"You'll what?" she taunted, her face flushed with anger.

"You take another step and perhaps we'll see *what*."

There was a chilling touch of menace in that low rejoinder. Kristy caught her breath in sudden awareness of her rashness in taunting Jason Thorne. She had been fooled by that deceptively light, teasing manner, but now instinct warned her. He was a dangerous man to taunt, too wealthy and powerful, and certainly too accustomed to having his will obeyed, to ignore a woman's scorn. She shrank back from the dark-haired giant who towered over her, his voice as hard and cold as ice chips.

"I'm not accustomed to being walked out on, Kristy."

"Nor of being defied, either, hmm?" she snapped. She turned to look into his hooded blue eyes, and he moved towards her, his steely grip tightening until one breast and hip met taut, muscular flesh. He held her there, saying nothing, and there was something riveting about his silence. She was powerless to move. The forces set in motion the moment she had met his man throbbed between them, deep and mesmerizing, and breathtakingly exciting.

The dark head dipped to hers, and for a dizzying instant, she thought he was going to kiss her again and she wanted him to. Her body helplessly softened against that male hardness, feeling the pull of him with shocking urgency. Enormous green eyes implored, but Kristy was thoroughly confused as to what they were asking from him.

He released her arm with a soft chuckle. "Neither being defied, nor taken for a fool. Keep in mind, little Mermaid, I like nothing better than a challenge, no matter how small," he said, very low. He relaxed, smiling again. "Now! Let's get back to business."

Limp with the sudden release of tension, Kristy sank down on the bench. "There's no business to get back to," she snapped, instantly combative. "You know perfectly well we couldn't work together five minutes without flying into each other!"

"I know no such thing—as long as you remember I'm the boss and therefore the only one with the privilege of letting fly," he retorted.

"And if you've got a grain of common sense, you'll realize that's not bloody likely! You're the most aggravating man I've ever met and I'd like nothing better than to pull out some of that hair!"

His joyous, completely unaffected laughter confounded Kristy. But then, Kristy confounded herself. *I would never grow tired of hearing that laugh*, she thought, eyeing the hair she would dearly love to pull.

Jason sat down beside her again, his relaxed sprawl requiring an amazing amount of leg room. Kristy tried to ease her thigh from his, but there was nowhere to go. Her vexed look was wasted effort. He settled into the tiny space and started talking again.

"Now hush up and listen—"

"You do like to give orders, don't you," she promptly cut in.

"Yes, I do—and I like it even better when they're obeyed," Jason said somewhat testily.

"Tough."

"Mermaid, I do have limits to my patience, and I know only one really effective way to shut a woman's

mouth," he warned. "Now. Since your uncle authorized a complete refurbishing less than a year ago—of
the main building, that is, that won't require much in
the way of redecorating. Odds and ends of replace-
ment, a few carpets, some paint. Whatever needs doing
in that area can be attended without disturbing the resi-
dent guests."

"It can?" Katie interrupted, surprised.

"It can if the decorating staff is experienced in this
area, yes. And mine is. And when I say mine, I mean just
that. Among other things, I own a highly skilled interior
design firm that specializes in hotels," he said shortly.
"Anything major can be done in that area after we close
down."

"Because you feel sorry for me!" Kristy said angrily.

Jason stared at her with mouth agape. "What on
earth are you talking about?"

"That's why you've decided to 'add me to your staff,
only temporarily of course'!" she mimicked. "Well, if
you think I want any favors from you, you're sadly mistaken! I have a job—I don't need yours!"

"Why in the world would anyone feel sorry for you?
The only thing I feel is a fervent urge to spank you and
I'll be dammed if I don't do just that if you—. One thing
you'd better learn is that I don't do favors, Kristy, not
when it comes to business," he said, hard as steel.

"Oh," Kristy said.

Jason made a strangled sound and rubbed his face.
"The east complex and the cottages, however," he val-
iantly carried on, "need a complete renovation."

"Well, I certainly agree with that. But I still don't see

how I—'' Kristy's voice ended in a gasp as he caught her chin and set his mouth on hers.

"Are you going to talk or listen?'' he demanded against her lips.

"Listen.''

"Very well. Dammit, I'm pressed for time tonight and your saying you're leaving tomorrow took me by surprise. It's imperative that we get this settled, so will you just let me *say* what I have to *say* and get done with it!'' he half roared, releasing her chin.

If his silencing tactics delighted her, the vexed male roar stroked pure velvet. Kristy's eyes widened with a highly pleasing discovery. Her quixotic mind could do something her skinny little body could not; Jason was eying her as if uncertain what to expect next, and this from a man who most assuredly knew what to expect from his women. She was so satisfied, she felt like purring. Throwing Jason Thorne off balance was a peculiarly sweet form of pleasure!

"Yes, Mr. Thorne,'' Kristy meekly replied.

Jason regarded her with what looked to be genuine bafflement. "Do you know, I've met several hundred like you.

"Kristy—'' Jason sighed and dragged a hand through his hair. "You're the only woman I've ever met who can make me forget what I was talking about. Where the hell was I?'' he muttered.

"The east complex. And the cottages,'' Kristy obligingly supplied.

"Yes. Since they've got to be done from stem to stern, so to speak, both the complex and the cottages

95

will be closed down at the end of the month. They're fairly well isolated from the main building, so renovation should pose no problem. Once this point is reached, we'll close down completely, during which time my construction crew will come in to do a little extra work—resurfacing the tennis courts, extending the pool area—I've some plans for the bar, too. As well as a few other changes, minor things, but important, I think.''

He turned to her, warming to his subject, his enthusiasm bouncing off her eager interest. "Like replacing the courtesy vans with limousine service, a common practice on the Island, by the way. And adding to the staff. Your uncle's economy cuts went a little deep in this instance. A first class hotel that charges first class rates must also provide first class service; an ironclad rule, Kristy.''

Watching his animated face and gestures, Kristy realized he was very much enjoying sharing his ideas with her. And that she was very much enjoying listening. The bantering tone had given way to quiet respect, he was speaking to an equal now. Kristy loved the way he used *our* and *we,* making her one of those who merited his esteem rather than a woman who seemed to fit somewhere between a precocious child and a spitting kitten.

She was suddenly, inexplicably, utterly at ease with him. When she unconsciously nestled closer, he put an arm around her and drew her into the curve of his shoulder. Not a lover's embrace, just warm and comfortable. Gradually her head moved to lay trustingly on his shoulder, her face upturned to his with a blissful inner sigh. The night seemed to surround them, enclosing them in a secure little world. Marveling at her deeply felt pleasure, Kristy listened with half a mind. How mercurial her emotions were when she was with him! And what a wild gamut they ran, from laughter to passion to anger and contempt, all in a few minutes span.

And now this heavenly sweet, soft closeness, more companiable than seductive. One of her hands had drifted to his thigh, a light, exquisitely sensitive touch that knew the strength of tensing muscles. She started to snatch back the straying hand, then let it lay. He wasn't at all shy about touching her—why shouldn't she enjoy the same privilege?

Hoping she had not missed anything, she gave him her undivided attention. "The Pearl has an impressive list of regulars, but I want it given priority with every travel agency I can possibly influence," he was saying. "We've already begun an extensive publicity campaign, advertising, classy brochures—"

"Complete with pictures?" she eagerly asked.

"Of course."

"I know you have your own publicity department, but maybe I could help with the pictures. I'm quite skilled at photography. I also do my own processing. I've a darkroom at home, in fact. Black and white only, of course, color requires a lab, but I've done a little pro work for local businesses, fashion layouts and such."

The soft pride in her voice evoked a smile from Jason. "Um, maybe I've underestimated you, Mermaid," he replied, indulgently.

Her mood flip-flopped again. "Don't patronize me. I am good, and I don't need a condescending male to pat me on my cute little head," Kristy coldly rebuked.

"And I don't need an amateur photographer," Jason retaliated.

"Quite right," came her succinct agreement. "Nor an amateur decorator, no matter how diverting. I don't know the first thing about hotels, I've only worked with private residences, and even then, only as an assistant. I've never done anything on my own," Kristy said with blunt honesty. She stood up. "In fact, I've still got months of school before I'm qualified to do anything other than carry out someone else's instructions."

"Sit down, Kristy. Please, hear me out?" His hand laid gently on her wrist, his voice quiet and courteous. Kristy sat. He looked at his watch. "To return to the subject, and without further interruption, if possible; when we close down completely, we'll be working on a tight schedule, tight because our reopening date is absolutely inflexible—barring a major calamity. We've got three months from start to finish. At the end of that time, we endure a grand reopening party—VIPs, Kristy, newspaper and television, travel agency reps, minor celebrities. All public marks and all brought over at my expense. And irksome necessity but standard procedure in launching my hotels. However, that's not your concern."

Bemused, Kristy shook her head. It all sounded tremendously exciting, but to even think of being a part of it struck her as ridiculous. "And what is my concern?" She went along with it.

"The cottages, specifically, the entire renovation in general. You'll be working under excellent supervision, who will, of course, have the final say in every decision. But given your experience in this area, I foresee no problems. As you can see, it really doesn't cost me all that much to give you a chance."

Kristy stared at him. Was he serious? She never knew how to take him. "But why would you want to give me a chance—even if it doesn't cost you anything? And it will, I don't work free. In fact, I command a rather nice salary. I've spent nearly five years of my life working under a very fine decorator, starting as a clerk in her shop and working my way up to a member of her personal staff. I'm not entirely a neophyte," she said proudly.

Jason's hand eased into her hair. "Not in that area, no," he gave gentle agreement. He touched her startled mouth and lazily stood up. "Well, I must go, I've wasted too much time already. Shanna is going to be breathing fire," he said accusingly. "If I'm not around, my staff can clear up any questions you have. As for your salary, we'll settle that matter after you've shown some positive results. Meantime, you can draw advances as needed."

"This is utterly insane," Kristy commented.

"Please do not remind me of that. Hopefully, it's only a temporary aberration and I'll come to my senses, but meantime, I'm taking a chance on you."

"But why?"

"Yours is not to reason why. Just bow to superior judgment," Jason teased.

"When I find some, I will. Now if you please—why this grand gesture?"

"I've told you why, to my satisfaction, at least." Jason walked to one end of the bench and set a foot on it. "Your uncle and I had a little talk after you left," he casually tossed out.

Kristy's eyes narrowed. "I see. So it was my uncle who forced you to—"

"No one forces me to do anything," he said so flatly, she could not disbelieve him. "You start in two weeks, Mermaid."

Under that velvet tone Kristy heard the command, devoid of arrogance or hauteur, soft with the complete certainty of obedience. Her reaction was automatic. "Oh?" she said coolly. "And what if I've decided to go home during those two weeks?"

Jason leaned down to her, tipping her chin up with one finger. Kristy forgot to breathe as intense blue fire engulfed her face. He smiled. "Why then, I'll come after you," he said. "Aloha, Mermaid."

His abrupt dismissal left Kristy open-mouthed and mind awhirl. She watched the tall figure striding down the path until he disappeared. The idea of him coming after her was too silly to contemplate. *She wasn't the sort of woman men lost their heads over,* thought Kristy wryly, not to that extent. Just recalling his reaction to their kisses was a hot flush of shame. She set that aside as irrelevant—his job offer took precedence over a meaningless kiss or two.

This needed talking about. She reversed her course and was shortly in the lobby inquiring as to her uncle's whereabouts.

"He just returned, Miss Loring. But I think he went home," the desk clerk informed her.

Alex's house was located just down the road, accessible through a crushed shell path which connected the two properties. Lights shone in the windows. Kristy crossed the shadowed yard idly wondering as to his financial status. Even if the hotel had become unprofitable, he must have gotten a lovely chunk of money, enough to fulfill that long delayed dream and then some. He was only fifty-five and a good looking man for his age. Could be he'd find some smart young woman who knew a prize when she saw one.

A little disturbed at that, Kristy knocked on the door, then stepped inside the kitchen. Alex was frying eggs. He promptly dropped two more into the skillet and asked if she wanted milk or tea.

"Tea," said Kristy. She waited until they were comfortably settled at the table before telling him of Jason's startling offer.

Alex looked pleased. "Well, that works out fine, doesn't it! What're you looking so fretful about? Seems to me you got your wants," he said.

Kristy eyed him suspiciously. "But don't you think it's a trifle odd? After all, I just recently met this man— and even he's not sure he's doing the right thing."

"Jason Thorne is always sure about what he does."

"Well, he called his offer a temporary aberration— that doesn't sound too positive to me," Kristy retorted.

"Don't you think it's a little crazy?" she asked, exasperated at his noncommittal shrug.

"Why? He asked me if you were any good and I said certainly you were. After all, that's what you told me," he said with one of his rare grins. "Less'n you're intending to go back to that polecat you told me about, I see nothing to prevent you from staying here and enjoying yourself. You are going to do it, aren't you?"

Kristy winced. She didn't like thinking of the man she loved as a polecat. Apt description, though. "Oh, I don't think . . . well, I really haven't had time to think. I came straight here after he left. I'd really like your opinion, Uncle Alex."

"Do what you want. You're a grown woman, even if you don't act it sometimes," replied Alex, and wasn't that helpful, though! Trying to frame her urgent question, Kristy frowned at him.

"Alex, did you have anything to do with him offering me a job?" she asked baldly.

He shrugged and pushed back his chair with a quick glance at his watch. "He heard you say how much you loved this place—maybe that man's got a heart. Listen, would you mind clearing up? I'm supposed to meet a friend for a drink."

Kristy eyed him with a resigned smile. "Yes, I'll clean up. You didn't finish your eggs."

"I'm a terrible cook," Alex admitted.

"Goodnight, Alex. And you certainly were a big help," she called to the closing door.

She cleaned the kitchen and went back to her cottage. Apparently Jason's offer was legit, as crazy as it seemed. And what *was* she going to do about it? Kristy found herself clad in a short white nightgown without any awareness of undressing or even brushing her teeth. As she lay wide eyed in the fragrant darkness, the smell of him clung to her nostrils, the taste of him still tantalizing her wet mouth. Annoyed at the flush of heat, she stripped off her gown and stretched out nude, wondering, intensely, if he slept so.

Her breasts felt heavy and tender with the insidious warmth flowing through her like a steady current. She got up and turned on the air conditioner, gave her pillow a good thumping and cuddled back down again, frowning at the memory of a hard male body pressed thrillingly into her softness.

Not that this in any way influenced her decision, she sternly told herself, it would not happen again. Jason's expertise with love-making came from vast experience, of that she was angrily certain, and she had no intention of being added to a list which included a fire-breathing Shanna. What the devil did a Shanna look like? Itched by voluptuous images, Kristy doggedly dragged her mind back to more pertinent topics; Jason Thorne, and what she was going to do about him.

There were so many puzzling things about that offer. None of which made a marked impression, Kristy admitted with scalding honesty. Charity or kindness, she wanted it more than she wanted her next breath. Because of Jason? Had such a pleasing opportunity been offered by a neutral party, would she find it so difficult to accept or reject? She could not afford the luxury of involvement, no matter how superficial, with another man. Not right now and not *this* man.

Since she seemed to be going round in circles, she set Jason aside for another, far more troubling factor—her cousin, Flora Ramsey. There was in Kristy a deep, unquestioning loyalty that would never permit her to put self before duty. Quiet, retiring, infinitely compassionate Flora had done more than merely step in as temporary caretaker when Kristy lost her mother. Flora had become a surrogate mother, providing not only the two parent stability a child so desperately needed, but a gentle, dependable source of love and caring that had molded more than two-thirds of Kristy's life. Their roles had subtly reversed during the last few years, and Kristy had become the caretaker.

Not that Flora was incompetent, not by any means. But she did need someone to look after her, or so Kristy thought. And to abandon this responsibility . . . .

It was nearly dawn before Kristy drifted into uneasy slumber, and after ten before she came groggily awake. Noting the hour, she shook her head in wry disgust. How she was ever going to regain her early rising habits after this wallow in self-indulgence—

Jason. Like a mocking wind, the name cut through her drowsy mind. She closed her eyes, shivering as it came rushing back, the feel of his hands on her body, the heady taste of his kisses on her lips. Disgruntled at her vivid power of recall, she bounced up and headed for the shower, pausing for a quick look in the mirror enroute. She thought her mouth looked bruised. The purple splotch on one hip required a closer inspection—funny that it hadn't hurt when he touched

104

there last night.

She had just come out of the shower when someone rapped on the front door. Pulling on a robe as she walked, Kristy derided the swift spurt of excitement. "Who is it?" she called.

"Room service," answered to her tart inquiry.

Katie opened the door, her eyes widening with surprise as a waiter stepped in, bearing a silver-toned salver. He opened it with a flourish to reveal the lucious feast sent by—who? Alex? There were juicy, piping hot sausages, crisp cottage potatoes, a puffy omelet redolent with mushrooms and flaked crab, an icy pitcher of pineapple juice, succulent wedges of same mounded with enormous strawberries, fragrant hot rolls and spiced mango preserves. And a note tucked into the heart of a soft pink hibiscus.

The smell of coffee weakening her knees, Kristy sat down and watched the waiter lay her coffee table with snowy cloth and napkin and heavy silver, holding onto her unread note until he left with a cheery farewell. She settled back with a cup of coffee and opened the note, frowning at the unfamiliar handwriting.

The greeting sloshed hot liquid over her fingers.

Good morning, Mermaid! Breakfast on me this morning. Eat it all—you need it. If there are any complaints, do not hesitate to make them known. My hotel aims to please, in every way. Jason Thorne.

"Oh Jason!" she whispered. The sprawling signature was as bold and masculine as he. Kristy studied it, then crumpled it in her fist, anger dueling with pleasure. *His* hotel. A mocking gesture, she felt, but the food was delicious and she was hungry. She poured a glass of juice and thirstily drank it, then smoothed out the note, regretting that she had crumpled it. She had always been a sucker for a romantic gesture, Kristy derided.

Mermaid. Written in that heavy, masculine scrawl, the name conjured up images of the mythical creatures who had tantalized men for centuries. *Seductive sirens*, she thought, her mouth relaxing in a soft, pleased smile, half woman—half fish!

Immediately after breakfast she put in a call to her cousin, stretching the telephone cord to its limits, her hand flying in illustrative gestures as she regaled Flora with the details of Jason's audacious offer, although she omitted the kisses. No use shocking Flora beyond recovery. To her amused chagrin, Kristy's notion of being indispensible was briskly disputed and open to charges of vaunted self-importance. Naturally, Flora took it for granted that she had sense enough to stay on in Hawaii.

"I'll give it serious consideration," Kristy promised, but once she'd replaced the receiver, there didn't seem all that much to consider. Thinking that she could be of some real assistance to Jason was hogwash. What did she know about hotels? Jason had his own highly competent staff—he didn't need her amateurish efforts. Why had he asked her then? He hadn't asked, he'd *ordered!*

She rang the restaurant and crisply requested the charges for her breakfast, room service and tip included. During her stay here, she had paid for all her meals and drinks, and preferred to continue that practice.

A brief call to Alex alleviated another source of aggravation. Kristy got dressed, then set her restive hands to packing. Jason owned this cottage now, and she would not be indebted to him for even one night's lodging.

Chapter Six

Kristy followed her uncle with a quietness far removed from this morning's tempest. *No use unpacking yet,* she thought dully, watching Alex bring in the last piece of luggage. Inscrutable as an oriental, he stacked her bags in the spare bedroom and showed her where clean linens were kept. As was the way with Island homes, his was airy, light, open to the prevailing breezes. Brilliant red poinsettias banked her bedroom window, like an accumulation of Christmases past. Waist high and enormous, they bore little resemblance to the tiny potted plants she bought each holiday season.

A sense of unreality set her down on the bed. Flora had said it was cold and rainy in Texas, unseasonably so, but so. She had also said that the roof needed repairing, an expensive job. They did not personally know any roofing firms, and Flora hated handling it alone.

Alex came back into the bedroom with two frosty drinks, lemonade sprigged with mint. A bed of the fragrant plants grew round his back steps, planted by his wife, many years ago. Kristy's heart hurt. She looked at him with a somber gaze. Did he never feel the aching need to love and be loved? Did Jason? Perhaps the two men were alike in one respect. Alex's quiet reserve deflected love, and Jason fended it off with teasing banter.

Surprised at her insight, she raised her gaze to Alex again. "You make wonderful lemonade, Alex," she said for lack of anything else.

"Used to make it for Lanie after she got sick . . . . While you're here, you might do something with this place," he said, casting a critical eye around the shabby room. "Six years of bachelorhood doesn't do much for a house, does it."

Kristy suddenly laughed. "So I'm definitely staying?"

"Of course you are," said Alex, and just like that, it was settled. So absurdly easy, Kristy felt abashed at all her agonizing.

Her feeling of unreality increased as events moved swiftly on, carrying her with them like a drifting leaf. That night they attended the overwhelmingly warm party given by his day staff. Nightshift personnel who could spare a moment flowed in and out, adding to the poignancy of her mood.

Without prior warning, Jason stopped by for a brief time to formally meet his new staff and briskly explain his plans. If he noticed her standing quietly aside in her simple white gown, he gave no noticeable sign of it. The impersonal blue gaze touched upon her with only the briefest of glances. He was dressed in sports shirt and slacks, but there was no doubt as to who he was tonight, Kristy reflected, listening more to the resonant voice than to his words. He was all business, and totally serious about that business. That she could be included in it was more implausible than ever.

And that he could have kissed her with that searing passion, she thought wonderingly, her eyes filled with the tall, dignified, supremely attractive man. Infinitely masculine and infinitely desirable. *Way out of my league,* she wryly conceded to herself.

With quiet and moving dignity, Alex concluded the short ceremony on a few words of praise for his former staff, the two men shook hands, and Jason took his leave. *Not even a private word for me,* Kristy thought. Telling herself she didn't care, she got another glass of champagne and gaily joined in the toasts showering over Alex.

The following week, they flew into Honolulu to meet the dream that would take him to sea again, a forty-foot sloop so beautiful and trim, Kristy wished she were going with him. While the vessel was being prepared, they toured Honolulu, and a surprisingly witty, lighthearted Alex emerged at times to delight her heart. This had been her father's way, she remembered, a rather stolid manner studded with nuggets of droll whimsy, all the more precious for their rarity.

"Is Jason's office located round here somewhere?"

she asked as they strolled through a canyon of sky-scrapers.

"Just over there," Alex said, pointing to one of those skyscrapers. "Want to go up?"

"Oh no, I was just wondering—idle curiosity," Kristy hastily demurred. "Besides, you promised me Pearl Harbor before dinner," she reminded. Strange to think she was in the same city as he. Or maybe not; Alex said Jason traveled extensively, usually by private aircraft. She wondered what he was doing on the Air Hawaii flight that night. She wondered why she was even wondering. This time with Alex had been pure pleasure, and yet, just below the surface pulsed a tumid sense of waiting, like an extra note concealed in a symphonic interlude.

The day of Alex's departure, she felt embarrassingly near tears when he gifted her with a small, ornately carved sandalwood box. She opened it with an audible gasp. Nestled in white satin, the lustrous pearl shone with an unearthly blue-grey sheen. Alex placed it around her neck and fastened the delicate chain without comment. The pearl lay a shimmering drop of sunlight and water on her ivory skin.

"Thought it was kind of symbolic," he said in his best laconic manner.

Speechless, Kristy stared at her adored uncle. He was vibrantly alive, his eyes sparkling, a jaunty spring in his step these days. Had he hated running a hotel so very much?

"Aloha, Uncle Alex, aloha," she said. That marvelously versatile word covered it all. The first was thank you and a simple farewell, the second was love.

Alone, she caught the evening flight to Kauai. She sat by the window, staring at spun sugar clouds and a sky as blue as his eyes. She was bewildered by her constant thoughts of Jason. She had known him such a short time, and yet she was unable to get him out of her mind. She told herself that it was ridiculous. She tried to rationalize by putting it down to simply physical attraction, the lingering emotional confusion inflicted by Steve's perfidy, the natural pleasure of having a sound reason for staying on in a place she dearly loved. The man was totally immaterial beyond the fact that he was her employer, she assured herself.

And knew she was lying.

By the time Kristy arrived back at the hotel, Jason's plans were already set in motion. His decorator staff had arrived and were seemingly invisible as they went about their tasks. Everyone knew exactly what they were doing. Everyone except Kristy, that is. Wondering if she could possibly look as dumb as she felt, she deserted her drawing board for the bathroom. With her neatly coiffed hair, navy sailcloth skirt and white cotton knit sweater, she thought she looked reasonably intelligent, but the brain under that golden hair was blankly empty.

Nervous fingers plucked at her sweater. A tiny white frill of lace edged the rounded neckline, hugging the curves of her breasts, dipping into the softly shadowed cleft where lay the silvery blue pearl, the most precious thing she had ever owned. Clasping it lightly, she went back to her sketches. After days of concerted effort, she had absolutely nothing to show for her time. Not that she had anyone to show it to. According to the superintendent, Jason had gotten tied up with other matters, and meantime, they were to proceed on schedule.

Kristy had met the crew, discussed at length her assignments, and was, supposedly, proceeding on schedule. She got on well with Dayton, the formidably competent designer who headed this small platoon of experts. Kristy's own genuinely respectful manner accounted for part of that harmonious accord, but either Dayton was above petty rivalry, or she was not quite certain just where this greenhorn fit into the scheme of things.

Dayton had graciously suggested that Kristy concentrate on the cottages, and submit some original concepts which would, she assured, be given honest evaluation. In addition, Kristy was to direct the painters, carpenters and such who would, she knew from experience, parade in and out of her life with wearying irregularity. And during all this, of course, she was to be jotting down the inspired ideas which simply throng every creative mind.

"About as inspired as a cricket!" she muttered, looking down at her most recent brainstorm. In a burst of frustration, she wadded it up and hurled it across the room which mocked her even while she slept.

"I'm so glad to see you're doing so well, Miss Loring." A husky voice poured tons of oil upon her troubled waters.

Kristy whirled around to stare at the man leaning

against the doorframe with a compassionate smile smeared all over his handsome face. An eyebrow tilted. "Aloha, Mermaid," he said.

There he stood; tousled jet black hair and seablue eyes sooty-lashed and gleaming, his superb physique garbed in a crisp green and white striped shirt open deep at the throat, and the suggestive maleness of tight denim jeans. Kristy was unprepared for the raw jolt of reaction. Mentally backing away from it, taking a firm grip on her dancing senses, hoping she looked as composed as she sounded, she said, "Aloha, Mr. Thorne," a ridiculous amount of effort for three little words!

Jason strode across the room and stood smiling down at her. Silhouetted against the sun, he seemed ten feet tall. Her eyes became hopelessly entangled with his deep blue gaze. "Just Jason, please? Have you been properly welcomed back to the Island?" he asked huskily.

"I . . . well, I think so," she stammered.

"If you only think so, then you haven't," he chided. Swiftly the dark head bent to her upturned face, and his mouth set sweetly on her gasp of surprise. At some point his hands moved from her shoulders and pulled her roughly into his arms, his kiss becoming a hungry taking that rocked her senses. She clenched the hands that ached to lose themselves in his hair, closed her lips to the sweet probe of his tongue, but he held her for a timelessness that had nothing to do with reality.

When his mouth lifted, Kristy's lashes fanned up in reluctant acceptance. After three weeks' absence, she had been sure her guard was secure, but his kiss had just proved otherwise. She took a vitally needed breath. "This is an Island welcome?" she asked unevenly.

"Oh yes, an old tradition!" he assured. He caught the curl nestling in the hollow of her throat and rubbed it between his fingers as if gauging its honeyed texture. His eyes moved over her in mesmerizing slow motion, tracing the contours of her mouth, the tipped nose that wrinkled in puzzlement, wandering down to the curves swelling above the comfortably low neckline of her sweater. When he touched the pale grey pearl, his knuckles grazed her skin.

"This is lovely. Your uncle gave it to you?" he demanded. She nodded. "It suits you . . . have dinner with me tonight, Kristy?"

Distrustful, unable to distinguish whether of herself or him, Kristy increased the distance between them with a subtle sway of her body. "I thank you, but it would be easier for me if we kept this a business relationship, at least until I find my footing," she said, hating the qualifier, but helpless to prevent it.

Jason shrugged and dropped the curl he held. "As you wish," he said.

"It's just that this job—well, it's all I can take on right now," she felt compelled to explain.

Eyes as cool as blue crystal set on her flushed face. "Kristy, I wasn't asking you to 'take on' anything, it was merely a dinner invitation. I thought perhaps we could get to know each other a little better, that's all."

He looked and sounded bored with the whole business. Kristy flushed. "I don't think we need to know each other a little better in order for me to work for you," she said stiffly.

"And that's why you stayed, to work for me, isn't it," he observed.

"It is," she said firmly.

A sardonic smile touched his mouth. "Yes, of course. Please forgive me for insulting you with a dinner invitation, Kristy." When he inclined his head and abruptly turned to go, she held him at the door with her soft voice.

"Jason? It wasn't an insult. Thank you for the welcome."

"Well, your manners are much improved," he said in pleased surprise. "I hope it's lasting. And you're welcome, Mermaid."

How lovely to hear that absurd little name again! "Jason, wait a minute, please? I truly didn't mean to be ungracious about your invitation, I—" She hesitated, seeking words that would convey what she wanted, without leaving her open to misconception. "What I meant was, the only kind of relationship I want is friendship." She smiled, relieved that he didn't pounce. "I guess what I'm asking is—can't we just be friends, Jason?"

A look of surprise stole over his features. "Well, that's a first. I can't recall ever having a woman ask just to be friends," he said as if mulling some curious new idea.

"What's so strange about that?" she snapped, smarting at his reaction. "Men and women can be friends, you know, without resorting to bedroom gymnastics."

"Can they?" He shrugged. "Well, I'll take your word

116

for it."

"Perhaps we'd do just as well to forget it," she said curtly. "One more thing, please. Will you tell me exactly why you gave me this job?"

"I thought we went through all that."

"We did, but the reasons given didn't quite satisfy."

A sardonic grin curved his mouth. "You're still looking for an ulterior motive, hmm?" Jason drawled. Hooded blue eyes wandered over her with lazy amusement. "Some dark, sinister designs on your body, perhaps?"

A blush tinted her. "I meant no such thing and you know it," Kristy rebuked. "I would assume a man like you prefers sophisticated women."

"At least a *pinch* of sophistication," he dryly agreed.

It was Kristy's turn to shrug, and she did it with a *pinch* of anger. "I'm devastated that I don't meet your requirements," she said with more sarcasm than she liked. "However, all I really wanted to know was if it had anything to do with my uncle."

He looked annoyed. "I like Alex, so perhaps that did in some small way influence my decision. A very small way; I seldom mix business with sentiment. I guess you'll just have to be satisfied with the reasons I gave you, Kristy. At any rate, welcome aboard. I'll leave you to carry on with—" His eyes went to the wadded sketches laying in the corner of the room. "With whatever you were doing."

As Jason strode out the door, Kristy's weakened knees dropped her on the couch. *This is ridiculous,* she thought, watching the tremor in her fingers. Naturally I was a little anxious about our first meeting. Jason Thorne isn't exactly your average boss—but still, what happened just now was no big deal. A welcoming kiss, that's all. And an invitation to dinner . . .

Kristy gave a sheepish laugh. One thing she excelled in was making mountains out of molehills! And just because Steve had proved to be an unprincipled heel did not necessarily reflect on Jason's character. "Beware of blanket judgments, Kristin. Could be Jason's a genuinely nice, decent man," she reproved her suspicious self. But that naive self had thought that Steve Brady was a genuinely nice, decent man, too.

Fortunately, one of her errant workmen, a plumber this time, inadvertently wandered through the door just then. Inadvertently, Kristy was sure, because he was due two days ago. She led him to the bathroom and pointed out the problem, the bathtub faucet that dripped incessantly. Which would, he informed her, require a whole new set, which he happened to have in his truck. And which would, she learned, mean tearing out a section of the wall since he could not possibly install it through that tiny trapdoor.

The expensive project gave her pause. She was not certain she had the authority to sanction this, but Dayton was in town and if she let this jaunty independent go, no telling when she'd nab him again. "Tear it out," she said, a decision that was, thank heavens, later approved by Dayton.

Leaving him to it, Kristy returned to her sketch pad.

Curiously enough, Jason's prickly-pleasing welcome was just the impetus she needed. Kristy plunged into her work with new determination. Now, rather than fearing it, she found herself rising to the challenge with delicious enjoyment, and her sketches came to life as color and design flowed effortlessly from the vast storehouse of her mind. On paper, at least, the cottages looked absolutely lovely. And if her spirits flagged, she had only to touch the symbol of her uncle's affection, the perfect blue pearl that lay warm as life against her skin.

Glimpsing Jason striding about the hotel grounds with lordly demeanor always caused a skip of her heart. The next time he spoke to her was an infuriating reprimand. Chill blue eyes pointedly checked out her jeans, and the shirt-tails tied beneath her breasts as he irritably inquired, "Kristy, you're not a construction hand. Is it necessary that you dress like one?"

He's the boss, Kristy reminded herself, and choked down her hot retort, replacing it with a suspiciously polite, "No sir. Sorry."

His gaze traveling over the untidy ponytail tied with a snip of yarn, Jason twisted the knife a little deeper. "I hope so. Right now you look like something someone forgot to bring in for the night. I don't mean to be rude or hypercritical, but I do have a sharp aversion to messy-looking females.

The arrogance of this took her breath. He wore a deep blue shirt and darker blue trousers, and he was madly attractive. Every long line of his body radiated a vibrant, all-pervading maleness, a sense of dynamic power yet held in restraint. Kristy felt dizzied by the force of that power. *He was so alive,* she fumed. And just a little frightening. She hadn't forgotten that glimpse of glacial steel.

A smile thinned his mouth as he awaited the explosion. She remained silent, but the cost was plainly revealed by her stormy eyes. This was her employer, she stoutly reminded herself, and one does not fly into one's employer, no matter how much he deserves it, nor how badly one needed it!

Jason's amusement visibly deepened as he watched her struggle with her unruly nature. "No comment, Kristy?"

'Sorry,'' she said sweetly.

"Accepted," he said sweetly. "Now come have lunch with me. Not a social occasion, Kristy this is business," he sternly added when she declined.

It was not, by any stretch of imagination, a social occasion. They went to his office and Jason poured over reports, flung questions at her concerning her progress, talked on the telephone while instructing a workman, and somehow managed to devour a platter of sandwiches without missing a beat. Being in his presence was like standing in the center of a whirlwind, and Kristy was relieved to escape him. Yet she found herself anticipating their next meeting before she had finished this one.

A week without seeing him was an oddly colorless seven days. The few moments he spared for a greeting when she did encounter him again were unsatisfying and resented. He did not come to the cottage again, nor did he display interest as to what she was doing with her time. A sign of confidence, perhaps, but Kristy felt increasingly piqued that he could so easily resist—was he devoid of normal human curiosity?

Contrarily, when he did finally stop by to see her, she felt a flash of resentment, as if he was checking up on her. Bored with television and the silence of Alex's house, she had returned to her former cottage after dinner and become so engrossed in what she was doing, no heed was given the late hour. It was nearly midnight when he interrupted her. Watching him mount the steps, a sliver of moonlight gilding his ebony hair, Kristy suddenly doubted her lofty sentiments of friendship between members of the opposite sex. The warmth gathering low in her stomach was not engendered by friendship.

"Is that coffee I smell?" he asked, pausing in the open door.

"Yes, I keep a pot handy—I'm a coffee fiend when I'm working," Kristy lightly replied. "The pot's on the counter, and there are some clean cups. Help yourself."

Jason sat down on the one remaining chair. "How about you getting me a cup? I'm beat."

"You think I'm not?" Kristy replied tartly.

Jason propped his chin in hand and musingly regarded her. "Jeans again," he remarked.

"Jason, I've been working like mad to remove a hundred coats of paint from this door frame. There's a beautiful tapa wood design under all this glop, and I think whoever authorized painting over it should be hanged . . . which is my uncle, I guess. At any rate, the coffee is on the counter."

"I'm a coffee fiend too, when I'm working," Jason

121

agreeably remarked, making no move to get up. "One thing I've always believe is that it's a woman's place to serve her guest—or her boss—coffee. Rather a natural function, you might say," he went on. Those little devils were dancing in his eyes again, hot gold sparks that tickled and teased. Actually, Kristy had been taught the very same thing and took pleasure in doing it.

"Your coffee, Mr. Thorne. Do lean back and enjoy it," she invited.

"Thank you," Jason said. He took a sip and frowned. "You ever hear Tallyrand's formula for perfect coffee? Black as the devil, hot as hell, pure as an angel, sweet as love."

"In other words, you would like some sugar?"

"If you please," he said, holding out the cup.

Gauging her rising temper with unease, Kristy resorted to the old formula—*he's the boss.* "How many lumps?" she asked resignedly. "Of sugar, I mean."

"Two will do. And next time, you might make it stronger," Jason suggested.

Not for the first time, Kristy wondered if he was deliberately trying to provoke her. He seemed to take a perverse enjoyment in doing so, and before she knew it, she was furiously combating his taunts. Afterwards she was plagued by shame at being provoked to temper, and vowed it would positively, absolutely, never happen again. Until the next time.

"I'll keep that in mind. Did you want anything in particular, Jason, or are you just here to aggravate?" she asked sweetly.

"Hardly the latter. I wanted to inquire about this receipt for, quote: twelve clamshell basins, unquote. You have an explanation?"

"Certainly. I ordered them to replace the basins in all the cottage bathrooms. The man had the necessary quantity in stock, so I decided then and there to take them. He said they were easily adapted to the existing plumbing, and could be installed with no complications whatsoever. And they're relatively inexpensive considering the lift they'll give these rather plain facilities. I assume I did have the authority to do so?"

"Actually, you assumed wrong, but we'll let it pass this time. Since Dayton concurs with your opinion," he said sourly.

Bless you, Dayton, Kristy thought. She walked back to the counter to fill her own cup, her thoughts tumbling on. She would have liked a word of praise on what she had accomplished so far. The plans she had submitted to Dayton had undergone some alteration, of course, but Kristy was exhilarated at how much of her original ideas were accepted. "Bright, colorful, practical," was the pleasing compliment bestowed upon her, and while that was morally uplifting, a simple word or two from him would be appreciated.

Like; *Kristy, you're doing fine.* Or; *Kristy, you're doing rotten,* for that matter. But no, nothing—neither praise nor criticism, when he must know what it would mean to her. And now, she thought hotly, he was questioning her authority on a paltry matter like a dozen clamshell basins!

That he had a perfect right to do so was no deterrent. Kristy whirled around, green eyes flashing. "Perhaps you'd better explain just how far, *precisely*, my authority extends, Jason," she suggested, dangerously soft. "Exceeding it was not my intent, I assure you."

"I never implied that it was," Jason mildly reproved. "But before you purchase in bulk, I think you should *perhaps* check with Dayton. She is, after all, the final authority when it comes to matters of this sort. Since she's worked for me for eight years, she's well aware of budgetary limits."

"Fair enough," said Kristy.

Jason set aside his cup, his smile sardonic. "I'm glad you agree. And I didn't mean to criticize your appearance. Actually, those are quite nice jeans. But don't we have someone more suited to taking goop off wood?"

"I was only testing some small spots to see if it's worth the effort before I get someone in to help. Would you like a refill on that?"

Moodily he watched her crossing the room. The jeans she wore clung to firm young thighs, and her breasts stood high and proud against the tailored white shirt that cupped them. When she leaned down to get his cup, a lock of red-gold hair fell on his bare arm, soft pale fire laying on his skin.

Glancing at him, Kristy noted the brooding quality that quietened his gaze. Something had changed in their relationship—if you could call this velvety conflict a relationship—and she was unsure in just what way. They were basically relaxed with each other, yet there was always this prickling between them, no matter how casual, curt, professional or friendly his manner at any particular time. He didn't tease her anymore, and she missed that.

"I saw some of the pictures you took," he said abruptly.

Kristy forgot about the cup. "Oh, the ones I left in the office? I was showing them to someone—forgot to pick them up when I left."

"They were very good, Kristy. I apologize for that condescending pat on your curly little head," he said with obvious sincerity.

She glowed—no other word for it—she simply glowed! She shrugged. "Apology accepted," she said airily, then spoiled it with an eager, "What ones did you particularly like?"

"The ones of the hotel, of course. You put something in those pictures my own photographer missed. Maybe a little love, hum?" he smiled gently. "And the picture of the iliau plant. It was exquisite, Kristy the colors, the . . . the composition, I guess you'd call it, was more like a work of art than a snapshot. Have you ever thought of a career in that field?"

"Yes, now and then. But I sort of fell into this interior design thing," she laughed, and reached again for his cup. "More money, I guess. Refill or not?"

"Just half a cup," Jason growled. "I haven't been sleeping well lately."

She straightened. "Then you shouldn't have any more coffee."

"It isn't coffee that's keeping me from sleeping," Jason muttered. His arms suddenly curved around her hips. Kristy stiffened. He rested his chin on her stomach and looked at her, and grinned, that sly, devilish grin that twisted her heart. "You're still too skinny," he sighed.

"Please don't, Jason," she said, low and strained. Her hand had already found its way to his hair with a passionate wish to caress.

Jason studied her for an uncomfortable moment, his arms locking tightly around her hips. "Are you afraid of me Kristy?" he asked softly.

"I—I don't think so. Not you especially, just . . . I got hurt pretty bad in that grand love affair, as you called it. I thought we were going to be married." She shook her head, her fingers curving into the softness of his hair. She brushed back the lock tumbling across his brow, then dropped her hand.

"So what happened?" Jason prompted.

"As I said, it went sour," Kristy said dismissively. When she pulled against his clasp, Jason immediately released her.

He stood up and looked around the nearly barren room. "Thanks for the coffee. How much longer with all this?" he asked, a wave of hand encompassing the dropcloths and paint containers scattered about.

"A few more weeks, if all goes well, meaning if deliverymen, plumbers, carpet installers and the like keep their schedules," Katie said wearily. "And you're welcome for the coffee. By the way, I've been meaning to ask—did I ever thank you for this job?"

Jason scowled. "Come to think of it, you didn't."

A smile lit her face. "In that case, thank you, Jason," she said softly.

"You're welcome," Jason said, looking even more irritated. "Why the devil are you so tired?" he barked. "Do you make a habit of working this late?"

"No, of course not. Well, I have been burning the candle at both ends," she conceded. "In the evenings, I work on Alex's place. He's got some really lovely things; a bronze mantle clock by Tiffany and Company of New York—I couldn't find a date, but it must be very old. And an Edwardian etagere so heavily inlaid, it looks like it should be in a museum. And an exquisite Tabriz rug . . ."

Noting Jason's impatient shift, Kristy spread her hands. "Sorry. It's just that I love beautiful things and we were always a leather couch and slatetop table family, so it's a pleasure just to live with these lovely things."

Her voice faded away as they stood staring at each other, an uneasy moment that spun out on shimmering motes of time. Shaken, Kristy turned aside and pushed at her tumbled hair. "Well," she said briskly, "time for home and bath and bed. I've an early flight to Honolulu in the morning. Goodnight, Jason."

He looked at her with that dangerous tenderness that melted bones. "Goodnight, Kristy," he said softly, laying the back of his hand on her cheek. Then, with that same delicacy, he cradled her small face and kissed her. Not a lover's kiss, not even a man to woman kiss; just a soft, warm, friendly kiss.

She wanted more, much more. As if sensing this, he embraced her, holding her with one hand deep in her hair, her face pressed into his shoulder. He smelled so good. She put her arms around his back and closed her

127

eyes as he drew her closer. The beat of passion pulsed slow and steadily, like his heartbeats, needing only a kiss to set it to pounding. *There's nothing wrong with this,* she told herself, *we're just taking comfort from this, just strengthening each other.* She looked up at him and his mouth found hers before she could draw a breath.

Her heart hammered against her stomach, the rapid breaths that scorched her lips. She was lost again, lost in this hot, sweet flood of passion . . .

Jason raised his head and gave her an angry look. "Get some rest tonight," he commanded. With that, he strode from the cottage, leaving Kristy groping for breath.

She went into the bedroom and sat down on the mattress. It was new, still wrapped in plastic. She ran a trembling hand over the slippery surface. "Might have been a trifle uncomfortable," she murmured, trying for humor, for sarcasm—anything to soften awareness of her urgent need for him. For his kisses, his caresses, she corrected—not the man himself. Sex, pure and simple. She felt disgusted with herself. And as ever, and possibly forever, confused. She had never needed Steve like that. The man would have been her husband and the father of her children, but she had never lost touch with reality when Steve kissed her. Some small, inviolate part of her had always stood aloof, refusing to risk total committment.

But tonight she had been appallingly vulnerable. Jason could have asked, and received, anything he wanted of her.

Kristy got up and turned out the lights. "Fortunately for you, he didn't want anything," she scolded as she walked out into the velvet night.

Chapter Seven

Morning dawned with the soft, misty hues of a water-color. Still in her robe, Kristy walked out to the terrace to collect her hand laundry, pausing for a moment to savor the clean, sparkling air of Kauai. She felt strong and capable this morning, at ease with herself. *Last night's madness was merely a temporary lapse in discipline,* she thought comfortably, nothing to fret about. Gathering the lacy undergarments from the line Alex had affixed to the terrace posts, she went back inside to bathe and dress.

She had just stepped out of the shower when the telephone rang. Dripping water, she snatched up the receiver with a sharp, "Hello?"

"Good morning," Jason said, his sardonic smile visible in his voice.

Rattled, Kristy suddenly set her wet bottom down on the bed. "Oh. Jason."

"Um hum, Jason. What time's your flight to Honolulu?" he asked lazily.

"Ten oclock."

"Well, cancel it. I'm leaving in a few minutes and you can ride with me."

"With you? But how?" Kristy blurted.

"I've got a plane," he said. *Of course*, Katie thought, *doesn't everyone?* "Will twenty minutes be enough time?" he asked.

She agreed it would, and promised to meet him in the lobby. Replacing the dark blue dress she had laid out for the trip, Kristy chose a creamy white suit of crisp linen and a lavishly bowed, soft blue dacron blouse. The slim jacket sleeves displayed full blue cuffs fastened with ivory cufflinks, and the puffy bow collar made a voluptuous splash against severely cut lapels.

She smoothed the slender skirt over her hips, admiring the provocative flash of silken leg as she stepped to and fro. Several minutes of her allotted time were given to wondering if it was too provocative, and another hefty slice of time spent taming her hair into a sleek coil at the base of her neck. Kristy added her mother's antique ivory earrings, and anxiously studied the results. "You don't have time to dither around like this!" she muttered, annoyed at her uncertainty. Deciding on her one good pair of alligator pumps, she changed handbags, and hurried to meet Jason.

She had forgotten to cancel her reservation. Jason

sourly instructed the desk clerk to attend to it before escorting Kristy to the white Cadillac. Not a rental car, then. She looked up at him and he suddenly smiled, their thoughts briefly merging.

He did indeed have a plane, a sleek white Cessna that accommodated four passengers. The two men who joined them at the airport kept Jason engaged the entire flight. Curling up in her seat, sipping the coffee Jason poured from a silver thermos, Kristy kept to her own affairs and they were in Honolulu in a surprisingly short time.

There was a car and a driver waiting at the airport. Jason dropped her off at her requested designation with a brusque order to meet him at Horatio's for lunch. Kristy barely stopped herself from snapping a salute in defiance of that curt voice. Contenting herself with a cool, ''Yes, Mr. Thorne,'' she gave the other two men a sweet smile and swung off down the avenue.

Although Kristy's purpose for the trip was strictly professional, she managed to find time to stop by a photographer's shop and leave the iliau negative, with precise instructions as to its treatment; a twenty-four by thirty-six inch print with a medium gloss, silicone finish. Using the original picture as a guide, she selected a mat and frame with orders to have it completed and shipped to Alex's house.

Unfortunately, she became so absorbed in the process, she was fifteen minutes late getting to the restaurant. *Jason would doubtless be seething at her tardiness, but he would just have to seethe a little longer,* she thought crossly, ducking into the powder room. This

132

was their first public lunch and she had to look halfway presentable.

Jason was standing by the door chatting with one of the fetchingly costumed serving *wenches* when Kristy emerged. She approached him with far more composure than she felt. "Sorry I'm late, Jason," she said lightly, her heart beating too fast for comfort.

"Quite all right. I've never found women to be the most punctual creatures," he said, sardonically. He smiled, his gaze gliding over her from the top of her golden head to the tips of her alligator pumps. Kristy had taken off her jacket, and the soft blue blouse clung to her proud young breasts, the trim skirt outlining svelte hips and thighs. There was a touch of masculine pride in the possessive hand he slipped under her elbow.

"Come along, I've a table waiting. Some friends are joining us for lunch," he said, guiding her into a beautifully decorated room. Very much aware of the eyes drawn to the tall young executive and the small woman who walked before him, Kristy lifted her chin with imperious hauteur. The restaurant was modeled after an old sailing ship, the *H.M.S. Victory,* and Jason's table was in an area charmingly called the *Lieutenant's Wardroom.* The three men waiting there, two bankers and an attorney, Kristy subsequently learned, rose to their feet as she approached. Poised as blue blazes, Kristy greeted them and made small talk while she worked at controlling her erratic pulses.

Jason had, somewhere, changed his casual attire for a superbly tailored suit, and looked every inch the formi-

133

dable executive. He acted much the same way with her, courteous, impersonal, leaving no doubt in his associates' minds that she was merely an employee in town on business. Kristy appreciated that; at least these impressive gentlemen would not be speculating on her presence here.

In his formal gray suit, Jason was a disturbingly unfamiliar man. *Even his hair conformed to formality, laying smoothly in place, the enchantingly tousled look she preferred evidently tamed by superior will,* she thought, smiling at the notion of Jason sternly forbidding a single hair to leave its assigned place. At his suggestion, she ordered an avocado salad and chicken Florentine. This was proceeded with a cup of clam chowder and a basket of crunchy bread so good, Kristy mentally slapped the hand reaching for another piece.

Once the main course was served, she concentrated on her food and left the men to their talk. It was obscurely satisfying just to look up and see Jason sitting across from her. He held his own with these imposing older men, and she was fiercely proud of him, proud of that easy confidence, the articulate conversation that excluded her simply because of its complexity. The flood of prideful emotion was fully as strong and riveting as the passionate need she had felt for him last night.

Nonplussed at this new awareness of him, Kristy reflectively spooned up her chocolate mousse, scarcely tasting the rich confection. She had been proud of Steve, of course, but then, a woman was supposed to take pride in her man. Jason was not her man and never would be, yet what she felt for him at this moment transcended logic.

After the thoroughly satisfying lunch, the four men parted at the door with handshakes all around and pleasantries for Kristy. Then she and Jason were alone, and she was immediately uneasy again. She cleared her throat, glancing up at him as they emerged into the bright afternoon sunlight.

"What time will we be returning to Kauai?" she asked lightly.

Jason drew her aside, out of the flow of pedestrian traffic. "I won't be returning, I've a social engagement here tonight. However, my secretary has reserved you a seat on the six o'clock flight," he said matter-of-factly.

Color flushed her cheeks. "I'm sorry, I just assumed . . . well, thank you for the lunch. It was most enjoyable," she said with stilted courtesy.

There followed one of those moments of taut silence. Oddly enough, they both exhibited signs of feeling uneasy with one another. She wondered what sort of engagement—a date? Jason was looking annoyed, and she felt too flustered to break the lengthening silence.

A man passing by gave her a thorough once-over. Noting Jason's sour look, Kristy suddenly laughed and held out her hand. "Well, all right then—aloha, Jason! Have a good time tonight!"

Jason took her hand in both of his and idly examined the small, reddened palm. "I usually do . . . why do you have blisters on this palm?" he asked abruptly.

Startled, Kristy stammered, "Well, I—felt a need for some physical exercise yesterday evening, so I found some clippers and trimmed the shrubs around my cottage. They're quite overgrown," she explained, wrinkling her nose at his frown.

Jason dropped her hand. "We have gardeners for that express purpose. I'd prefer that you confine yourself to less punishing forms of exercise. Come on, I'll get you a cab," he said pleasantly, but Kristy sensed an inner annoyance.

At that moment, a long black Lincoln parked a few feet behind them honked impatiently. Jason paused, undecided as it honked again. "Sorry, that's for me," he said with an apologetic shrug.

"That's okay—I'm capable of finding my own cab," Kristy crisply assured him. "Thank you again for the lunch," she added, but Jason had already turned towards the car. He walked around to the driver's side. Through the rear window, Kristy caught a glimpse of a woman's lovely face, the flash of dark eyes as she slid over to give him the wheel.

As the Lincoln eased onto the street, a glossy dark head drew close to Jason's, and a slender hand with poppy red nails slid up the back of his neck. Streaks of sunlight caught the bluewhite fire of a diamond bracelet glittering against his black hair. Kristy felt a pang of something peculiarly like jealousy. She turned in the opposite direction and hailed a passing cab.

It was only late that night, laying in bed in darkness as soft and seductive as velvet, that Kristy's stubborn resistance caved in to a stronger force. Who was the woman with Jason, she wondered with a strange, desolate hurting. Was he with her now, smiling at her with that engulfing tenderness, touching her with hands that knew so well how to please a woman, holding her against his aroused body, coming to her until they were one . . .

Kristy bit down on her knuckles to stop the protesting cry that welled up from a bewildering depth of feeling. She had been so proud of him today, had seen him, for the first time, not just as a man, but a person, a fine decent person she was honored to know. She had not realized how very much she liked and trusted Jason Thorne until today.

But what had that to do with the fact that he was very likely in another woman's bed at this very second! Kristy's nails sliced deep into her palms. *Nothing*, she gritted, *absolutely nothing*. How he spent his leisure time, how many women he had, what he did with them, was none of Kristy Loring's business.

* * *

The next three weeks were hectic ones for Kristy, too filled with activity to ponder the long range effects of that relatively unimportant lunch with Jason. Yet by virtue of that strong surging pride he aroused in her, it was the pivotal point of their relationship. Deep down, safely out of range of examination, she was hazily aware of more and more of an inner resistance giving way, of the steady erosion of protective walls erected at such painful costs, but the press of work smoothly

137

covered this.

However, another, more profound realization emerged during her restless nights. Thus far, the time she had spent on Kauai had been a leisurely getting acquainted process for she and Jason, not the artificial, best foot forward acquaintance two potential lovers would project. Rather, it was a natural, down to earth acknowledgment of freely revealed character flaws without too much concern for the other's opinion. Bickering and disagreements, spontaneous laughter and the pleasure of a common goal, had forged a friendship neither had expected. It was the kind that, if given a chance, would outlast passion and withstand any adversity—a priceless thing.

Although she did not consciously think of their relationship in this way, Kristy felt it, and since she had been taught that friendship was as important as love to a good marriage, her subconscious mind placed a high value on what they shared. But at the moment, hurrying through her shower and rushing to re-dress, she was concerned with more direct thoughts. Three of the cottages, including the one so special to her, were ready for Jason's inspection, and his opinion was of paramount importance. Failing him was unthinkable; it was as if this vast outpouring of her time and energies was a primitive offering to the man who dictated her days and haunted her nights.

This feeling was invisbly linked to the trust inherent in friendship, and vaguely frightening to a woman who was determined not to play the fool again. Her bitter resolve undermined by this subtle softening towards Ja-

138

son, Kristy often found her emotions in conflict without understanding the reason. The only thing she could do was fight it, as she had fought the crushing charges hurled at her by another man whose opinion she had once deeply respected.

It hadn't been easy, Kristy reflected, without pinpointing the exact substance of that *it*. But the overwhelming pain she had brought to Kauai had shrunk to a hard, tight knot and she was deeply thankful for this timely blessing. Pausing in front of the mirror, she critiqued her dress, a crisp strawberry linen color-cued to her lips and nails. It looks so dressy—perhaps she ought to change to slacks and shirt . . .

"Oh, the devil with it!" she muttered. She tucked a stray curl into her neatly coiled chignon, then left for the hotel.

In the bright May sunshine, The Blue Pearl slept like a restless giant. Kristy skirted the mound of soil scooped from what would be an enormous, free-form pool, and waved at Ben Soames, who stood surveying the gutted east wall of the bar.

"Aloha, little one! Your usual?" he mischievously called. Kristy laughingly accepted a cup of icy pineapple juice from his thermos, then continued on her way after a brief chat with the genial giant. And now to find the not so genial giant. Of late, a Jason Thorne preoccupied with business was often a forbiddingly brusque encounter. Noting the continued expansion of a crack in the swimming pool's south wall, he had summarily decided that a patch job would not be satisfactory, and even though it meant canceling the advance guest list

139

and closing down the hotel ahead of schedule, he had elected to remove the defective wall, a crash program that entailed a dawn to dusk work schedule for his construction crew.

Expedience, not choice, had dictated his actions, and Jason's mood reflected it. Tingling at the prospect, Kristy hunted him down with decreasing eagerness and mounting excitement, an absurd combination, she derided as she strolled into the lobby. She had not enjoyed a moment alone with him since the night he came to her cottage, and a quick assessment of that brooding profile assured that she wasn't going to enjoy this one either.

Kristy noted the handsome alligator boots on his slender feet, the khaki shirt and slacks that were several shades lighter than the rich gold of his skin. His thick cap of glossy black hair was unmercifully rumpled by the restless hand thrusting through it. He was deep in conversation with two other men, and she had to touch his arm to attract attention.

Jason looked down at her. "Yes?" he asked curtly.

"I was wondering if you had time to come inspect some of the cottages," Kristy said.

"Has Dayton okayed them?"

"Yes, but I thought . . ." Kristy paused—what had she thought? That he could at least spare a minute to look at the results of her exhaustive effort! "I would like your firsthand opinion." she said, that stubborn little chin coming to a point.

"All right—but not right now." Jason looked at his watch. "Twenty minutes, okay? I'll meet you there,"

140

he said dismissively.

Sensing the tension emanating from that long, taut frame, Kristy simply nodded, and returned to her cottage. She paused at the door to assess the impact of first impression, then walked slowly to the bedroom, her gaze critically appraising. Airy and spacious, the cottages had, she felt, come into their own as luxury suites, no longer identical except in the most basic structural sense. If she never accomplished anything else in her life, she had this to remember.

And yet, her green eyes were anxious as she gazed around the bedroom. Deep opulent pinks in the velvet chaise lounge, sunsplashed carpet and walls, touches of stamen yellow and rich leaf greens in the covered windowseat. The room pleased every atom of her beauty-sensitive soul.

In the living room, practical materials and honey-hued rattan were luxurious in visual effect. The pair of deep green velvet chairs were for color, as were the flowerlike cushions on the couch; delphinium, fuchsia, rose, jonquil, misty lemon and lime. She thought it all enchantingly lovely, but what about Jason? Nibbling on a nail, she tried desperately to see it through his eyes. A basket of Vanda orchids mingled with ferns and a cunningly curved branch of pale green *kukia* centered the small glass and bamboo table. Was it too pretty? Darkly amused at her anxiety, she shook her head. Dayton didn't think so, but Dayton wasn't Jason Thorne.

''Hello, Mermaid.''

The soft, husky voice brought her wheeling around to confront the smiling man lounging against the doorframe. Sapphire eyes sparkled up and down her pretty dress. Evidently his mood had much improved, and it was contagious. Kristy suddenly felt too good to adopt the meek manner which both amused and annoyed him.

"Hello, boss!" she said liltingly. What had changed his mood? He was laughing, dimples flashing dazzling white teeth against his tanned skin, flatly irresistible to Kristy. Striving to bring her soaring spirits down to earth again, she asked primly, "You ready to inspect?"

Jason strode through the livingroom, into the bedroom, and back to the living room, a most cursory inspection, at best. "Very nice," he said.

Disappointed, Kristy repeated, "Nice?"

"Um hmm," Jason blandly affirmed, "nice." Those little golden devils were dancing in his eyes. With a shout of laughter, he caught her up and whirled her around. "Congratulations are in order, Mermaid! I am now the proud possessor of a baby sister, who is, I'm told, an absolutely gorgeous, blue-eyed, black-haired princess named Julia Elizabeth Madonna Robinson Thorne! A mouthful, I grant you, but the little lady bears it royally, says Dad!" Jason joyously declared.

"Oh, Jason!" Kristy squealed. She was kissing him—he was kissing her—holding her to his chest, laughing between these short, hard, utterly delightful kisses. "So that's why you've been such a grouch lately," she said, her voice softening with compassion.

His eyes deepened to the clear blue of April hyacinths as Jason met her gaze. "Yes, that's why. It's been rough going for Mother. I've had a plane and pilot on standby

142

for the past damn *year*, terrified that I'd be called home at any minute. Well, maybe not a year, but God, it seemed like it, Kristy, it did seem like it,'' Jason groaned, burying his face in the satin of her hair.

Her arms wound round his neck. ''But all's well now?'' Kristy whispered.

''Oh yes, all's well now. I got the call right after you left.'' Jason put her down, looking a little embarrassed at his emotional outburst. ''Well, I guess it's back to work,'' he said briskly. He gave a quick laugh and shook his head, setting that enchanting lock of hair atilt again.

Kristy brushed it back. ''Yes, back to work,'' she agreed.

''Be damn if that's so!'' Jason promptly disagreed. ''Go change into slacks and meet me in the lobby in ten minutes,'' he commanded.

''Yes, sir—but what for?'' Kristy asked, bemused at these mercurial changes.

A mischievous grin transformed his sobering mein. ''We're playing hookey, Mermaid,'' he said in a conspiratorial whisper. He swung out the cottage door with a jaunty wave, leaving her again standing in open-mouthed surprise.

An unbecomingly short time later, Kristy burst into her bedroom to shed her dress for white slacks and a red and white striped polo shirt. She ought not to feel so excited at the prospect of spending time alone with him, but there was no getting around the fact that she did. Her eyes were sparkling with it, huge and luminously green in her flushed face. Well, she genuinely

143

needed a break, Kristy offered as an excuse, and a few hours of playing hookey would be marvelously restorative, especially if she lent herself to his escapist frame of mind.

Kristy unfastened three buttons and tucked the lovely blue pearl into the shadowed cleft between her breasts, stroked perfume to throbbing pulse points, combed out her hair and tied it back with a silk scarf folded to a band and unearthed her battered sandals. Then, feeling as happy and carefree as a child, she skimmed the distance to the lobby on winged feet.

Jason was engaged with a group of workmen, his long finger stabbing a blueprint as he cleared up a point of confusion. Kristy waited at the door, disinclined to advertise their outing. Considering their employer's lusty virility, Kristy could not blame Jason's crew for their furtive speculations, but she was careful not to encourage it. Referring to him as Mr. Thorne had become second nature by now, and she never flew off the handle in public. Even if it meant biting through her tongue, she managed a respectful *no sir* or *yes sir*, which she believed Jason enjoyed no end. Jason was frowning as he walked towards her, his expression absolutely severe—except for the madly dancing eyes.

"You ready, Mermaid?" he murmured as they walked sedately to his Cadillac.

"Ready for what?" she murmured back.

"Just trust me, Kristin. Remember I know best," Jason adjured.

I trust you far too much already, thought Kristy, but the rueful thought winked out under the force of that

144

outrageous conceit.

Before she had her seat belt fastened, they were heading down the road at an unnerving speed. When Jason heard her strangled gasp, he murmured, "Sorry. I get carried away at times. Fast cars are one of my pleasures."

"And fast women?" she flashed, enboldened by his good humor.

"Um, those too," he said with a sidelong glance and that maddening grin. "But fear not, I handle both with excellence."

The remark was so audacious, she burst out laughing. "You're dreadfully conceited, Mr. Thorne," she sniffed.

"Nonsense, Mermaid, just terribly honest," he reproved, and she was helplessly laughing again. "And when are you going to cease with this Mr. Thorne stuff, hmm?" He shot a scowl her way.

"And when are you going to cease with this Mermaid stuff, hmm?"

"It fits so well," Jason sighed. "I've heard that a real mermaid is one of the most difficult of women to catch, and then to tame. A tantalizing, maddening creature, often reputed to drive men out of their minds. And often thoroughly disagreeable, too," he warned, cutting her a glance.

Having no suitable reply for his most startling descriptives, Kristy merely laughed. She leaned her head back against the seat and turned a fraction, to study him from under shielding lashes. He had exchanged his khakis for a white terry pullover and worn denim jeans, yet that exciting air of authority was clearly there. *What a complex man he was*, thought Kristy. She had sat quietly at staff meetings and marveled at the way he handled his people. He was unmistakably a leader, hard, shrewd, exacting; capable of icy reproof at incompetence, yet warmly bestowing praise when praise was merited. A totally dominant personality, she had to admit, taking in the determined line of jaw, the strong, tanned hands on the steering wheel. The Cadillac responded to his touch as obediently as a woman.

She was startled when he suddenly reached over and pulled the scarf from her hair. "Gorgeous hair is supposed to blow in the wind," he admonished, grinning as the red-gold mass whipped wildly around her face. Kristy caught it back and tried to scowl at him, but he was looking too pleased with himself, and she felt too wonderful. Suddenly they were both wonderfully relaxed with each other, and this simple joy spilled laughter through her lips.

"You think I have gorgeous hair, do you?" She hated it as soon as it was out—it was coy female begging for a compliment. Tossing her head, she stretched out her legs and smoothed her slacks over firm hips, hoping he would let it pass. A forlorn hope.

"Yes, Mermaid, gorgeous hair you've got." But nothing else, his tone said. She blushed furiously. He roared with laughter, then pointedly eyed her pouted lips before letting his gaze trail down to the creamy swells of her breasts.

"Keep your eyes on the road," she ordered severely.

"Yes, ma'am," said Jason.

146

It was all delicious fun. Casting aside his recent brusque manner, Jason had once again become a heart-catchingly attractive man, the one who laughed and teased and charmed a woman into a puddle of servile feminity begging to kiss his long, slender feet! Kristy tried desperately to maintain the guard she automatically erected whenever she came into his presence. But she was itchingly conscious of his dark, powerful virility, and the handsome face, alight with enjoyment, played havoc with her senses.

She had learned, through newspaper items and the usual staff gossip, that he was solidly established in the higher echelons of Island society, that he was thirty-three and the youngest of three brothers, and that his business acumen was respected nearly as much as his expertise with lovely women. The latter had come from Ben Soames, more jest than not. She had tried, casually and with utmost discretion, to pump Ben for information and gotten nowhere; Ben respected a person's privacy, too. She ought to, but womanlike, the paucity of her knowledge pricked her. More than pricked her, she admitted, the need to know all about Jason Thorne was curiously like a craving. To *know* the man concealed behind the softly cynical smile . . .

"Cousin Flora would love this!" she said to cover her thoughts.

"Would she! Tell me about Cousin Flora," he commanded, and she spilled over with more than he could ever want to know about Cousin Flora. Looking sheepishly aware of it, she stopped in mid-sentence. Jason laughed and squeezed her hand, seeming not at all put out about this flood of personal details concerning a stranger.

"She sounds like a lovely person," he said.

Absurdly pleased, Kristy said proudly, "She is a lovely person. We're much alike." She blushed at his grin. "I mean, we're much alike in size and appearance. My mother was tall and slim and very beautiful. Oh my goodness, what a lovely tree! what is it?" She gushed so wildly, he smiled.

"A plumera," he gravely answered, knowing full well she already knew this. "Your cousin resembles you?"

"Yes, she's tiny and has blond hair, but her eyes are gray. I have my father's eyes . . . and Uncle Alex's," she said faintly.

"So I noticed. And does Cousin Flora have your terrible temper?"

"Uh, no, she's very quiet and mild mannered—but I don't ordinarily display temper, Jason. It's you. Sometimes I think you deliberately try to provoke my temper."

Jason looked at her with astonishment. "Why, Mermaid! I assure you that's the furthest thing from my mind."

As they wended their way through the beautiful valley, they laughed and joked and parried, and the pleasure of it played on her spine like caressing fingers. Suddenly made aware of having opened a sealed-off part of herself to him, Kristy felt a quiver of fear. She glanced at the strong profile. It would be appallingly easy to fall in love with such a man. And utterly disasterous, she reminded her fluttering heart. Thank heavens she was immune.

Jason turned to her with a smile just then, and her immunity fell ten whole points. "Have you lunched yet?" he asked.

"No, I forgot lunch," she confessed.

"Mermaid, I keep telling you, you can't afford to miss a meal,' he scolded with a worried glance down her skinny little body.

When they entered the small restaurant he chose, Jason was warmly greeted by the owner, and led to a choice table secluded by palms and tall, pedestaled urns holding an extravagance of flowering plants. Assuring them she would prepare a feast worthy of his presence in her humble establishment, the triple-chinned proprietress floated across the floor in her spectacular muumuu like a flow of lava.

"Worthy of your presence?' Kristy leaned close to him and murmured.

Jason cocked an eyebrow and looked stern and noble. "Certainly. Do learn from that, Kristy," he urged.

They had avocado halves stuffed with delectable crab salad, succulent prawns sauteed in garlic butter and dill, and an enormous medley of crisply cooked vegetables, *laulau*—which were spicy bits of pork, fish and taro shoots steamed in *ti* leaves and utterly delicious, and effervescent streams of laughter, which were even more so. They ate until it was impossible to hold another morsel, but when Jason requested the check, they received instead two hefty slices of passion fruit chiffon pie, *manawahi* (gratis) from the enamored proprietress.

"I can't possibly eat that," Kristy groaned.

"You have to. Would you offend our charming friend?" Jason hissed. "Eat. It goes down like a breath of air—you'll see." Scowling at her rebellious pout, he picked up her fork and forced a bit between her lips. It went down like a breath of air.

As they left the restaurant, a forlorn sliver of sanity squeaked for attention. Kristy felt rather sorry for the puny little thing. She knew herself utterly incapable of resisting the sheer delight of this day.

Chapter Eight

After crossing the Wailau River, Jason turned onto King's Highway with no sign of stopping. "Do we have a destination?" Kristy finally asked.

"Un hmm, we do, several of them. Be there shortly." Jason chuckled as her enjoyment splashed all over his car. The ridge-hugging road overlooked a breathtaking vista. He drove slowly, pointing out points of interest, and detailing the intriguing history which accompanied them.

"You certainly seem to know the islands," she complimented.

"I should. I was born here, as was my father before me, and his father before him," he said lightly.

"A *kamaaina* family," she said so knowingly, he

chuckled. "Your parents—where do they live?"

"They've a home on Molokai . . . near Kaunakakai. It's a lovely place," he said absently.

Kristy waited. "Well, go on," she demanded. She listened, curiously entranced as he obliged. His family were indeed *kamaaina*; his maternal great-grandfather had built a portion of that lovely manor home on Molokai. As he described it, Kristy's imagination kept pace, until she could almost envision the many cool, shadowed rooms with their teakwood floors and hand-carved ceiling fans, the verandas encircling it, the lush green lawns sweeping down to a private lake complete with swans. He told her about the stables they maintained, the sleek stallions and mares gained through generations of select breeding, the lovely morning rides through miniature jungles sparkling with sunshine on dew-wet foliage. Then there was the sailboat three young boys steered through impossibly rough seas, the outings to the summer cottage located on the west end of the island on a private beach of white sand checkered with jagged outcroppings of black lava. Casually, he mentioned the servants, the private schools, the thoughtless vacations in Europe and the splendor of an eighty-foot yacht they enjoyed for many years before it broke up on reef in the Bahamas, never to be replaced, much to Jason's regret. It was a lifestyle beyond the scope of Kristy's imagination, and light years removed from her own middleclass existence.

Too absorbed to notice their surroundings, she was surprised when Jason stopped the car. "Here we are, Wailau Falls. I think you'll like this," he ordered.

152

"You think right," Kristy whispered as she gazed at the eighty-foot cascade which spilled down with singing abandon on the rocks far below. It dwarfed her private waterfall to a mere drip from a faucet.

Like the man beside her, it was both fascinating and frightening in its awesome power, Kristy thought. Jason stood tall and quiet, his dark face somber as he gazed at the perpetually flowing waters. When she shivered in the moist wind blowing off the falls, his arm encircled her shoulders. Feeling keenly alive, Kristy leaned back into his casual embrace.

"What's next?" she eagerly inquired when they returned to the car. "The Fern Grotto, complete with boat ride," Jason promised the sparkling green eyes.

The enchantment of this day spun into a golden web that held Kristy enrapt. From its starting point at the Wailua Marina, the flat-top boat glided between green river banks festooned with a glorious tangle of vines and trees. Kristy lamented aloud—several times, in fact—her stupidity in forgetting her camera. Although the captain spun some fascinating legends about the area, Jason's soft, running monologue was much more interesting.

"*Pili* grass," he identified the lush greenery carpeting the bank. "Once used for Hawaiian houses, you know; *The little grass shacks of Oahu!*" His sing-song voice delighted Kristy, as did the roguish grin that accompanied it. What she wanted just then, achingly, was to reach up and hug him. Oblivious of the affection flooding through her, Jason pointed to the caves in the high bluffs they were passing. "Royal burial grounds,"

153

he murmured.

A sobering thought. Turning from him, Kristy gratefully touched earth again. But not for long. He was simply too appealing. Why? *Oh, who cares!* she thought, impatient at her constant hedging, and turned back to him with open enjoyment.

At the upstream landing, Jason took her arm for the short walk to the Grotto. Again she marveled at her reaction to his most casual touch, a tingling warmth which seemed to radiate through her body from that central point. She wondered if he felt it. Apparently not; when she glanced up at him, his gaze was on the dense jungle growth which enshrouded the narrow trail.

Aptly named, the Fern Grotto was a cool, damp cave roofed with ferns. Kristy was already exclaiming over the monstrous fishtail palms which screened the entrance when she stepped inside the naturally formed amphitheater . . . her gasp of astonishment tickled Jason into a soft burst of laughter. She shivered, perhaps from the cool dampness, perhaps for another reason. At any rate, Jason wrapped his arms around her midriff and pulled her back against him.

Shocked at her unseemly lack of caution, Kristy nonetheless permitted this intimacy. When a Hawaiian chorus began to serenade, her head tipped back on his shoulder, and his clean-shaven cheek lay gently against hers for a moment. At first she enjoyed the feel of him pressing lightly against her. But when his arms tightened, she began to experience an amorphous sense of panic, and remembered she never had been too fond of

154

caves. Finally she suggested they leave before the others.

Jason was agreeable. When they emerged from the shadows into sunlight, he smiled at her and said, "We have time to explore if you'd like?"

Feeling a little ashamed of her incipient panic, Kristy gave a vigorous nod that set her hair to bouncing. Jason grinned and took her hand, lacing his fingers with hers as they began exploring the surrounding area. She was enthralled by the lush, tropical vegetation. All around them were shimmering bursts of color; red, pinks and yellow, and a fluorescent orange that turned out to be the center of a bromiliad with infinitely tiny, neon-blue flowers studding its vivid funnel. "Oh why didn't I bring my camera!" wailed Kristy.

Jason's delighted laughter rolled forth. When he caught her waist to lift her over a lichen-covered log, he held her off the ground and lightly kissed her. "Now it's *de rigueur* for this spot," he said quickly. "Every woman who comes here must be kissed, or else be sacrificed to Pele!"

"I thought Pele was the goddess of the volcano," she said suspiciously. "Her influence extends this far?"

"Oh yes, anywhere there's fire," Jason blandly assured. His hands slipped into her hair and drew her lips to his again, in a long, sweetly tender kiss. Kristy permitted it. It simply went with the moment.

Her lashes fanned up as he drew back. "Pele again?" she asked breathlessly.

Jason's gentle smile completely disarmed her. "No, Kristy, me this time." He knelt and picked a salmon

155

pink flower and ceremoniously wove its long stem into her hair. "There," he said with such vast satisfaction, she laughed aloud.

"Is this *de rigueur* too?" she mischievously inquired.

"Certainly. A woman with no flower in her hair is suspected of having an evil nature, which would, of course, shrivel the flower immediately and proclaim to all the world her shrewishness."

"You're making that up!" Kristy accused, frowning at the tall, slim man whose sideburns curled in damp little wisps.

"I am not," Jason denied. He peered worriedly at the flower stuck in her hair. "I think it's beginning to wilt already!"

Oh God, how lovely this was! So happy it scared her, Kristy stuck her pretty little nose in the air. "Ha! Let's just see how quickly it wilts in your hair," she retorted. Taking the flower from her hair, she held it to his. "Oh my goodness, it's wilting in mid-air!" she said so incredulously, he laughed and scooped her up again.

"Men are never shrewish, Mermaid," Jason scolded. Kristy lost her breath as she gazed into dancing blue eyes now level with her own. She wound her arms loosely around his neck. "Of course not. Only quarrelsome, aggressive, pugnacious, cantankerous—"

"Come along, we've seen enough here. We're going to miss the boat," Jason said sternly. Placing her sedately aground again, he steered her back towards the trail. His arm curved around her waist to tuck her into his side, and again, Kristy permitted it. Knowing she was behaving too freely did little to correct it. *When*

156

she was with this man, she stepped into another dimension not subject to the laws of the natural world, she thought wryly.

Laughing, hand in hand, they ran the last few feet to the landing. Jason looked so young and carefree, and she was so headily responsive to it, Kristy made an effort to bring herself down from this dangerous height. Part of her knew the danger she was courting, but the other part whispered—LET IT COME!

Withdrawing from him, she leaned against the rail and silently watched the river. A warm brown hand covered hers. Kristy, in a confusion of feelings, smiled at him and moved closer until his lean, hard thigh braced hers. The sensuality between them flowed with the slow, invisible sureness of an underground stream.

Once back in the car, their next stop mystified her. After several miles of lazily quiet driving, he turned into a curving lane and drew up before an obviously new house. Reaching behind the seat, he took up a roll of banded blueprints and opened the car door. "Come along, Mermaid," he commanded when she made no move to join him.

Kristy followed him inside the structure. Waving a hand about the imposing entry, he smiled and said, "My home, Kristy."

"Your home! You're building this house?" Kristy exclaimed.

"Yes, I am. Would you like to see it?"

"Very much," Kristy said. She thrilled to the lovely, contemporary dwelling, all clean lines and graceful angles, with soaring banks of windows taking advantage of the magnificent hilltop view. The towering wall of glass at the rear of the den rose nearly sheer to a sixty-foot peak. Square in the center of this peak was an exquisite brushed-chrome and stained-glass chandelier suspended on a twenty-foot glass chain, the whole of it shaped like a circular cascade of irridescent water.

"What do you think of that?" Jason asked as they stood gazing up at this stunning object.

"I think it's the most beautiful thing I've ever seen," Kristy reverently replied. "Anything that lovely doesn't actually supply light, does it?"

Jason laughed softly. "It does. Or will, when the time comes. I have a friend who specializes in this sort of work. I designed it, he created it."

"Then together, you and your friend created a masterpiece," Kristy assured. Her heart was pounding out the question: Who would live with him in this lovely home? Shanna? Had he designed the chandelier with her in mind?

"And this is my study," Jason said, towing her into a darkly paneled room. Two walls were lined with floor to ceiling bookcases, the third a solid expanse of glass, but the fourth wall was bare. Kristy knew, with absolute certainty, what should go on that empty wall. The picture of her *iliau* plant. It had arrived last week and it was breathtaking, an impossibly complex simplicity of shape and color, stark, voluptuous, as diametrically opposed as velvet and iron. She had chosen an inordinately expensive, very thin, chased aluminum frame at the time, and now she knew why. For this room! For this man! She would give to him the day she left Kauai,

158

Kristy instantly decided.

Shaken by the intensity of her pleasure, she teasingly asked, "Do you smoke a pipe? This rooms demands it, you know."

"I'll learn," Jason said. "Come along, there's lots more to see."

They explored the fifteen room house, every nook and cranny of it. Kristy's febrile imagination added the missing appliances in the sunny kitchen, filled the three cornered window above the sink with African violets, draped the four multi-paned dining room windows in the filmiest of pale yellow dacron, mentally carpeted and painted and papered—another woman's house.

The master bedroom suite was immensely pleasing, the jacuzzi equipped bathroom a designer's dream of marbled elegance. She finally stopped exclaiming and walked quietly beside him, nodding as he pointed out details.

If it were mine, I would put the bed between those two east windows, capture the sunrise with mirrors, . . . ran her private thoughts. But it wasn't hers. Strange how much that stung.

"Would you like to see the architect's sketch?" he said with a charming touch of diffidence. Then, without waiting for a response, Jason steered her outside again, heading towards an enormous tulip tree which had showered the grass with glistening red blossoms. Wild red ginger fanned out around it, a romp of sweet smelling, white panicled clematis made of the spot a natural bower. Disregarding possible damage to her white slacks, he pulled her down beside him and spread out the sketch.

"It's so beautiful, Jason," Kristy said softly. She leaned closer, their shoulders rubbing as his finger moved over the accompanying blueprint, pointing out with endearing pride his own personal touches. Kristy stayed close to him, asking questions with unfeigned interest, although never the one that clamored for release.

Time drifted by as effortlessly as the evening shadows falling upon them. A knowledgeable engineer in his own right, Jason grew absorbed in explaining to her the many hidden strengths of his house, and Kristy's lively interest spurred him on. At length, he re-rolled the blueprints and slipped on the heavy rubber band. Kristy wrapped her arms around her knees and lay her cheek on them, her eyes soft and reflective.

"Why are you building a house? You have that condo on Kauai," she said.

"Yes, I do. I maintain residences in several cities," Jason said matter-of-factly. "But they're condominiums, apartments, hotel suites—investments, in the long run. But this is a house—a home." His eyes crinkled, and her reaction was as inevitable as that boyish grin that could melt vital connections. "I may take up gardening, or raising goldfish in my ornamental pond which will be right down there, complete with fountains. You like fountains?"

"I adore fountains. I also adore gardening. But I can hardly picture *you* taking up gardening, or even raising goldfish," she laughed.

"And how do you picture me?" Jason asked.

"Hard work and hard play, one as structured as the other . . . certainly not the goldfish type," she teased. The deep cleft in his chin captured her eyes. She wanted, desperately, to place her mouth just there.

"Oh, I have many hidden traits, some no one knows about," Jason countered, laughing, but the crystal blue eyes were somber.

Kristy idly gazed about. At the extreme rear of the lawn, adjacent to a large flagstone terrace, she spied a deep excavation. A pool, she supposed. Her voice was musing. "And this house, do you plan to stock it with anything besides goldfish? Like a wife, for example."

"Um, that's possible. A man needs a wife, I'm told." He grinned in that inimitable way. "Personally I haven't figured out exactly why, but I bow to my superiors."

Kristy stretched out her legs and gazed off across the valley. The question she itched to ask came out a very watered-down version. "You don't want to get married?"

"Of course I do. Just as soon as I discover a reason why," he drawled.

"I'm serious, Jason."

He shrugged. "It isn't something I've sat and pondered, Kristy. I guess I've gone on the assumption that when it happens, it happens. Sort of a natural function . . . like getting bald."

"Have you any candidates? Like your fire-breathing Shanna, for instance," she said, casually.

"An odds-on favorite, according to various people," he said dryly.

An ambiguous reply, at best. She glanced at him with affected amusement. "Is she the only one?"

He laughed deeply and plucked a tiny white flower, twirling it around by the stem. "Ah, Mermaid, a man has to sample many flowers before he decides which one to pluck and keep, don't you agree?" Cynical blue eyes gleamed between his thick, sooty lashes. "How else is he to know which is the sweetest of all?"

He just wasn't going to be serious, Kristy conceded. "I reckon so," she said.

"I reckon so," Jason softly mocked. "My oldest brother is working on his third marriage . . . up to his ears in alimony," he added with a twist of lips.

"It doesn't have to be that way," Kristy quietly refuted.

Jason shrugged. "Perhaps not. My other brother, Rand, has been married twelve years to the same woman . . . two kids . . ." His eyes darkening, he studied her quiet face. It was nearly dusk, and the hazy blue stillness around them was almost palpable as they stared at each other. The tension building between them set her blood to racing. Kristy pushed at her hair.

"Perhaps we'd best be getting back. It's getting late," she suggested.

"We have plenty of time," Jason said huskily. Gentle fingers grasped her chin, overcoming her token resistance, sliding up to cradle her face in an infinitely tender gesture. Kristy froze to utter stillness as his mouth came to her, lightly, testingly. And again. On a swift, indrawn breath, Jason pulled her roughly into his arms.

"No—stop it, Jason," she said, twisting her

face aside.

"Why, Mermaid?" he murmured. "Don't you like my kisses?"

"To be blunt, no, I don't," Kristy defensively lied.

His mouth brushed her ear, easing under her hair to taste sweetly sensitive flesh. "Ah Kristy, I'm having a hard time believing that," he chided.

The tremors rippling under her skin were telling testimony to his doubts. Aggravated at this wholly involuntary reaction to his caressing mouth, Kristy sought to steady her reserve, but the tantalizing kisses traveling up her throat evoked a shaky breath rather than the stinging reprimand she truly meant to make. She wanted to pull him to her . . . to push him away—

Jason's mouth caught hers with breathtaking urgency. Turning her unresisting body to conform to his, he lowered her into the velvety grass.

"Jason—Jason, don't," she half moaned. Acutely aware of the urgent pressure of his body, Kristy spread her hands flat out on his shoulders in chaotic denial. He responded to her protest with soft, tiny kisses on her face, her neck, the wildly pulsing hollow of her throat, moving down to the neckline of her sweater. He nuzzled under it, kissing deeper and deeper. She felt his tongue slide between her breasts, heard his thick whisper. "Oh Kristy, you taste so good, so good . . ." When he raised his head and looked down at her, she experienced again the dizzying sensation of sinking deep into the depths of his eyes.

"Jason, please," she choked.

"So lovely," came his husky whisper. His eyes

163

touched her face with physical impact, caressing, dark with arousal. Slowly his mouth descended on hers.

Kristy felt in dire need of both breath and willpower. From the very beginning she had tried to deny this primitive response to Jason Thorne, and from the beginning, she had failed miserably, just as she was failing now. Steve's kisses had been stirring; Jason's were intensely passionate and demanding, and they simply shattered her senses. His mouth left hers. Dazedly she looked up at his intense face.

"Ah Mermaid, sweet sweet Mermaid, I want you," Jason whispered. He laughed, a soft, husky sound aimed at himself. "What have you done to me, Kristin Loring? I thought I was far past the age for making love in the grass," he murmured, and sought her lips again.

"Jason, don't," she said, turning aside.

"Kristy, why not? What's the harm? We're both adults, free to enjoy this," Jason coaxed. Wordlessly, she shook her head. Jason placed his mouth at the corner of her lips, a tantalizing torment as his husky voice vibrated on her skin. "Kristy, my fiery little Kristy . . . I know it's there, I've tasted it, felt it—felt your wanting," came his seductive whisper.

Kristy could close her eyes to his face, but she could not close out that erotic voice. "Not for you," she lied, fighting the fierce urge to turn in to his mouth.

"Yes, for me. Ah baby, don't be afraid of this, of me. It can be so good," Jason whispered. "Let me love you like I want, like you need to be loved. Let me show you, teach you—" his mouth slid over hers with sensual persuasion.

In Kristy's spinning mind, his seductive voice clashed with his careless words about sampling many *flowers* before he decided which to pluck and keep. That innocuous little description of his sexual pleasures was murderously enraging to Kristy. *What he wanted had nothing to do with love,* she thought bitterly. A flood of disappointment, unnamed but intense, stung her eyes.

"It isn't love you want to teach me," she said, low and fierce. Ignoring his startled look, she shoved at his shoulders. Fury spiraled up, fed by her own shame at being so responsive to his practiced kisses. "You don't know the first thing about love!" she spat with cutting scorn.

Despite her squirming, Jason held her easily enough. His eyes darkly blue, he regarded her stormy face. "Perhaps I don't, but I wasn't speaking of love, I was referring to something entirely different," he said softly.

His puzzled look reinforced Kristy's anger. Was sex so incidental and routine, so commonplace and meaningless, that he was honestly perplexed at her reaction? He sat up with a careless shrug, the dark silky head bent to conceal his face. "But if you prefer to deny us a great deal of pleasure—"

Stung to the quick, Kristy flared to boiling point in half a second's time. "A great deal of pleasure? That's a trifle presumptuous, isn't it?" She flung the contemptuous words in the face which suddenly snapped towards her.

Jason smiled thinly. "Well now, there's only one way to find out, isn't there, Kristy."

"I told you once that it wasn't worth the bother of finding out, remember? Really, Jason, what's so hard to understand about that? I simply don't want to make love with you. You're an attractive, exciting man, but it takes more than surface looks to—I just don't want you that much," Kristy snapped.

His eyes narrowed, intense blue lights as he stared at her. Jason suddenly laughed, a dangerously soft sound that chilled her blood. "Is that so," he said, very softly. "You're a poor liar, Kristy, remember I warned you about that? And didn't I also warn you about challenging me, hmm?"

"Oh, don't be absurd. I'm not challenging, I'm simply stating a fact," she snapped out.

His jaw tightened. "Are you? Let's just test that fact, Kristy," Jason said, still dangerously soft and mild. Catching her hands, he drew her arms over her head and held them with one big hand around her wrists. "That's enough, Jason!" Kristy flared. "Ah no," he whispered. Holding her with one arm across her midriff, Jason bent his head and set his mouth on hers in a punishing kiss.

Kristy twisted against his clasp, but that arm was a steel band curved across her body. Hoping to defeat him with passive resistance, she went limp for a moment, but the urge to respond to him was overwhelmingly strong. Jason released her hands, smiling against her lips as her fingers promptly curved into his hair. Kristy sensed that triumphant smile, yet despite her surge of anger, what began as a furious protest came out a soft, yearning moan.

She turned into him, and his kiss deepened into searing passion. She was powerless to resist the electric thrill of his mouth moving hungrily on hers. Rapacious, demanding, his tongue thrust in, probing the moist sweetness of her, plunging deep as their bodies melted together. The lean, taut length of him molded to her yielding softness, flowing into receptive curves and hollows, while his hands moved slowly down her, caressingly, curving around her hips to press her hard against him.

Drowning in erotic pleasure, Kristy wound her arms around him, her fingers thrusting deep into the thickness of his hair. Waves of warm, tingling excitement poured through her, and their passionate kisses went on until she was breathless and trembling under his marauding hands. Hands that knew her breasts, her hips, the soft curves of her inner thighs, caressing her desire to fever pitch, until she moaned and pulled him tightly into her, molding her body to the throbbing heat of his passion.

His ragged groan swelled through her as they came together in blind, seeking urgency. Caught up in the tumultuous sensations hammering at her senses, Kristy shuddered with pleasure, yet when Jason's searching hands moved to the waistband of her slacks, fumbling blindly at the double buttons which secured them, an icy shred of reason penetrated her passion-fogged mind, as shocking as an icicle suddenly pressed against her fevered skin.

Kristy's voice rose to a muffled scream as bitter awareness crashed in. Furiously she shoved at his shoulders, her hands balling into fists. "Stop it! Stop it, Jason!" she hissed, escaping his possessive mouth.

Jason's reaction struck her like a dash of cold water. He drew back from her and laughed, low and deep and vindicated, his jagged breathing the only sign of the passion she had aroused. Kristy sought something to say . . . anything that would wound him, shred that infuriating confidence!

"How dare you hold me against my will!" she gasped between hard little breaths. "You *took*—you weren't *given!*" she charged wildly.

"Now, Mermaid, are you trying to provoke me a-gain?" he chided, but something hard and dangerous moved in those glinting blue eyes. A muscle ticked in his jaw, slow and steady as he regarded her. He came to his knees, a thin smile curling round his mouth. Cocking his head, Jason managed to look both impressed and sardonic. "You play the outraged virgin very well, Kristy, a better performance I've yet to see," he applauded.

Gasping with shock, Kristy grappled with the fierce urge to slap that laughing face! But she would not be driven to such typical female behavior! "Let me go!" she gritted.

"Certainly," said Jason. Bounding to his feet, he looked at her with impatience, and something else she could not fathom. "Well, get up. It's time we got back to the hotel," he reminded. When she just lay there staring at him, her green eyes enormous with confusion, he caught her hand and roughly pulled her up. "Dammit, I said come on!" he grated.

The abrupt transition from insouciance to anger only served to heighten her confusion. Trembling with reaction, Kristy walked ahead of him to the car, her cheeks flaming and her hands tightly clenched. *Oh God*, she thought, *I've made a fool of myself!* And why was that so important? She had always coveted Steve's pride in her, of course, but on the main, his opinion didn't matter all that much—she knew what she was. But Jason's opinion mattered very, very much, and she ached to show him the sophisticated composure he knew in other women. Instead, she had reacted like a—*like an outraged virgin*.

Jason followed at a more leisurely pace. "You have grass stains on the seat of your slacks," she heard him comment. Heavily conscious of her swaying hips, Kristy made it to the car without exploding, and half fell into the seat.

Jason got in beside her. "I hope you're not going to sulk," he remarked.

Desperate to recoup her dignity, Kristy smoothed her disheveled hair. "Oh, of course not," she said crisply. "You forgot your blueprints, Jason."

She stared straight ahead as he swore softly, then slammed the door and strode back to the tulip tree. How could he so easily dismiss what had just happened between them? Humiliated at his unperturbed manner, Kristy adjusted her rumpled clothing, wondering what on earth she was going to say to him when he returned.

Chapter Nine

She need not have worried. As they started back to the hotel, Jason reverted to the faintly sardonic manner that characterized their relationship. Although her mind kept straying like a rambunctious infant, Kristy followed his lead, and their conversation was free of personal inflections.

But beneath her stoic calmness, confusion was having an orgy. Hurt and anger jockeyed with distrust, uncertainity, self-disgust . . . Oh God, what a grand potpourri of emotions! Kristy felt a wild urge to giggle. Instead she turned her face to the window and closed her eyes as Jason withdrew into brooding silence. *If she'd only relinquish her blind anger, things would fall into perspective,* Kristy told herself. After all, what had happened? Jason had wanted to make love; she had not. That's all. See how simple it is, Kristy? Nothing hard to understand about that. As Steve would say, no big deal—what are you getting so worked up about?

Steve's face flitted across her mind, amused, scornful, pained. *For God's sake, Kristy, grow up!*

Overreacting, pure and simple, Kristy, she lashed herself. And she was so mad her teeth hurt.

"Kristy, you aren't still upset, are you?" Jason asked quietly, and Kristy, exceedingly upset, said she wasn't upset at all.

"I'm just tired," she said after another silence. She had not realized how tired until now. Dispirited, she watched the hotel come into view with a deep sense of relief. Getting away from Jason without further embarrassment was top priority right now. She still felt explosive and in no mood to be sensible about anything.

She glanced at Jason's inscrutable face with a kind of bitter envy. How lovely it must be to feel nothing deeply, to react with annoyance and actually feel that way when someone hurt or disappointed you! Oh, that wasn't fair, Kristy grudingly admitted, remembering his concern about his mother. Wearily she raised both hands to her face and brushed back the damp wisps of hair.

"Let me out near the cottage, please? I left my handbag there," she said.

When Jason obligingly stopped beneath the banyan tree, he stayed her move to the door. "Did you enjoy the drive?" he asked, mildly.

"Yes, very much. Up until today, I've stayed so busy,

I really haven't seen much of the area," Kristy calmly replied. "Thank you—it was a lovely day." *My, how grown up, Katie,* she thought sourly.

A wry smile thinned Jason's mouth. "Yes, a lovely day. Could have been even lovelier," he murmured as if to himself.

Green eyes flashed. "Jason, let's get one thing straight right now! I will not continue working for a man who has no respect for—" Incredulous, Kristy listened to her rising voice. She was going off *again!* How could he so easily infuriate her? Wasn't it enough that he stalked her dreams, that he was in her bed every blasted night of the week! Blushing hotly at this unfortunate phrasing, she glanced at him, and choked on a shriek of fury. Jason was struggling with the laughter twitching his mouth, and it was quite possible she would slap him if she remained in this car another second. *This blasted temper of mine!* she thought wildly.

Katie groped for composure. "Jason, I'm a lady and—"

"Yes, you are. And someday you might even become a woman," he assured her gravely which drove her over the edge.

"That does it! I quit!" she half shouted. "You can take this job and—and—" Furiously she scrabbled for the door handle. "I shall be on the plane for Texas first thing in the morning."

"Mermaid, I reallly do not have time to go to Texas to abduct fiery little women," Jason drawled.

Astonished, she stared at him. "Why would you even want to?" she asked in mad confusion.

His smile vanished. Kristy was looking into steel blue eyes which gave no quarter. "Because *I* say where anyone goes and when, Kristy. You made a verbal contract, which is, to me, just as binding as a written one. You will *not* quit, you have a job to do and you're going to stay here and do it. Is that clear?"

"It's perfectly clear, but on condition. You will not just grab me and kiss me whenever you feel the urge," she said just as flatly.

"Afraid, Mermaid? Not so invincible after all?" Jason taunted softly.

"Not at all," she flared. Mustering her wits about her, Kristy tried to make a sensible statement without sounding abrasive or hysterical. "Jason, as an employer, I find you satisfactory. As a person, I like you. But as a man, I . . . Your kisses are neither desired nor feared, I simply find it repellent that they seem to come with the job, and I'd rather walk out on a contract, verbal or otherwise, than put up with your uninvited passes. Please don't feel you're being singled out. I've had to handle similar situations with the same ultimatum. I mean it, Jason. There will be no more of it."

Unwavering, she held the flat blue gaze. *She must have scratched his ego,* she thought, his skin was tinged with gray under his tan.

Jason shrugged. "Very well, Kristy, no more of it. I think I can survive the strain." Insolently, his eyes raked over her. "Can you?"

"I'm quite certain I shall be able to restrain my wild yearnings," she said, acidly amused. "Then it's settled?"

"It's settled," he said lightly. Leaning around her, Jason opened her door, then drew back with his face just inches from hers. The smile that thinned his lips did nothing to cut the chill set of his features. "Until you provoke me, of course. Then I can't be held accountable, can I."

"I do not deliberately provoke you—"

"Oh, yes you do, Kristy, oh yes you do," he said very softly.

His breath brushed her face as hooded blue eyes probed like searching fingers. The small space separating them was suddenly charged with electric tension. Alarmed by something she did not understand, Kristy made a small sound in her throat. Jason sat back and flexed his fingers around the steering wheel, that odd little smile still lifting the corners of his mouth.

"If so, I assure you it is unintentional. Thank you for the drive," Kristy said with mechanical courtesy. She was beyond confusion.

Another shrug. "Anytime, Kristy."

Fighting the urge to run, Kristy walked stiffly from the car. The proud carriage she affected was a natural defiance to the eyes she sensed following her slim figure. She was walking too fast, struggling with tears; she saw Ben in the most peripheral sense and turned her to smile at him. The familiar sharp wrench of pain sent her stumbling to her knees, too fast for the instinctive outthrust of hands that would break her fall. Her head glanced off a sharp stub of a twig as she rolled to one hip.

Katie groaned deep in her throat; what a time for that

174

treacherous ankle to turn on her! Balanced on one hip, she groped for the source of stinging pain, and whimpered at the blood on her fingertips. Dazedly she looked up at the two tall forms looming over her. There was Ben's concerned voice, and Jason's sharp oath. Then his incomparable scent as strong arms lifted her, cradling her close to his chest; her hair cascading down his shoulder. Jason swore, softly, fiercely, under his breath.

"Put me down, I'm all right," Kristy protested. "Oh, will you put me down!"

"Stop squirming, dammit!" Jason snarled. He carried her to a bedroom and laid her down on the pale coverlet which would be terribly stained and she tried to tell someone that, but that someone angrily told her to shut up and lie back down. Only then did Kristy realize that she was in her beloved cottage.

"Here, let me, I've had some experience with wounds. It's just a small cut," Ben said as he gently probed through her hair. His face leaning close to hers, he asked softly, "Why were you running, honey?" Kristy heard something odd in his voice, but she could not pinpoint it.

"Miss Loring and I had a disagreement," Jason coldly supplied.

"I asked Miss Loring, didn't I," Ben mildly countered.

"Just feminine reaction to a . . . disagreement, Ben," Kristy said. "I'm all right."

"Certainly you're all right," Ben agreed.

"There's a first aid kit in my car," Jason said.

"Then get it. But first, wet this," Ben ordered, handing him his handkerchief. *If she could die and do it gracefully, she would,* Katie thought with grinding humor, but as it was, she closed her eyes and let whatever was going to happen, happen. She heard the sound of running water, then Jason's footsteps pounding from the bedroom, and impossibly quick, returning again. She felt Ben's tender touch and the wetness of his handkerchief sponging the tiny cut. Jason left again. Ben dried the wound and touched it with disinfectant.

"Ouch!" Kristy said. "Oh, hush," Ben scolded. When he had completed his task, he stood aside in belated deference to Jason, who sauntered back in with the blackest of scowls. Kristy's eyes promptly closed against it. She had felt foolish many times, but this took the cake.

"I'll handle things now," Jason said.

"All right. Kristy, I'll be around if you need me," Ben said, and touched her cheek. He left the room with Jason and she heard them talking in low voices, then the sound of the front door closing.

Reluctantly, she opened her eyes to meet blazing blue ones. "Jason, I'm sorry for this fuss—"

"What the hell were you trying to do, kill yourself?" Jason snarled. "Wasn't one attempt enough? Must you go leaving pieces of Kristin Loring all over my hotel? Dammit, how do you feel? Should I call a doctor?" he asked angrily, striding back and forth beside her bed, a hand savagely rumpling his hair, looking for all the world like he would very much like to spank her.

"I appreciate your concern, but I don't need a doctor, I'm fine. I bumped my head is all—and this ranting and raving isn't helping much!" Kristy flared.

Blue eyes showered sparks all over her. "I've got a right to rant and rave! What the hell good is a dead or injured decorator going to do me! If you hurt yourself again, I will personally take you to that waterfall and fling you over the edge—is that clear?" Jason roared, purpling with fury as she glared right back at him. A hand rambled over his head, rumpling with abandon. Kristy tried to prevent it, but the tiny giggle escaped her lips in spite of herself.

Jason swung around like an enraged buffalo. "I see absolutely nothing funny about this, Kristy! I feel like— COME IN!" he bellowed as a tap on the bedroom door interrupted his splendid tirade.

Kristy's eyes widened as a young woman entered the room. She was draped in a simple length of blue cloth, and her hair flowed down her back like streams of blue-black lava. Her ample, rounded hips and melon breasts were as temptingly sensuous as a Gauguin painting. Tilted black eyes met Jason's with a soft, melodious laugh.

"Aloha, Ja-son," she murmured, "I got here as soon as possible."

Jason curved his arm around the tawny shoulders as he introduced the beautiful young woman. "Kristy Loring, this is Meleia. She will stay with you tonight—" He looked into the enchanting face nearly level with his, and said something in a language Kristy could not understand. Whatever it was, the woman tipped her head and delightedly laughed. He ruffled her satiny hair and smiled at Kristy with an odd glint in his eyes.

Kristy promptly sat up and swung her legs over the side of the bed. The swirl of dizziness took her by surprise. She grabbed the coverlet to steady herself. "I don't need anyone to stay with me—"

"Lie down!" Jason commanded.

"I'll do no such thing!" Kristy retorted. "Now I'm going home to my own bedroom before I mess this one up any further . . . and you can take that hand off my shoulder, Jason!"

That hand laid her back down as effortlessly as placing a feather. "You're staying right here tonight. Ben's going to sleep in the hotel tonight also, so if you try to sit up again—" Jason drew a deep breath. "I've never spanked a woman, but it's never too late to learn," he grimly warned.

Still embarrassed, and a little delighted by all this attention, Kristy yielded with a weary sigh. She did have a headache, and doubtless a few bruises on tender spots. She closed her eyes to the overhead light. This day had been a mad jumble of crystal-edged feelings, all separate and distinct, yet changing so swiftly that her mind resembled one of those old fashioned kaleidoscopes.

"What time is it?" she asked like a querulous child.

"A little after nine," Jason said. The woman Meleia murmured something, and he leaned his head to hers to listen. His eyes on Kristy's face, Jason gave a brief chuckle of agreement. Meleia's gaze wandered over Kristy as she murmured again.

Like a mountain stream, Kristy thought crossly. Who

was this exquisite woman, and what was she to Jason? Another one of his *flowers?* If so, a young one then—she couldn't be a day over twenty.

Jason drew away from Meleia, laughed and nodded. "Meleia sent Ben to get you a nightgown and such. She'll stay until midnight, just to make certain that you're sleeping naturally, then she'll leave." He smiled sardonically again. "Goodnight, Kristy. Do stay in bed—there might be a bump in the carpet, a menace to your fleet feet—" He ruffled Meleia's hair again. "Aloha, Melly," he murmured.

Kristy kept her stony gaze on the ceiling until he left the room. She considered getting up—it was ridiculous to spend the night here when she had her own bedroom just down the road. Oh, why bother! Angrily she nibbled her lip as she watched Meleia settle on the chaise lounge. It made a striking frame for her dusky beauty.

"How old are you?" Kristy abruptly asked.

"Nineteen last month," came the melodic response. Meleia had a beautiful voice. Also a keen sixth sense. "Jason and I are very old, very good friends. Perhaps I'll soon be his mistress," she languidly remarked.

Kristy stared at her. She was only a child, a lovely child. No, a beautiful child, precociously self-assured. It was impossible to take any of this seriously. As her sense of humor asserted itself, she eyed the girl with a dry smile. "Does Jason know that?"

"Ah no, not yet," Meleia placidly replied. "Did you know I'm to be the featured singer when we reopen? Jason promised. And when I am experienced, he is going

179

to help me become a star. He knows the right people," she explained.

"Wonderful," Kristy tonelessly assured. She was suddenly, numbly exhausted, leaden-limbed and swaying as she stood up. Her head throbbed. She meant to go home, but it wasn't worth the effort.

She bathed, then donned the white satin gown Ben had brought. It felt wonderful on her aching body. And how lovely to be sleeping here again. How much she loved this beautiful little cottage. *Silly,* she thought, sinking down on the enormous king size bed, people don't love hotels . . .

"You sleep now. Jason knows best," Meleia firmly assured.

"Jason knows nothing," Kristy muttered, but she found Meleia's assurance, as well as her innocent manner, oddly soothing. "How long have you known him?" she asked curiously.

"Since I was born," said Meleia simply. "You sleep now. I'll be in the living room." So saying, she turned off the light and glided out of the room.

Sleep was impossible, of course. Kristy lay staring at the moonlit ceiling, smiling as the scent of *piake* filtered in to drench the darkness. The two brass light fixture ceiling fans she had installed swept a soft current of divinely cool air through the cottage. Kristy turned on her side and snuggled deeper into the silken linens.

Gradually her anger at Jason seeped away, replaced by more sensible emotions, an amphorous sense of shame predominating. What had happened between them was nothing more than a run-of-the-mill seduction attempt. And who to blame but herself for that? She had loosened up with him, given him ample cause to think she would welcome his love-making. The intimacy of shared laughter and pleasure, the yearned for touchings freely given and received—She was experienced enough to know the soft, subtle signals a woman sends out. Jason couldn't have known that she had done so in all innocence, yielding to a feeling that this sweet pleasure was simply another integral part of their time together.

Kristy's thoughts winnowed the darkness. What had possessed her to respond so wildly to his kisses? Physical attraction—raw sex? Yes, certainly that. She still tingled from his kisses, the lovely, lovely feeling of his body pressing hard against hers. She had wanted him, had ached to know the excitement that throbbed through that lean, taut body. Jason had aroused her far beyond anything Steve Brady was capable of, the force of it raw and elemental and totally new.

Why had she stopped him then? A brief affair—just what the doctor ordered—wasn't it? No. A casual fling would be a lighthearted, fun affair, but Jason Thorne would be a shattering experience. Was it just him? Or was it only that she was incapable of shallow involvement with a man? Other women managed it without going into a tailspin. But not Kristy.

What if she hadn't stopped him—what would she be feeling right now? Something a lot more dreadful than this confused shame. It was damnably difficult to consider Kristy Loring as a momentary flash of masculine excitement, approximately as memorable as the wilted flower Jason had picked for her hair . . .

It was here that Kristy fell into the dreamless sleep of exhaustion. Meleia was gone when she awoke next morning. Kristy lay in bed for a time, thinking, feeling curiously detached from her surroundings. Then she got up and redressed in the stained slacks and sweater. There was a hairbrush in her purse. No pins, but she found the scarf and folded it to contain the soft, curling mass of hair. All thoughts of yesterday were carefully blocked out; she had a job to do, and this required all her attention.

When she stepped out the door and encountered Jason striding up the steps, she gave him a remote smile. "Good morning, Jason."

"Good morning. Why are you out of bed?" he snapped.

Her glance was fleeting, but it took in his tired face, and the faint circles under his eyes. *Yesterday must have been an enormous drain on his vitality,* she thought puckishly. "I have a job to do," she reminded.

"So you do—but a day in bed wouldn't hurt," he growled.

Amusement curved her lips. "Oh nonsense, I feel fine. I fell and bumped my head, Jason, nothing more. Children do it all the time without ill effects." She chuckled. "Unfortunately, so do I. Oh, please thank Meleia for me?"

"Meleia is to be our new singer, she's got a fabulous voice," Jason snapped.

"Yes, she told me," Kristy replied. As she walked down the steps, a lacing of hurt, another and another

182

began to puncture her composure. It was a golden day with a few puffy clouds, and a mild wind that teased her hair. *Perfect for exploring and laughing and light-hearted kisses,* she thought longingly.

Kristy walked on without regard to Jason. He caught up with her and placed a hand on her arm. "Your dedication is commendable, but it might also be foolish. I think you should rest today," he said curtly.

"I told you I'm fine, Jason."

He studied her with a hint of wearied defeat. "Very well, if you're sure you're up to it. Kristy, about yesterday—"

"Please, nothing about yesterday? I'm a little embarrassed by how it ended, and I'd appreciate just dropping the subject. Up until the time we went to your house, it was one of the loveliest days of my life, Jason," she said honestly. Green eyes raised to his. "As for my rather adolescent reaction to your love making, the reason I got so upset was because I . . . thought perhaps that you might be already be committed to another woman ... ." She paused, giving him a chance to deny or confirm.

Jason did neither, merely slanted her a look and asked, dryly, "And that caused your reaction? You're sure it wasn't that blighted love affair of yours?"

Kristy flushed. "That too. I don't want to get involved with another man, no matter how meaninglessly, until I'm totally over that one."

"I've always found it directly the opposite, myself. Another woman can easily erase memories of the last one," Jason carelessly commented. He shrugged. "But I

183

suppose you know what works best for you."

"I reckon so. At any rate, I apologize for the ruckus," Kristy ended with an embarrassed laugh.

Jason sighed and ran a hand through his hair. "I think I'm the one who should be apologizing, Kristy. But alright, let's forget it then." He looked at his watch. "We have a staff meeting in fifteen minutes. Be there."

"Yes, sir!" Kristy saluted.

Jason's smile did not reach his eyes. He turned in the direction of the pool, and Kristy continued on towards the rear of the hotel. His dark hair shone in the sunlight, and his long, easy strides were a pleasure to watch. Kristy forced her gaze back to the path. While laying in bed this morning, she had made a promise to herself. Although she would not retreat to the silliness of formal address, still, she *would* retreat. Because she was frightened by the strength of her feelings for Jason, she would take back the trust she had given him that bright, lovely yesterday.

Crisp, friendly, coolly impersonal, that's the ticket, she thought, watching Jason pause by the pool. His long legs and lean hips were outlined by white denim, and he wore a shirt as blue as his eyes. That dark head arched back, and she caught the pleasing sound of his laughter. Kristy shivered. Keeping her promise might be more difficult than she had anticipated.

It was summer, and in Kauai, it came with frangipani blossoms strewing the verdant grass with five-petaled stars, and drifts of perfumed air on hazy purple dusks. At odd moments, Kristy stopped to savor this extravagant beauty, but her main awareness was of the solid fact that she had never worked so long, so hard, and with such frantic dedication to the task, in her entire life. The tempo of activity about the hotel had swung into high gear, stretching around those involved like a live electric wire hissing with energy, invigorating and exciting and she loved it.

Jason was as deeply involved in the final stages of renovation as she, and he rarely had time for more than a few brief words concerning business. Their rare lunches together were invariably shared with another staff member, and there was no intimate sharing of looks or the deceptively innocent remarks which so delighted and incensed. At times she closed her eyes to reality and pretended that she was again with the laughing, teasing, utterly charming man who had taken her to the Blue Grotto and kissed her free of Pele's wrath, but a few moments in the presence of the impatient executive soon set thing in proper perspective again.

Her days were filled with frenetic activity, but once the whistle blew, time passed as slowly as a season. Kristy often felt lonely in the long evenings after the hotel emptied of life and silence rang around her. Sometimes the night watchmen stopped and chatted, and now and then Ben spent an evening with her, but usually her after dusk hours were as quiet as the deserted hotel.

On one such evening, she was sitting in solitary splendor watching the sunset from Alex's veranda, when Jason suddenly appeared and smilingly wished her a happy birthday. She was practically misty-eyed that someone other than Flora had remembered. The elaborately wrapped gift he extended delighted her, but then, she wryly acknowledged, the gift of a pebble from Jason Thorne would delight her.

Eagerly she had unwrapped the rather large box, then released her breath in a long sigh. Carved from a single piece of green jade, the tiny sculpture she lifted out was nothing less than enchanting. From its gently molded base rose a reed-like stem topped with a water-lily pool. And perched on one exquistely sculpted petal was a winsome, elegant, delicious little mermaid. Her face was tipped to an imaginary sun, a Mona Lisa smile on her impossibly lovely face, the waterfall of green hair spilling to her naked little breasts.

The green eyes of another mermaid lifted to Jason's. "Oh Jason, thank you! It's too lovely for words," Kristy softly exclaimed.

Jason had looked amused. "It's just a trinket, Mermaid, hardly anything to merit such excitement."

Kristy would hardly call anything so beautiful a *trinket*, but to a man of his means, she supposed a jade sculpture was as trivial a gift as a box of chocolates. But Ben's soft whistle when he saw it confirmed her suspicion of its value, and she'd lost count of how many times she'd wondered at the why of this gift.

Certainly not affection, she grumpily admitted. Jason seemed determined to obey her stinging ultimatum, his behavior exemplary to the extreme. Kristy reciprocated, but a gnawing discontent eroded her spirits to the point of tears, at times.

Like now. Kristy dashed at her eyes. She hated weepy females—she hated seductive summer evenings!

"Oh, blast!" she muttered, flinging her shoe at the door. It was warm and lovely and she was hungry for some fun and excitement! What did she ever do but work and eat and sleep?

"Speaking of work," she sighed aloud. The hotel was finished, and to all practical purposes, her job was finished with it. What now? She ought to actively probe the question. Instead she lay down on the couch and closed her eyes. Jason was pleased with the results of her labors, which meant that she should be pleased and happy, but why wasn't she?

Gingerly she faced the reason. He had not touched her since that day at his house, or even acted like he wanted to, and while this was what she had wanted, had insisted on, in fact, she felt hurt and unhappy that he ignored her femininity and concentrated exclusively on her professional talents. Maybe such contradictory reaction was natural. Jason had once proclaimed that a woman confounded a man simply because even she was never sure of exactly what she wanted. As much as she hated to admit it, he did have a valid point.

Thoroughly put out at her ambivalence, Kristy got up and collected her mail, a postcard from Alex with the routine, *Having great time—wish you were here.* She wished she was too. And a letter from Flora. She sat down and read it with her usual twinge of guilt. Kristy had stopped sending postcards to Flora. Now she sent rafts of pictures and carefully worded assurances that she was feeling wonderful, enjoying her job, etcetera. Nothing about the long, empty nights filled with fevered longing, the haunting fear that she had again become infatuated with a man who possessed the same ability to hurt her.

She put on her swim suit and slung a towel over her shoulder, adding a pair of sunglasses to cut the bright sunlight, then her bathing cap. The hotel was alive with delivery trucks and people bustling in and out the service doors. She didn't know where Jason was and wished she didn't care.

From a distance, Meleia gaily hailed her. Although Kristy had dismissed that adolescent claim to bedding Jason, she was still undecided as to the role this nubile Island girl played in his life, thus her manner was cool and reserved with the sweet, friendly Meleia. Perhaps she really was merely the featured singer—certainly there were classy posters proclaiming this—*but Meleia had to be the sexiest woman she'd ever seen,* Kristy thought, lifting a casual hand in greeting, and Jason hadn't shown any spectacular immunity to sexy women.

Jealousy and common sense warring in her breast, she flung herself into the rough trail Jason had bulldozed to the waterfall's lovely pool. He had ruined this too, she fumed, soon there would be hordes of tourists trampling through here in their Bermuda shorts and atrocious shirts and Instamatic cameras. Lord but she was in a rotten mood!

Stepping into the ferns which fringed her pool, Kristy flung down the towel and checked her new bikini. It left very little to the imagination, she sourly reflected as she tightened the ties of the tiny briefs setting low on her hips. Cramming her hair under her cap, she split the surface of the water with a clean dive.

Kristy flipped onto her back to float in dreamy enjoyment. Feeling the tension flowing from her body under the warm, rippling current, she lay so still, a dragonfly lit on her toe. She laughed and splashed it away, then struck out vigorously across the pool. Becoming aware of an intensely sweet fragrance, she waded through the shallows searching out the source, until she spied the vine entwining the trunk of a slender *wili-wili* tree. A flock of tiny yellow and peacock blue birds flitted through its branches, and the wind whispering through the ferns ruffled the petals of myriad wildflowers.

"Lovely," she marveled aloud. For a startled instant, she thought she heard an echo. Dismissing it as imagination, she lay on her back and drifted with the current. The sun beat down. Opening to it, pleasantly aroused by the heat, the honeyed caress of water, Kristy relaxed to the substance that cradled her body. Where was Jason, she wondered, and with whom?

Jason, she shortly discovered, was here, with her.

Chapter Ten

The hurtling body hitting the water was a streak of sun-bronzed skin. Kristy skrieked at the voluminous splash. Treading water, she watched the bubbling wake until a sleek, black head bobbed up. Jason grinned, then flipped over backwards in a graceful dive and came up on the other side of the pool. His powerful arms propelled him around the deep green lagoon as cleanly as a sea otter. Kristy watched him for three laps before turning onto her back again.

Jason glided smoothly up beside her. Floating lazily in the sun, they said nothing for a time. He finally broke the silence with a long sigh. "Are you as exhausted as I am, Mermaid?"

"I think so. But it's a good tiredness," she

murmured.

"Yea, I guess so."

He sounded so dispirited, she looked at him in surprise. "Surely you feel the same way? I mean, you must be tremendously proud of what you've done—"

"And what is that?" he interrupted sourly.

"Why, the hotel, of course. We open tomorrow and—my goodness, everyone's astonished at what you've done in so short a time!"

"What I've done? It wasn't me doing it, Kristy."

"No, not the actual labor, but you were the driving force behind it. Without you, we'd still be dithering along . . . but no one dithers with our benevolent taskmaster cracking the whip!" she teased.

The admiration in her eyes was genuine. Even though he had many other interests demanding his attention, Jason had managed to attend to them, and still supervise the renovation of his newest hotel.

As his gaze met hers, she blurted, "Jason, you aren't worried about the hotel, are you?"

"It's a gamble, just like anything else," he bleakly responded. "I've put an awful lot of the firm's money into this venture. Whether or not it pays off is anyone's guess."

His hard sigh touched her deeply. It seemed impossible that this man could know fear, Kristy thought him immune to the nagging anxieties that afflicted ordinary people. Something dependably firm and needed melted as their eyes met again. "I detest personal failure, Mermaid. It's the one thing that leaves scars on Jason Thorne's impregnable hide," he confessed.

191

"You won't fail. The Blue Pearl won't let you down, Jason," she said very softly. "It's special, touched with magic—don't you know that?"

Jason looked startled. "Is it!" Her infectious smile and firm assent elicited an answering smile. "Of course it is," he agreed. "And so are you, Kristy. You've done a fine job, far exceeding my expectations."

"You know the credit goes to Dayton. But I thank you for the praise, it was needed."

"You're most welcome, Kristy, and I do not give credit where credit is not due," Jason said severely.

"The question is, what do I do now? Return to Texas and rest on my laurels?" she mused to herself.

"Seems rather an uninspired vision," Jason observed. A smile shaped his mouth into a pleasing curve that she longed to kiss so badly, she was shaken. "I've been thinking, Mermaid," Jason went on.

Kristy smiled to herself. This switching from proper name to nickname was a sure barometer of his mood. "And what have you been thinking, Sir Thorne?" she asked. There was a provocative lilt in her voice that signaled a letting down of barriers.

He laughed. "A lot of things . . . but we'll omit the thoughts which might cause another disaster," he teased, laughing again at her rosy blush. A week after her second fall, Kristy had proceeded to tumble down a ladder with remarkable ease, resulting in nothing more than a bruised leg, and another furious tirade from Jason for being on a ladder in the first place. That she had been measuring windows was discarded as completely irrelevant, and he had threatened to throw her off the waterfall again.

"With your penchant for falling off things, it's rather difficult to fit you in here now that we're through re-decorating," he added with an ornery look.

Kristy kept her voice light. "Just what exactly could I do here? My vision may be uninspired, but at least it's practical. I can't just hang around the hotel, and I've no inclination to be a beach bum. There really is no need for me to stay in Hawaii, is there," she ended matter-of-factly.

Jason groaned. "Kristy, please don't ask me to make another decision? Give me just an hour of respite from problems? I don't even want to decide what I'm having for dinner tonight!"

"Poor man . . . typical example of an overworked, underpaid exeuctive," she crooned. "They ask so much of you!"

"You're very impertinent—has anyone ever told you that?" Jason inquired. Without further ado, he flopped over and dunked her.

She came up sputtering and hissing threats. Clinging to his shoulders while she wiped her face, Kristy scowled at him with surging delight. He was laughing, his eyes sparkling with devilment, sun-dried wisps of hair clinging to his brow. Catching him offguard, she grabbed that dark head and shoved it under, then streaked off across the pool with a taunting laugh.

She dove deep but he was after her. They played like two young animals, diving and surfacing, chasing and being chased, gamboling in the shallows and racing fleetly over the shiny black boulders, laughing with the innocent joy of children at play. But beneath that innocence ran a deeper, more erotic vein of enjoyment. After nearly drowning her—or so Kristy proclaimed—Jason curved an arm around her waist and performed a splendid, one-armed backstroke to shallower water. When her feet touched bottom, Kristy stood up and scowled fiercely at the beguiling man. He swept off her cap and delightedly helped the golden mass of curls to come tumbling down around her shoulders. As his hands became lost in her hair, sapphire eyes fastened hawklike on her face.

A black eyebrow tilted. "Mermaid, you know I'm going to kiss you. Are you going to hiss at me?" he asked hopefully.

As she looked up at his tensing face, fighting the drift into the glowing pools of his eyes, Kristy suddenly knew the reason for her initial reaction to Jason Thorne, and to all the confusion which came afterwards. *She loved him.* Overwhelmed at finding herself in such an ignominious position, she turned her face. *To love Jason Thorne was the height of idiocy,* she told herself, but her heart ignored logic and went on beating its tormenting refrain. *I love you, Jason—Oh God, I do love you!* With the ease of hindsight, she saw clearly that Steve had been the infatuation, and knew that she had always suspected that, deep down where thoughts grow and fester.

There was only a small tremor in her voice as Kristy replied, "I probably would hiss at you. It would be a deliberate infraction of our rules, Jason."

"Your rules, not mine," he huskily reminded. "Be-

194

sides, don't you find it enjoyable to break a rule now and then, hum?''

"I—I don't know, I've never broken any," she confessed.

His hands slid down her back. "You might find you like it, Mermaid.''

Kristy wanted nothing more than she wanted that kiss. His skin gleamed golden in the sunlight. The hair on his chest curled in dark little whorls that tickled her nose when she impulsively pressed her lips into the damp mat. All those nights of suppressed longing had left her terribly vulnerable. Deliberately blocking out thought, Kristy glided her hands over his muscled arms to his shoulders, up the strong column of his neck, while her lips followed the path of her fingers. *No rules, no yesterday or tomorrow, just now, just this.* She felt wild and explosive and intensely alive to the hands on the small of her back, pulling her closer until their bodies touched. Her head dropped back as she laughed up at him in this moment of joyous release.

"Yes, I might find I like it," she whispered.

"Mermaid!" Jason's groan brushed her skin as he eagerly sought her lips. She responded with mindless abandon. His back was silky smooth under her fingers, his mouth warm and demanding, taking hers again and again while he rocked her against him. There was nothing between their bodies but the briefest scraps of cloth. She felt weightless, boneless, filled with radiant warmth. Their kisses grew fierce and urgent, his breath gusting on her lips as his hands moved under the water. She was flamingly aware of the aroused body molding

195

to her yielding softness, the hard, demanding mouth devouring hers, of his hands gone rough and wild on intimate places.

"Kristy. Oh baby, I want you—you know how much I want you," Jason said thickly. His voice matched his straining body as he pressed her into him.

"Yes—yes, I know," Kristy said distractedly. She needed to think! "Jason, I think . . . oh Jason. . ." He kissed her again, and she lost the slender thread of sanity, but when his hands moved to the ties that secured her swim trunks, she made a tiny sound of protest. His hands stilled, then slowly glided upwards to her breasts. Unable to function in any other manner, she held her body close to his while his kiss went on and on, her nipples taut, hot peaks between his caressing fingers.

It took her a shockingly long instant to associate the sound of voices with the people coming up the path. Jason heard them first, and when his mouth abruptly left hers, she was chilled by the loss. Uncomprehending, Kristy stared at him, her hands still locked in his hair.

Looking at her hazed eyes and softly bruised lips, Jason gave her a crooked grin. "Saved by the cavalry, green eyes," he murmured huskily.

Only then did she become fully aware that they had company. Kristy pulled away from him and began wading to shore. Once she reached the grassy bank, her knees gave way, and she sank down into the soft ferns, abstractedly noting the tiny pink flowers crushed under his body as Jason came down beside her. He leaned back on his elbows and moodily watched the sleek young girl diving into the pool, followed a split second later by the husky boy. They were both dusky skinned and attractive, a natural complement to the lagoon-like pool.

"They look like they belong here," Kristy said wistfully.

"Do they? You're the only one I ever think of as belonging here," Jason idly returned. Kristy glanced at him but his face was expressionless.

The silence grew uncomfortable. Jason lay back and folded his arms under his head. Realizing her eyes were devouring the white trunks which molded his lean hips, she consciously looked away, then back at the long, long legs as he crossed his feet. Color burned her cheeks at how pleasing she found his beautifully formed body, so cleanly, arrogantly masculine, the manly bulk of him compelling her gaze until she felt on fire. What they had shared in the pool was an embarrassment to her. Was he going to mention it? She didn't have the nerve to bring it up, but she wished he would, just so she might glean some hint of its meaning. Or lack of meaning.

"Lie down, talk to me," Jason murmured.

Kristy stretched out on her stomach. "Okay. What shall I talk about? The hotel?"

"Anything on earth but the hotel," he said sourly.

She was silent, uncertain what he wanted. The evening sun tiger-striped his chest and glistened in the springy black hair. Remembering too vividly the feel of it under her lips, she gazed beyond him.

Jason tuned on his side and traced the contour of her

197

jaw. "Tell me about What's His Name, the blackhearted knave who broke your heart," he said, teasingly.

Taken by surprise, she cleared her throat. "His name is Steve Brady, and he did not break my heart. Nor is he a blackhearted knave," she replied in kind.

"Um. What is he then?"

"Just a man. And it's not a terribly dramatic story. I was twenty-one and he thirty when we met. He was tall, handsome, sophisticated, a worldly man. And I was—well, I wasn't nearly as sophisticated as I am now," Kristy said guilelessly. Catching his quick smile, she flushed and picked up a piece of bark to occupy her fingers. "We went together for awhile—"

"How long a while?"

"Nearly a year."

"And then?"

"Steve was very success-oriented, and he needed a wife with proper credentials—background, money, influence. Since I lacked all three . . . well, obviously, I wasn't suitable. It wasn't part of his plan to fall in love with me, he just had the misfortune to do so, he said. At any rate, I walked in one him and another woman one evening at his apartment, and I—I threw one of my famous little scenes. So . . . we broke up," she ended evenly.

"And then you ran off to Kauai to nurse your broken heart."

"I wasn't running. I just . . . in a small town like Rhyland, no one's business is private. I guess Steve and I were something of a fixture by then. Anyway, everyone had an opinion on what happened to us and it was more or less poor little Kristy time. As you might have guessed by now, I don't take well to pity. Or sympathy—whatever you want to call it. And Steve wouldn't leave me alone, he . . . I just felt a need to get away and sort it out without interference, that's all. It was all so confusing. . ." She studied the piece of bark. "Maybe, in a way, I was running, I don't know. I hope not, but maybe I was."

"And did your broken heart mend, or are you still carrying the torch?"

Jason's sardonic voice hurt. The bark snapped in her fingers as she vehemently replied, "I'm not . . . I don't love Steve Brady!"

"Okay, okay, Kristy, you don't have to snap my head off, do you?" Jason protested.

"No, I don't. I'm sorry. It's rather a tiresome subject to me, that's all. . ." Knowing he did not believe that too emphatic denial, Kristy shrugged. Maybe it was safer that way. "I'm hungry. You doing anything for dinner tonight?" she asked boldly. "Or are you not up to decisions yet?"

"I have a dinner date," Jason said briefly.

"Wish I did," she laughed. "That's the flaw in your island, Jason, romance is in very short supply. One more reason it'll be good to get back home again, I had things called dates there. Wonder if they still do that?" Getting to her feet, Kristy looked at him, then at the pool. "But since right now I have nothing better to do, I think I'll swim awhile longer. "Wondering if she had carried it off in a convincing manner, she smiled as he stood up and brushed off his trunks.

"Sorry. You should have asked me sooner, Mermaid," he said mildly.

"Yes, I realize I should have reserved the evening at least a month in advance. Have you ever thought of having yourself cloned, Jason?" she drawled. "Just think of the benefits to womankind!" *Her chiming little laugh contained the right degree of mockery,* she thought.

"I may have to give some serious thought to that," Jason laughed, but anger glinted in his eyes. "Well, I'd best get on back. Nice sharing your pool, Kristy, I do thank you for the pleasure." Touching her nose, he walked off in the careless saunter that gave back her mockery.

Kristy sat back down on the grass still bearing the imprint of his body. She stared blindly at the couple playing in the pool, refusing to acknowledge the ache in her heart, or her crushing disappointment at being turned down for dinner. There were more important matters demanding attention. Jason had deliberately ducked her question concerning her future, and since she believed him an essentially kind man, she was ready to put the blackest possible interpretation on his evasion. Not only was her usefulness here ended, a fact she should have readily accepted, but she had embarrassed him by trying to pin him down.

And behaved shamelessly in the bargain, she reminded herself hot-cheeked as vivid images raced across her mind. *Well*, came her acid thought, *that might be one reason he would like her to stay—so they could finish what they'd started in the pool.* A temporary position at best, conceded Kristy with black humor.

The boy and girl had left, and she sat alone in the lavendar dusk. Kristy felt her loneliness as something she could almost touch. Or was it self-pity? Angered at this possibility, she got up and began to walk back to the hotel.

Her feet found their way by rote as her mind churned with thoughts. Jason had asked her to act as hostess during the two nights of opening festivities, and after that, she would no longer be officially connected with the hotel. So. She would return to Texas and take up the threads of her old life, start her own business. Dayton had assured her she was good, very good. Hang up her shingle: Kristin Loring Interiors. . .

She was dismayed at the total lack of interest or excitement in that visualized sign. Without that creative spark, a designer was nearly as handicapped as an artist. Why wasn't she feeling the thrill of challenge?

Assuring herself it would come, Kristy put it aside with the aid of a startling new idea that did excite her. Flora's birthday was next month—why not a birthday gift to end all birthday gifts! A trip to Hawaii, a week's vacation at The Blue Pearl, compliments of Kristy Loring!

Delightedly she examined it as she made her way down the hill. Flora had never had a real vacation, had never been on a plane, and with her natural love of beauty, she would go crazy over this beautiful garden isle! The thought of giving such an extraordinary gift was deeply pleasing. By the time she entered Alex's house again, Kristy had it firmly settled; she would call Flora in a day or so and tell her she was coming to Kauai for a solid week of luxury and no *buts* about it! And then, they would go home together and from there. . .

From there was only grayness. Kristy slipped off her swim suit and sat down on the bed, remembering the interlude in the pool, the electrifying sensations that had pervaded her body, the touch of wildness that had swept her beyond reason. And she wondered. What would have happened had they not been interrupted? She hadn't the faintest idea of how far she would have gone.

The grand opening of The Blue Pearl was both a dreaded and eagerly anticipated event for all concerned, but particularly to Kristy. Jason was absent the next day, and although the new manager and his assistant were on the premises, it was to Kristy that staff familiars turned when a minor problem arose. She found herself deeply involved in every last detail, no matter how trivial, of readying the hotel for the inspection of hundreds of critical eyes.

Their verdict was crucially important; according to Jason, these people all packed an enormous amount of clout, and it would work to his advantage if they went back to their various careers thinking well of The Pearl. Kristy wasn't going to pretend she understood everything about this, but if Jason said it was important, then it was. Going on that premise, she was as tough and critical as any guest.

And there were already an abundance of them. The paying guests had begun arriving early that morning, by groups and pairs and singles, some bound for the less expensive rooms of the east complex, several more affluent couples booked into the luxurious cottages. Jason's non-paying guests were to be housed in the elegance of the main building, and these rooms were being readied with an awesome diligence to detail.

Kristy thoroughly enjoyed her vaunted importance. Taking care not to tread on managerial toes, she opted for the tasks she most enjoyed, such as situating the mammoth flower arrangements, and heaping the beautifully carved *hua* bowls with an array of exotic fruits as splendid as the flowers. These vessels were exquisite replicas of the great, sculpted island canoes, and she was proud of their artistry, as well as being responsible for discovering them.

Delightedly she looked around the elegant lobby. Late afternoon sunlight gleamed on shining teak floor, splashing gold over Philippine mahogany wainscoting and the great baroque doors guarded by a snappily dressed doorman whose cedar-hued skin glistened with pride. Orchids carelessly heaped in an enormous shallow basket, one for each lady guest, looked so sinfully extravagant, she had to resist a childish urge to call attention to her handiwork. Perhaps to a seasoned traveler, it meant nothing, but to her, everything was inexpressibly lovely.

After examining the elaborate buffet set up in the private dining room, she left to check the new pool. *Jason and his love of fountains*, she thought indulgently. The widest end of the pool was rimmed with closely fitted, huge black stones arranged in ledges, down which water splashed in a dozen singing cataracts. Pockets of soil behind the stones contained lush ferns and shade-loving flowers, and other plants were artfully concealed in huge pots to create a miniature Rousseau landscape.

She walked across the terrace to greet the bevy of young women engaged to act as hostesses for the evening. They were all attractive, and resembled a flock of brilliantly colored butterflies in their slender, sarong-styled dresses. Proud in her position of senior hostess, Meleia bustled about giving orders so efficiently, Kristy left them to make a final inspection of the cottages.

Where was Jason, she wondered? The fact that he was absent today of all days struck her as odd, but trying to figure out an enigma like Jason Thorne was beyond mere woman. Pleased at her mildly spiteful thought, she started home to bathe and dress, but someone was paging her.

Incredulous, Kristy listened as the manager informed her that she was to move into her cottage for the next two nights; Mr. Thorne's orders.

"Why on earth should I do that?" Kristy protested.

"Mr. Thorne's orders," he repeated, rather imploringly.

"But why would he want me to do that?"

"I have no idea," the manager said, looking at her over the half-rims of his glasses. "I'm simply repeating his instructions."

Yours is not to reason why, Mermaid, she could just

hear Jason saying. Only seven of the cottages were booked for tonight. Perhaps he simply wanted bodies in as many as possible to break that row of unlighted windows? Kristy shrugged. Seemed as good a reason as any, and she was agreeable. "Well, he's the boss," she said lightly. "Oh, will you send someone over to Alex's house in about ten minutes? I'm going to bathe and dress at home, and I'm not toting a bag back to that cottage."

By the time she reached her door, long black limousines were driving up the circular drive to hand their passengers to the doorman. *Leave it to Jason to do it in style,* thought Kristy. She packed a small bag and sent it and several hanger garments along with the bellboy, then ran a bath.

Everything she did tonight must be done with extreme care. Shanna Bouchard would be here tonight. Kristy had seen her name on the private guest list.

After a luxurious soak, Kristy stood naked, her skin giving off the perfume of her bath, brushing her hair until it shone with the flickering highlights of satin. Undecided as how to style it, she set down the brush and uncapped a tiny bottle of costly perfume. She touched it to her throat, her temples and wrists, between her breasts and behind her knees, then moistened her fingertips and ran them through her hair. Mirrored green eyes somberly watched this feminine ritual. She had tried not to think of anything disturbing, had half convinced herself that it was simply passion and not love she felt for Jason. Look how easily she had leaped to that conclusion about Steve, she remembered.

But what she felt for Steve was totally different, a purely physical thing, and this was mind and body and soul. . .

Discarding this dead-end line of thought, she put on a filmy half slip, and an expensive black lace bra that made of her breasts startling, uplifted mounds. The dress she took from her closet was as delicate and fragile as cobwebs, the softest of silk chiffons, a beguiling contrast for her sunkissed skin and golden hair. Dainty straps crossed behind her neck, leaving her back bare to the waist. The tightly clinging bodice was cut low, and the full skirt was uncountable tiny pleats in perpetual motion around her slender legs. It was a daring dress; chic, expensive, and tauntingly feminine, the first she had ever owned.

A bronzy lipgloss sufficed for makeup, the silvery blue pearl for jewelry. And now this lioness mane of hair. It looked quite fetching down, but when she swept it up, the effect was stunning. She had never considered herself more than pretty, but once she had secured her hair atop her head and fastened it with a single white orchid, she was awed by the woman who gazed back at her from the mirror.

Was that person little Kristin Loring? Thrilled to the tips of her toes, she preened in narcissistic enjoyment. *Once in a lifetime a plain woman feels beautiful,* she thought happily, *and this was her once.* It was the dress, of course, but anticipation added its magic until she glowed like an ethereal being clad in a black chiffon cloud.

As she gave a last, still disbelieving look in the mirror,

Kristy thought intensely of Steve for the first time in months. What would he think of his discard now?

She stepped out into the starry night with a sense of wonder. Sounds of laughter and music and festivity echoed about the lovely, old-new hotel. It was all exactly as she had dreamed it could be. What a shame Alex could not be here to see it! But she would savor every moment, and store it away like a treasure for his return.

Kristy walked more slowly as she felt her palms beginning to perspire. The knot of nervous anxiety tightening her throat was becoming downright uncomfortable. Soft lights and splendidly dressed people, flowers and music and the muted thunder of voices greeted her as she reached the lobby. Somewhat awed by its suddenly unfamiliar splendor, she hung back at the door. She was unaccustomed to glamor on such a scale, and the feeling of being an imposter was difficult to overcome.

A handsome young bellboy suddenly appeared beside her and offered his arm with endearing gallantry. Tipping her chin, Kristy allowed him to escort her to the private sector Jason had placed off limits for paying guests this night.

Jason's pleasing laugh brought her head swinging around in search. His back was turned, but she would know that wide-shouldered physique and proud dark head anywhere. His face alight with laughter, he half turned, and Kristy's heart leaped joltingly against the black chiffon. He wore a white dinner jacket and he was devastingly attractive.

Making an effort to calm her wildly racing pulses, she gave a perfunctory smile to the burly man eyeing her with salacious interest, then slowly let her gaze go back to Jason. He was sandwiched between two women, an attractive brunette with hard blue eyes, and the other, a tawny beauty Kristy recognized immediately.

Shanna Bouchard was bewitchingly French. The piquant tilt of aristocratic features was enchanting enough; the addition of a low, sultry voice so charmingly accented one strained to hear it, made her a seductive temptress without equal. A sleek cloud of dark red hair swayed around her shoulders, and her Italian ancestry was evident in the flawless cast of honeyed skin. A petulant mouth and restive hands bespoke a volatile nature which, Kristy spitefully admitted, would certainly captivate a man who knew himself male enough to tame a beguilingly witchy jungle cat.

A person ought not form hasty opinions, Kristy chided herself, but what she was feeling was hot, stinging jealousy, and it was impossible to think kindly of Shanna Bouchard. Unnerved by her intense reaction, Kristy focused her attention on the scene around her, but Jason remained the center of it. The white jacket played up his dark good looks, and he wore it with that unconscious elegance unequaled by any other man in the room.

Jason turned his head a fraction, and a startled look widened his eyes. Kristy stood with her head held high in proud challenge as those deep blue crystal pools took an eternity to complete their appraisal. His spontaneous smile set her knees to trembling again. Truly alarmed at her weakness, she placed a hand on the back of a chair to steady herself. Her breasts rose and fell with her excited breaths, and his blue eyes took note of this as he moved towards her. Kristy stood quietly waiting, to all outward appearances coolly composed, a quivering mass of jello inside.

Shanna walked by his side, keeping easy pace with his long strides. She wore a clinging white gown with a diamond and emerald collar around her long elegant swan neck. Instantly outclassed, Kristy donned a smile as carefully as she had donned this dress. Her heart pounded violently as he neared. She found herself wishing desperately she was back in her cottage imagining how wonderful this night was going to be.

The introduction was brief. Shanna gave her a smile and a careless, "So nice to meet you, Miss Loring," before turning to Jason with a different smile. "Darling, let's dance—this is boring, all this meeting and greeting. And please don't introduce me to any more of your hired help!" she pouted so winsomely no one could possibly be offended. Her eyes touched Kristy again. "Your bartender, your chef, your receptionist, your decorator—*really*," she scolded as she towed him off.

The speculative glance Shanna flung over her shoulder stung Kristy like a nettle. Her chin came up in quick defiance, but she had already been dismissed as irrelevant.

Chapter Eleven

Dancing was on the flagstone terrace which backed the dining room and circled the pool. This area had been turned into something quite glorious, with thousands of tiny, twinkling white lights and the heavenly chic of pink and white calla lillies massed in a border that defined the off-limit boundaries. Waiters passed among the crowd bearing such dainties as tiny new potatoes stuffed with pate, and elegant white mushrooms mounded with crumbly black caviar, among other things Kristy found distasteful.

"Potato-chip and onion-dip, Kristy," she cheerfully sniped at her uncultured palate. Kristy drifted through, charmingly, or so she hoped, playing out her role as hostess. Many of the guests were already attacking the buffet and seating themselves at the pink-linened tables, while others elected to prolong the enjoyment of the fantasy drinks prepared by Ben and two assisting bartenders. The pretty hostesses were everywhere, and Kristy could see how effective they were. She laughed and chattered with studied ease, welcoming the press of duty that blocked painful thoughts.

Jason was the perfect host, and Kristy inwardly smiled at the power of his charm. Shanna flitted about like an exotic flower, no doubt helping his cause immensely. Another spiteful thought. Kristy put on an extra coat of niceness to counter it.

"Here you go, Mermaid," Jason said, suddenly appearing at her side with a pretty drink.

"What is this?" Kristy asked, eyeing it suspiciously.

"Fresh orange juice, vodka and Blue Curaco. Ben calls it Green Eyes—I thought it appropriate," he said, laughing.

Kristy sipped it. It was prettier than it tasted. "Thank you, it's delicious . . . I think," she said so doubtfully, he laughed again.

"Quite welcome. It's going well, don't you think?"

Instantly responsive to the faint note of anxiety, she warmly assured, "It's going splendidly! Everyone's having a marvelous time, and I've heard nothing but how lovely this all is." She raised a hand to her hair as she spoke, a subtly provocative gesture. Jason smiled at her and moved away. Did he remember yesterday? Kristy turned to the gentleman on her right. His face was vaguely familiar, and she supposed he was a celebrity of one sort or another. She put on a smile and gave him her undivided attention for the required length of time.

Eons later, Kristy stood at one side of the shadowed terrace listening with distant enjoyment to the music played by a famed native band. When the tempo changed from haunting softness to a throbbing, pounding jungle beat, her blood leaped to answer the thunder of those pagan drums. Suddenly she felt as savage as the primitive sound tearing apart the night, a smoldering excitement that fanned to flames as she looked across the dimly lit terrace, her gaze nakedly seeking.

Gleaming blue eyes met and welded with hers. She was oblivious to the jetblack gaze, the possessive hand on Jason's white-clad arm that sought to detain him. Kristy's entirety of self was focused on the tall, powerful man who came towards her as unerringly as a magnet drawn to its lode.

"Let's take a break," she heard him say from some uncalculable distance. Returning to reality was a shock to every nerve she possessed. Drawing a trembling breath, Kristy managed a nod. She felt literally stunned at the force that had so briefly, and so completely, taken possession of her senses.

Threading their way through the faceless throng, Jason guided her to the private terrace at the side of his—the manager's—office. Kristy leaned against the rail, still trembling inside, acutely conscious of the now muted drums, and the rustle of his jacket as Jason came up behind her.

"Tired already?" he asked, mistaking her slow release of breath for a tired sigh. His arms suddenly curved around her and drew her back against him.

"A little. It's been a strain. This entire day has been . . . a little wild. . ." Kristy faltered as he dropped a light kiss on her nape. The warm security of his arms was utter bliss. What would it be like to be held like this for the rest of her life, to be loved and cherished as wife to Jason Thorne. . .

Pipedreams, she jeered, romantic fantasies brought on by a full white moon and the piercingly sweet glory of a jasmine scented night. And a love so deep, it clamored to be told, she bleakly admitted. Reeling with the confusion that seemed to have taken permanent hold of her, Kristy leaned her head back into the warm solidity of his shoulder and wove her fingers with his.

"Well, Jason, playing with the hired help again?"

The amused feminine voice went through Kristy like an icy dagger. Jason's arms dropped so swiftly, she stumbled backwards with clumsy lack of balance. Shanna's low, cutting laugh was only another tongue of flame adding to the inferno of embarrassment.

Shanna was tapping a long, elegant foot, her eyes belying her vast air of amusement at Jason's little foibles. When she drew a hissing breath, Kristy was terrified that the woman intended making a scene—and with all those reporters around! Wishing desperately that she had the sophistication to cope with this, knowing she did not, Kristy said tightly, "Excuse me, please," and walked from the terrace.

Locating a bathroom by blind instinct, Kristy delayed only long enough to splash water on her burning face before returning to the party. With considerable trepidation, she paused at the door, her eyes scanning the milling throng, searching for signs of she knew not what, but terribly fearful of finding them. Everything appeared normal. Shanna had Jason tethered to her side while she gaily related details of her recent trip to Lisbon.

For what seemed an endless time, Kristy went back to hostessing. Ben, roguishly handsome in his crisp red jacket and black bowtie, was a popular attraction. She caught his eye with a smile for his obvious success, then slipped away to the opulent powder room for a breather. Her mouth ached from smiling and her eyes were suspiciously bright. Jason had studiously ignored her after that galling incident on the terrace. *Guess Shanna set him straight on fooling around with the hired help,* Kristy thought with no little bitterness.

The powder room was jammed with chattering women. Recalling the private bathroom in the manager's office, Kristy went there instead. At one time her uncle's private domain, the handsome old office touched her heart with its familiarity. It was empty, and she appreciated that. Taking the time needed to restore her hairdo and paint another gloddy smile on her lips, Kristy stitched some steel into her limp spine before leaving the bathroom.

She had need of it. The office was no longer empty. Shanna Bouchard lounged on the brown leather couch, smoking a cigarette and looking languidly at ease.

Kristy paused by the desk with a tight little smile. She thought about apologizing, then decided against it; as far as she knew, Jason was a free man. Waiting for

214

Shanna to speak first, she laid her evening bag on the desk and unconcernedly straightened her dress.

Shanna was an expert at waiting. Kristy's palms were damp by the time the sultry woman broke the silence. "Miss Loring, you intrigue me. I've been wanting to meet you for ages . . ." She paused for an indulgent chuckle. "But Jason wouldn't permit me to set foot in his precious hotel until it was all prettied up."

"I hardly see what's to intrigue you, Miss Bouchard. I'm sure Mr. Thorne's told you all about me," Kristy quietly probed.

"Of course he has—that's just the point!" Shanna said, looking prettily puzzled. "You must admit it's rather an unusual situation, one I enjoyed in a way. It's the first time in his life Jason's ever been forced to accept both an unpleasant and an impractical situation, just to obtain what he wanted. You should have *heard* him going on and on about it!" she said with a tinkling laugh. "Jason's usually so cool and collected . . ." Shanna laughed again, looking delighted at his upset.

"I'm afraid you've lost me, Miss Bouchard," Kristy confessed. "Just what unpleasant and impractical situation are you referring to?"

"Why, you, of course." Shanna's eyebrows rose in surprise at Kristy's baffled look. "Don't you know why he hired you?" she asked incredulously.

Kristy shook her head. "I *thought* it was because he was kind enough to give me a chance to prove myself, but obviously, I was wrong."

"Oh really, Miss Loring! Jason's not given to charitable impulses, I assure you! And while you are attractive,

215

you're hardly the sort of woman to drive a man temporarily insane," Shanna sweetly reproved.

Kristy stifled a natural urge to strike back. Besides, she was minus the weapons to make an effective rebuttal, she wryly admitted. Serenely poised, Shanna ground out her cigarette in the seashell ashtray, and clasped one knee. "You really don't know why he hired you, do you," she said curiously.

"I assumed, of course, that my uncle had something to do with it, perhaps asked it as a favor. I mean, he knew how much I had grown to love this place."

"Yes, Jason told me about the pathetic way you carried on when you found out he was buying it," Shanna said, beautifully compassionate. "But I—perhaps I'm speaking out of turn, I just assumed that you knew the conditions. . ."

Shanna's discomfort was too suspect to be taken seriously. Kristy looked at her and said, "Miss Bouchard, I would appreciate it if you'd speak frankly.'

"It's really quite simple. Jason naturally wanted the entire estate, not just the hotel alone. I'm speaking primarily of the acreage that surrounds the waterfall, of course." An amused smile tilted her lips. "Charmingly referred to as *your* waterfall. At any rate, your uncle was willing to, and did, sell the hotel to Jason, but aquiring the waterfall property hinged upon fulfillment of your uncle's terms, mainly that you remain here in some official capacity, until the renovation is complete and the hotel reopens. Jason does want that land, and when Jason *wants,* Jason *gets.* I'm proof of that. I was quite comfortably married when Jason decided he

216

wanted me.''

Sickened, Kristy betrayed no visible sign of it. ''I see,'' she said softly. ''Thank you, Miss Bouchard.''

Shanna stirred. ''Thank me? You've surprised me again, Miss Loring. I expected any reaction but that.''

''Why?''

Caught off balance, Shanna's mouth tightened, throwing into bold relief two sharp lines at the corner of her lips. *She must be near thirty,* Kristy thought. ''Well, from what Jason said, I. . .'' Resuming her light, offhanded manner, Shanna relaxed, smiling again. ''According to dear Jason, you have enough stiffnecked pride to outfit a regiment of Marines,'' she said. Kristy didn't respond. ''I would think that—well, knowing he was forced to hire you. . .'' Shanna made an impatient gesture.

''True, that's unpleasant, but mainly what I see is my uncle's loving concern for my welfare, my feelings. That's very precious to me, Miss Bouchard, and so, I thank you.''

''Oh. Well, you're welcome,'' Shanna said dryly. ''Then I suppose we can say that a potentially unpleasant situation turned out for the best, didn't it. Jason got what he wanted, and you'll have some very prestigious references to take back with you. By the way, when are you returning?''

''Very soon.''

''A wise decision,'' Shanna approved. ''I was afraid you'd be silly enough to hang on, hoping. . .'' Shanna was also an expert at leaving things hanging.

''Hoping for what?'' Kristy asked evenly.

Shanna crossed her legs and lit another cigarette, regarding Kristy through the streams of blue smoke rising lazily from her nostrils. "Oh come on, Miss Loring, what do you take me for? That wasn't precisely a friendly little hug I saw, was it."

Hearing the feline hiss behind that honeyed voice, Kristy stiffened. *So we get down to it,* she thought, eyeing the languid beauty on the couch. Shanna was a tall woman, and those long legs were sheer silken elegance. It was simply too farfetched to impart jealously to the woman's remark. However, she did have a point, Kristy conceded, uneasily recalling what Shanna must have seen.

Kristy perched on the corner of the desk and lazily swung her foot. "Miss Bouchard, if you've a point to make, then make it," she suggested. Shanna's curling smile set off skyrockets of temper. Kristy's voice flattened. "I assure you I am not sleeping with Jason, if that's what you meant to imply. I simply work for him." *And whatever else I do for him is none of your business!* The unbridled viciousness of that thought shocked Kristy deeply, but she had held her ground.

Shanna's mouth bowed into a pout. "No cause to get nasty, Miss Loring. You can hardly blame me for being a bit miffed when I saw Jason hugging you. I've been wondering for quite some time just what was going on between him and his newest . . . employee. But after seeing you, I must admit I may have leaped to unfounded conclusions. You're so far out of our class. . ."

She made a little *moue* of apology for her frankness. "However, Jason does forget himself now and then, a

218

form of self-indulgence, I suppose, the perpetual male urge to conquer," she continued with a laugh that invited Kristy to join in. She remained silent, her mouth twisting as ashes flicked on the shining floor. "But he soon tires of it and comes crawling back to me," Shanna said with a careless shrug.

"I can't imagine Jason *crawling* to anyone," Kristy coolly reproved.

Shanna's smile took on a wintry cast. "*I* am not anyone, Miss Loring, I'm his fiancee—" Following Kristy's quite glance at her ringless left hand, Shanna chuckled. "Oh, it's not official yet, but he is mine. We've had an . . . understanding . . . for over a year now. Our parents are old friends, you know. They approve the match—quite vocally, too!" she said with another tinkling laugh. *Like crystal windchimes,* Kristy thought distractedly.

Shanna flipped her cigarette on the floor and abruptly stood up. "Jason and I are two of a kind, Miss Loring. We understand each other, you see, something you could never do. And I overlook the weaknesses because they never last long. Once he's had his fun, he loses interest."

"I would suppose that Jason is no different from other men when it comes to weaknesses," Kristy said with an inner bitterness, but her voice was noncommital. "However, to be blunt, I'm not interested in Jason's personal life, his failings, or anything else, for that matter. As I said, I simply work for him."

Shanna broke into a celestial smile, her voice drawling with amusement. "I didn't mean to imply anything to the contrary, Miss Loring. It's just that . . . well, we women have a sixth sense when it comes to gauging another woman, don't we? To put it tactfully, I don't think you've had much experience with men, and Jason is—well, we know what Jason is! Quite enough to turn silly little heads, to say the least.''

"Fortunately for me, my head is not that silly," Kristy replied, dead level.

"Perhaps not. At any rate, I would hate seeing you get hurt. And when you play a game without knowing the rules, that's exactly what happens. But it seems you've sense enough to realize that. Well! I'm glad we could settle this in a civilized manner. I hate getting nasty," Shanna confided with well-bred distaste. She paused at the door. "Oh, if you're agreeable, I'd prefer Jason not know of this little discussion," she requested, her eyes warm and twinkly again.

Repulsed by that calculating warmth, Kristy shrugged. "I'm agreeable. As you said, I'm a sensible person."

"Good for you," Shanna said succinctly. She raised an elegantly casual hand in salute and sauntered out the door. The lamplight caught in her hair, turning the clouded mass to dark, rubescent flames before she disappeared from view.

Realizing that this arrogant woman would likely share Jason's bed tonight produced a surge of nausea. Too well trained to ignore the cigarette still smoldering on the floor, Kristy stooped and picked it up, her mouth twisting with distaste. Duty called, she heavily reminded herself, but the ordeal of resuming her bright, smiling role of hostess was beyond her capabilities just now. She ducked out the side entrance for a breath of fresh air.

The moon was high—it must be past midnight, she thought, rubbing her temples. All her sustaining excitement had evaporated, and she felt drained of energy. She leaned against the wall and closed her eyes.

A hand suddenly gripping her arm startled her into a soft cry.

"I'm sorry, I didn't mean to startle you," Jason said quickly.

"That's all right," Kristy said dully. "Jason, I'd like to be excused now, I've got a headache and I don't care for anymore of—of anything."

His hand dropped. "Of course you're excused. The party is officially over, anyway. Kristy, I apologize for any unpleasantness you may have endured tonight. I'm truly sorry if—well, I deeply regret it if you were made to feel uncomfortable in any way," Jason said with quiet sincerity.

"No apologies necessary. I had a lovely time. Goodnight," she politely replied. *A lovely time.* Her soundless laugh came through her nose.

"Goodnight, Kristy," Jason said, husky-voiced.

Kristy looked up at the shadowed face, wondering, as usual, what emotions that bland mask concealed. Giving him a perfunctory smile, she walked on to the cottage, examining only her feelings concerning the stipulation that blocked Jason's aquisition of the waterfall. It was a tossup between joy and humiliation, she decided, and one was as strong as the other.

The sounds of festivity faded into blessed quiet as she reached her door. She paused to pluck a fragrant white blossom from the nightblooming cereus by the steps, and laid it on her night table, then wearily stripped off the black dress and ran a bath, her mind ranging far beyond the green and gold bathroom. Tonight was over-filled with confusion, and she had to sort through it.

Her mouth atwist as she recalled Shanna's well-bred arrogance, Kristy stretched full length in the warm water. She went over and over their conversation, and changed her mind a dozen times. Part of her believed nothing Shanna had said. Unfortunately, the other part believed every word. The latter was composed of mostly scars inflicted by Steve Brady, thus distrustful and thus suspect, which left her all the more asea.

If one accepted Shanna's words as truth, then one likewise accepted as fact that Jason possessed the same calloused indifference to the sanctity of marriage. Kristy didn't want to ascribe to Jason the same character flaws Steve had revealed, yet, who should know better than Jason's fiancee?

Having reached an impasse, Kristy got out of the tub and briskly toweled. She would believe that Shanna Bouchard was Jason's fiancee when Jason said so, and she would retain her belief in his basic good character until proven wrong. And if the truth be known, she didn't think all that highly of Shanna's character. "Could be a little biased there, kiddo!" she advised the snapping green eyes in her mirror. She could also be a fool, but what else was new?

She took a white muslin lounging gown from the

closet. An extravagant froth of ruffled lace trimmed the wide neckline setting just off the curves of her shoulders. The flowing sleeves were edged with the same exquisite lace, and tiny pearl buttons closed the bodice. It was an outrageously romantic gown, clinging seductively to her breasts and hips, falling to her ankles in a cloudlike drift. Kristy gave it but a cursory glance. Ordinarily she would have been pleased with such prettiness, but she was too disillusioned, too drained, too spent to care about anything but getting to bed.

And yet, this was not a nightgown. Plagued by a sense of waiting, she bypassed the bed and stopped before the mirror again. Her hair felt hot and heavy on her neck. She piled it carelessly atop her head and pinned it without regard to appeal, yet some secret part of her applauded the charming effect. She picked up the white flower and held it to her nose, inhaling the lovely fragrance. Where had she smelled it before? On Shanna Bouchard. . .

Kristy started at a knock on her door. As she passed in front of the lamp, her body glimmered pinkly beneath the thin white gown, but she was too eager to take note. Only one man knocked on a door like that. She flung it open without hesitation.

"Hello, Mermaid," Jason said.

He hadn't gone to Shanna! "Hi, Jason," she said softly.

"You have pollen on your nose," he grinned. He brushed it off, smiling down at her, setting her heart to thumping with incredible ease. "May I come in?" he politely asked.

"Oh! Well, I—it's very late and I'm not exactly dressed for company," she stammered. Her heart was now in her throat, threatening to escape.

"You look fine to me. Quite fetching, in fact," Jason said, easing past her. He sat down in one of the green velvet chairs, and Kristy took the other one, perching on the edge of it as though poised to flee. Flushed with warmth, she folded her hands around the flower she still held, and waited. When Jason glanced down at her bare feet, she hastily tucked them under the hem of her gown.

"Do you know, this is my favorite of all the cottages," he said idly, gazing around. "It has an air of cool cleanness, yet it's warm and inviting . . . like a lovely woman holding out her arms in invitation," he continued lightly. He slipped off his brown suede loafers and flexed his long legs.

"Yes, it's my favorite too," Kristy helplessly agreed. "Why are you here, Jason?" she asked bluntly when he just smiled again.

"I was concerned about your headache. You've had several falls in recent weeks, and a headache of any kind should not be taken lightly," Jason stated with great authority.

She smiled. "Thank you for your concern, but this was a normal headache and it's gone now. I took a long bath. . ." This polite conversation was too insane to continue. "Why did you tell Miss Bouchard about how you came to hire me?" she blurted.

Jason looked at her keenly. "Kristy, I was feeling rattled that night. Shanna noticed my abstraction and nat-

224

urally she questioned, so I discussed it with her. If that offends you, I apologize. Did Shanna say something offensive?" he asked in a hardening tone.

She evaded his true question. Telling him she knew about the waterfall seemed to serve no purpose. "No, she just mentioned it, that's all. She's really a beautiful woman."

Jason concealed his relief very well. "Yes, she is that," he lightly agreed. Piercing blue eyes wandered over her. "You're not bad yourself, Mermaid. You looked quite pretty tonight. It stunned me for an instant when I looked up and saw a vision in black chiffon. Isn't it amazing what a certain dress and a little makeup will do for a woman!" he teased.

"I don't wear makeup," Kristy said coolly. How could any woman resist him, she wondered with a kind of soft despair. Sitting in the rich green velvet chair, his hair rumpled, the soft, v-necked polo shirt revealing a glint of gold around his tanned throat and a sprinkling of black hair on his chest, he radiated such compelling maleness, she unconsciously crushed the petals of the cereus.

The need to go to him and tell him of her feelings was overwhelmingly strong. Wouldn't that amuse him, though! Kristy looked down at her hands. She had shredded the lovely white flower.

Rising abruptly from the chair, she realized, once erect, that she had no idea of what she meant to do. Jason came gracefully to his feet and closed the distance between them in one long stride. She could not look away from those blue eyes. They gleamed with dancing

225

gold lights, like tiny sparks of flame on her face.

To hide her tumult, she said, "Everything went well tonight, don't you think?"

"Yes, I think. . ." His voice deepened. "But let's not discuss it, Kristy. I've lost interest in tonight's affair."

When she looked up at him from beneath her lashes, his eyes were on her breasts. Despising her puny resistance, she turned swiftly and walked to the window to collect herself. His forceful presence dominated the spacious room, filling it with vibrant life. Her heart began to hammer as he came up behind her. Never had she felt so completely vulnerable to a man!

She gasped softly as his lips touched the curve of her neck and shoulder, trailing slowly down her tender nape. "Like silk . . . warm, honeyed silk," he whispered. A heaviness enveloped her limbs as he drew her back against him and curved his hands under her midriff. Her breasts rested on his wrists, and she felt deeply the yielding pressure of rounded flesh.

"You looked so lovely tonight, so sweet . . . innocence in black chiffon," Jason said with caressing huskiness.

A weapon of seduction, Kristy strove to keep in mind. "But Shanna was beautiful," she said flatly.

"Was she? Beauty is in the eye of the beholder, sweet Mermaid," he murmured. He turned her around and dropped his lips to the pulsing hollow of her throat. Trembling with longing, she stood mute while he made silent love to her with that caressing mouth, touching slowly, tantalizingly, down to the swells of her breasts.

He said, his lips on her skin, "You smell like flowers

and sunlight and woman. . ."

"It's merely perfume, Jason, it comes from a bottle," she flatly replied.

Jason gave a husky laugh. "Not this, honey, this doesn't come from a bottle." He drew back and took the pins from her hair, letting it tumble in rich profusion around his wrists. "I love your hair, Kristy. I think how it would feel on me, spreading over me. . ." Smoldering blue eyes charred her skin as he gathered up great handfuls of gold, and drew her lips to his.

"No, Jason, don't start something, please," Kristy said before he could kiss her. Where she got the strength she would never know! "You have a certain physical attraction which I admit I find hard to resist, but I—it's my nature to resist the irresistible, just as it's yours to pursue a challenge," she ended coldly.

"Ah Mermaid, maybe we could break the pattern, hmm?" he chuckled.

Thrills of delight tingled her from head to toe as his whispering mouth moved over her face. She wanted to hold him, to come in to him and cling like a limpet on a river stone, to love him until this feverish excitement no longer tormented! She stepped away from him.

"Jason, I have to know. Are you . . . is Shanna your fiancee?" she asked baldly.

"No," Jason said.

The relief flooding through her stilled her voice. "Come here, Kristy," Jason said, softly, commandingly, seductively. Kristy went eagerly into his arms. He kissed her fiercely, passionately, his tongue thrusting into her willing mouth. Long, slim fingers, as pow-

227

erful as steel, as gentle as velvet, moved to know her body. Kristy's response was given without hesitation, yet something still held back from what she knew was surely coming. But when Jason suddenly wrapped her in his arms and swayed her back and forth, slowly, his face buried in her hair, the depth of that surrendering gesture conquered totally.

"Jason," she said. That's all she said, but that's all she needed to say. Jason picked her up and carried her into the dimly lit bedroom. He placed her on the bed with infinite gentleness. He pulled off his shift, then his hands went to the waistband of his slacks, but they stilled there as Kristy held out her arms. Her hair spread out over the pale pillow case in a tumble of coppery gold, the huge green eyes faintly uneasy. He came down beside her. She was so slim and small against him, a soft, rounded warmth he gathered close with a groaning of her name.

He kissed her, with soft hunger, with increasing hunger, with hot, demanding, passionate hunger, exploring the sweetness of her mouth until they were both gasping for breath. He found the buttons to her gown and unfastened it to the waist, his hands curving around the uptilted globes, his mouth quickly following to devour the tight pink peaks of excitement. *A firestorm was racing from his body to hers,* Kristy thought wildly, yielding to him, holding his head to her breasts. *Nothing like this, never before anything like this.*

Her fingers dug deep into his smooth golden back. She wore nothing under her gown and his hands had found that delicious nothing. She had never been touched so before, and it shocked her. "Jason . . . please, Jason, stop—" her chaotic gasp of sound was all but smothered by his burning mouth.

"No, darling, not now. Kristy, love me, love me, darling," Jason said thickly. She was stunned with the ecstasy flooding her senses. *Love him?* She loved him so much there were little explosions of dazzling light bursting in her mind and body, as acutely felt as if they were tangible substance. It was beautifully right and natural that his hands should know her, that they should have this weet, sweet fulfillment.

His mouth moved forcefully down her throat to her breasts. "Sweet, sweet," he whispered, his mouth greedy on her skin. His kisses roughened, his hands claiming a lover's rights. He took her mouth again and pulled her roughly, tightly, against him, pressing into every soft, yielding hollow, kissing her into singing rapture. He turned her on her back and came down upon her with such care, Kristy knew he was fearful of his weight. She pulled him down and gloried in that weight, the hard, firm press of his big man's body. Her body began to move in an age-old movement as he kissed her. He groaned and raised his head to look at her.

"Kristy, now—I want to love you," he said thickly.

"Yes—oh yes," Kristy whispered.

Chapter Twelve

The words she spoke were total surrender. Kristy's only desire was to be one with the man she loved above everything and everyone, to share with him this intoxicating rapture. She was a willing slave to his drugging kisses, her passionate moans accepted and begged for his rough caresses. She wanted both his tenderness, and his harsh male need—she wanted *him*. Floating on a cloud of love, it was with sick dismay that she felt the sense of wrongness creeping in, a tiny thinking part of her mind ruthlessly demanding attention.

Nothing special, just one more in a tormentingly long list of conquests. He always loses interest once he's had his fun, Shanna's voice whispered, *the perpetual male urge to conquer . . . nothing special . . .* It was a coldness that gradually crept through flesh and bone, chilling passion's heat, denying, stinging until she groaned. Feeling torn in a dozen different directions, Kristy struggled with her desire, and the now equitable need to reclaim herself from this man's careless hands. Oh God, how could she stop him now! *Nothing special,* her demon taunted, *just another woman who aroused his male lust . . .*

She wrenched her mouth from his. "Don't, Jason, that's enough," she half groaned.

"How can you say that's enough! Kristy, darling—" Jason sought feverishly to reclaim her lips, but she obstinately avoided his kiss.

She wasn't reasoning, she was *feeling*, a wild, insane mix of emotions spinning through her heart like a tornado. He didn't love her—he simply wanted her—a body, a thing! Oh God, she hated him!

"Don't call me darling! Not until you mean it—not like you do with your other women!" she spat venomously. Her fury was laced with scalding selfshame and it blotted out everything but this overwhelming need to escape him. "Leave me alone, Jason, get out . . . get out of my bedroom!" she cried.

Jason groaned deep in his chest as her hands shoved hard and furiously at his shoulders. When he raised his head, the vulnerable, confused expression on his face abruptly quenched her anger.

"Oh Jason, I'm sorry. Oh darling, don't look at me like that!" she implored. She was flooded with an indescribable need to succour this beloved man. It was not just passion that compelled a woman to give to the man

231

she loved, Kristy realized with raging joy, this consuming tenderness was fully as powerful an incentive to surrender. Feeling dizzied with her new knowledge, she held him and gave him everything but the physical part of her love.

It was only the latter he wanted. It didn't matter. Cradling his dear head on her breasts, she stroked his hair and kissed it, inhaling deeply its clean male scent, letting her love for him flow through her fingertips. To hold him so was her only reality.

Jason shuddered deeply, then raised his head and stared at her, his face a tight mask. "Is this one of your favorite games, Kristy? You get your kicks from driving a man to exploding point and then stopping him? Just how many times do you think I'll permit you this nasty bit of fun?" Jason asked savagely.

Her face mirrored her confused hurt. "This isn't a game to me, Jason—"

"Isn't it? Perhaps you'd best look a little deeper. You might be surprised at what you find," he said with cutting scarcasm. Jason jerked from her arms and stood up, watching with contempt as she fumbled with her open bodice. She could not manage the tiny buttons. Kristy sat up and pulled the sleeves back over her shoulders, looking up at him with wide, darklashed eyes, deep hazed with confusion.

Jason grabbed her shoulders. "I despise that look," he grated. "You turn me inside out and leave me aching—and then you look at me like that!" He flung her aside and strode to the window, clenching his hands to tight muscled fists.

Helplessly, Kristy stared at him. He was still shirtless, and in the soft lamplight, his skin took on the gleam of polished gold. She loved him with a physical hunger that defied logic. He turned back to her, and she saw the dark desire still smoldering in his eyes. But only desire, came her desolate admittance. There was no love in those hard blue eyes.

She clutched at her bodice and brought the edges together, her hands trembling with weakness. "I'm sorry, Jason. I know you have a perfect right to feel this way, to feel cheated, but I—I guess I have a hangup about sex. I can't take it as casually as you, if love doesn't go along with it, I . . . just can't." Soft green eyes raised to his with a look of quiet anguish. "And there was no love, no deep feelings at all. Just this physical attraction, so common, so worthless."

Her voice died away, her eyes dropping to conceal the hungry yearning she dared not express. She knew he could not mistake the look that shone there, and she was momentarily incapable of concealing her love for him.

Jason averted his gaze. When he spoke, his voice was devoid of emotion. "I see."

Kristy searched that dark, closed face. What did he see? Perplexed, she reached out a hand in appeal, but he glanced at that trembling little hand, scorned it. Kristy used the betraying gesture to brush at her hair. What she had done was reprehensible, she knew that as well as he.

"I'm sorry," she said again, tonelessly. "I didn't mean to—to lead you on and then—stop." The upward glance she dared revealed an uncompromising face, eyes dark and hooded, the clenched jaw, the muscle that ticked there. She would give anything to know what he was thinking, feeling . . . besides that anger coming white across his features! She shrank back from it as he crossed the room. There was no hint of the gentle man who had made that pivotal gesture of surrender such a short time ago.

His lip curled with contempt. "Oh yes, you meant to—you knew what you were doing. From the very first, you knew. Tantalizing, promising—" His voice roughened. "But when it comes to *giving* what you promise . . . there's an old but apt name for it, Kristy, but I'm sure you know that too."

She knew. Red splotches of color flared in her white face. He laughed with harsh amusement, his cynical gaze roaming over her, stripping her naked and defenseless. "Maybe you misconstrued your . . . lover's reason for breaking off your affair, honey. Maybe he just got bored with your little game."

Kristy shot to her feet. "That's a lie! I don't—I didn't play any games with him, I—"

An eyebrow quirked in hateful irony. "Oh? Well, maybe what you finally delivered didn't live up to its promise, hmm?"

Such crudity stripped her of control. "Get out of here—GET OUT!"

"Did I touch a sore point, Kristy?"

A blind urge to hurt made her voice provocatively spiteful. "Or maybe *I* did, Jason? Maybe you just don't like to admit you struck out. After all, failure is the one

234

thing that leaves a scar on Jason Thorne's impregnable hide, isn't it?'' she taunted wildly.

Jason's violent recoil astonished her. It seemed impossible that her pathetic taunt could strike so deeply. Bewildered, she blurted, ''Why are you acting like this? Surely not just because I refused to have an affair with you!''

Jason began to laugh. Stung, she asked tightly, ''Is something funny?''

''Yes, I . . .'' He laughed again, an odd, choking sound that sliced through her flesh as easily as a razor. ''Do forgive me, Kristy, it's just that the thought of *me*, chosing someone like *you* to have an affair with—'' He shook his head with another spasm of laughter. ''My God, I'd have to be crazy!''

Someone like her? It hurt so much Kristy gasped for air that wasn't there. Hot tears crowded her throat and spilled through her lashes. She struggled to regain her sanity, knowing it was too late, the die was irrevocably cast.

''Why the tears?'' Jason asked with nothing more than curiosity. When she turned from him, his fingers settled into her arm with an iron grip.

''Let me go, please,'' Kristy said, low and toneless.

A cruel smile curved his mouth. ''But we aren't through talking yet,'' he countered. ''I'm loathe to abandon such an intriguing conversation.'' Hearing the savage edge in his voice, Jason caught himself with visible effort. ''But there's been a little misunderstanding which I think I should clear up. I wanted nothing more than a night or two of pleasure, Kristy, that hardly constitutes an affair," he said with mocking indulgence. "A few kisses, a romp or two . . . just a little casual fun between the sheets . . ." He shrugged, and waited for an answer that was not forthcoming. "Damn it, talk to me!" he exploded.

Utterly defeated, Kristy slowly raised her head. "Please go now, Jason." The mocking amusement in his eyes lashed her into dull anger. "Just get out of here and leave me alone. I didn't invite you here and I won't put up with any more of your insults. Now you get out of my cottage!"

His eyes gleamed with blue fire. "Whose cottage?"

"Touche. Then I'll go," Kristy said wearily.

When she started towards the door, Jason grabbed her arm and whirled her around to face him. "Come here," he grated. His hands clenched in her hair and forced her mouth to his in a bruising kiss. Kristy fought bitterly against what seemed to be an ingrained response. His hands left her hair and moved down her body with brutal pressure, stirring, arousing, shockingly hard caresses meant to convey a hateful message; he could do anything he wanted with Kristin Loring.

She was trembling when he released her. Jason wasn't even breathing hard. A thin, cruel smile taunted. "It occurs to me to question my failure . . . Kristy," he said.

That he could kiss her like that and be immune to it— that he could taunt her weakness! Suffused with rage, Kristy struck him across the face as hard as she could.

The sound of her slap echoed hideously in the silent room. Jason's body surged forward with barely restrained fury. Horrified at what she had done, she held out her hands in appeal. "Please, I'm sorry . . . I didn't mean—"

"Button your gown!" Jason rasped.

Flushing hotly, Kristy tugged at the folds of fabric until they overlapped, and managed to work two of the tiny buttons into uneven slots. The icy contempt in his eyes was tearing her to pieces!

"Jason, please," she begged. Childishly she wiped at aggravating tears. The marks of her fingers were red welts on his cheek. She still could not believe she had struck him. No matter the provocation, it seemed a terrible thing to do. "I apologize for hitting you. It was unforgivable—"

Jason emitted a short laugh. "And unique in my experience. I admit I am not accustomed to being hit, especially for merely stating a fact."

"It was not because you stated a fact! You—can't you understand? The way you kissed me—and then to laugh at my lack of resistance—naturally I reacted in a violent manner! Hitting you was uncalled for, but surely you can see—"

"I really don't care to hear this," Jason said. "To be blunt, I don't give a damn whether or not you had cause, it's immaterial to me. In fact, I think you're going overboard about it—men have been struck before, I hear it happens with appalling regularity. Frankly, I'm sickened by the whole idiotic mess. It isn't often I find myself in the middle of an utterly ludicrous charade! Goodnight, Kristy."

Kristy ran after him as he snatched up his shirt and

strode towards the door with long, furious strides, meaning to plead, to implore, anything to wipe that glacial contempt from his eyes. Her toe caught in the edge of the rug and she fell heavily against the coffee table. A shocked little cry escaped her as her elbow struck wood.

Jason was at her side in three long, agitated strides. He lifted her onto the couch, his face registering concern overlaid with black anger. "Are you hurt?" he asked roughly.

Kristy shook her head. This kind of hurt had nothing to do with physical pain. Jason straightened. "You're the clumsiest woman I've ever met!" he exploded. "You're quite sure you're not hurt? I wouldn't want any lawsuits for unattended injuries—"

"I'm quite sure. Please just go away," Kristy said dully.

He eyed her long and mercilessly. "Very well. I'm sorry I came here tonight. I'll be the first to agree my actions were out of line. However, I mistook . . . certain things, whether deliberately or not, I don't know. At any rate, I apologize," he said with a careless shrug. Kristy stood up and wiped at her eyes. "Well, is it accepted?" he asked impatiently.

Kristy's head snapped up. She would not beg again— never again! Green eyes flashed with resurging pride. "Yes, accepted. Now get out of here, if you please? Go back to your Shanna!" she spat.

"Maybe I'll do just that," Jason said thoughtfully. "Goodnight, Kristy." Kristy listened to the door slam violently behind him, and his footsteps echoing on the porch. She turned her face into the couch and wept without sound or restraint. When the well of tears finally dried up, she lay staring at the ceiling. *There was too much pain in love,* she thought. She was caught in a whirlpool and it would pull her down into a darkness that would destroy her. If she let it. She got up and washed her face, then took off the pretty gown.

Jason hadn't mistook anything. She had asked for what she got. Too numb and sleepy to function, she slid between the cool sheets. Her bed smelled faintly of Jason Thorne. She curled up and slept her haunted dreams.

Kristy slept late next morning. She showered and dressed in a genetian blue blouse and a white linen skirt with braid trim accentuating her trim hips, twisted her hair into a knot at the base of her neck, and thought about nothing the entire time.

Reminding herself to call Flora sometime today, she began making up her reddened eyelids with soft gray eyeshadow. Just because she felt like ground glass was no reason to deny Flora that vacation. Kristy wrinkled her nose. "My, how noble we are!" she said aloud. She strapped on sandals and left the cottage.

The stately row of royal poincianas lining the drive had burst into glorious bloom. Kristy thought these flamboyant, red flowering trees the most dazzling of all the island's tropical wonders, and her resiliant young heart lifted in response to such beauty. She felt icily calm. But the closer she got to the lobby, the faster her heart beat, producing a breathlessness that she sought to allay with several long breaths.

Was Jason still here? Probably so, he wouldn't leave until the evening's entertainment for their guests—correction, *his* guests—which was an authentic Hawaiian luau complete with flaming torches and native dancers. She dreaded facing him. She thanked heaven for that fierce Loring pride that gave her the courage to do it.

Kristy ran lightly up the steps with a gay smile for the doorman. The lobby was a flurry of activity. The pretty desk clerk thought that Jason might be in the manager's office, and Kristy hurried on down the hall and stopped with a hissing breath as Shanna strolled out the office door. One look at that plumy smile and Kristy knew where Jason had gone when he left her last night.

She betrayed no trace of the pain carving her heart. "Miss Bouchard."

"Good morning, Miss Loring!" Shanna lilted. "Going to see Jason?" She looked radiant. The full skirted voile frock swirling around her legs gave her the appearance of a long stemmed rose. An antique cameo on a black velvet ribbon circled her slender neck. Kristy allowed herself ten seconds of violent thoughts before she smiled and said, truthfully, "Yes, going to see Jason, though not by choice, I assure you."

Shanna leaned down for a conspiratorial whisper. "Careful, he's a bear this morning! Lack of sleep always brings out the beast in him. I'm sure he'll be relieved when this tedious bore is over and he can get back to routine. I know *I* certainly will!"

240

"I suppose we all will," Kristy said, impassively. She would give an arm to know the truth of what Shanna confided last night. Would Jason stoop so low as to seduce a married woman? "Excuse me, I'd best get on before the bear starts growling," she said pleasantly, and walked on, feeling pleasingly cold. One felt nothing when one was frozen.

Kristy paused in the open office doorway. Jason was sprawled in the big leather chair, gazing moodily out the window. Something about his darkly brooding face kept her hovering on the doorsill. He looked forbiddingly remote. *And curiously young and vunerable,* she thought in genuine surprise.

"Jason?" Her soft voice had a tremor in it. Jason looked up with a start.

"Ah, Kristy. Come in, please, we've things to discuss," he said.

Strictly business. Kristy listened silently, catching only snatches of his discourse as her mind raced. Last night might have never happened; he was detached, pleasant, brisk, an impeccably correct employer instructing an employee.

Realizing that she had actually held onto a fragile cord of hope, Kristy relinquished it immediately as she saw the incident for what it was. Regretable, but hardly earthshaking. Being, presumably, a mature, intelligent woman, she ought not be so shocked at that, but she could not take lightly what had occurred last night. Jason could, and she envied him that.

"I would like you to dress in a sarong tonight. Meleia will show you how. Flowers in your hair . . . the whole bit," Jason was saying.

Kristy nodded mechanical agreement. "Jason, could I talk with you a minute about something personal? It's about my plans. After tonight, my usefulness to the hotel will be finished, and I'll be returning to Texas."

Jason fiddled with the pearl handled letter opener. Tossing it aside, he asked brusquely, "Is that what you want?"

Lying did not come easily to Kristy. Forcing herself to meet his gaze, she said firmly, "It is. I have my career to consider, and with this marvelous experience under my belt, I feel capable of striking out on my own. I've invested many years into becoming a qualified decorator, and now, at least in my opinion, I am."

"Not only in your opinion. Rest assured there will be glowing references to accompany you," Jason said dryly. "When do you plan to leave?"

"Well, that's what I wanted to discuss with you," Kristy said. Her eyes beginning to sparkle with excitement, she told him of the birthday gift that she wanted for Flora. "So I thought I'd stay another week—as a paying guest, of course. Then we'd go home together. I plan to call her tonight and tell her. I can't wait to hear her reaction! I feel positively wicked at how much pleasure I'm getting out of it!" she wound up with a delighted laugh.

"That sounds like a fine plan," Jason said. "I'm looking forward to meeting her and I'll make it a point to visit the hotel while she's here . . . excuse me?" he finished resignedly as the telephone rang.

Kristy stood up. "Of course. That's all I had to say, I

. . . well, see you later." She made a little farewell gesture and left the office in a rush of excitement. It was all settled. *Flora would be here in a day or two and . . . Kristy would have another week of sunshine,* she thought wryly, Jason Thorne sunshine. Hoping her gift to Flora did not have such an ulterior motive, she resolved to examine this more closely, but right now she was still an employee and still on the job.

Late that evening, she stood half naked in her bedroom, working with the supple length of fabric in frustrated attempts to wind it correctly. Angrily she dashed it to the floor. There was a knack to creating a smooth fitting sarong! Glancing at the clock, she decided to call Flora without waiting for the rate change. As soon as her cousin said hello, Kristy launched into it with renewed excitement. When she finished outlining her wonderful idea, she waited eagerly for Flora's reaction.

Flora coughed. "No, honey," she said gently.

No amount of pleading could change Flora's mind. It wasn't only the expense. She was terrified of flying, an illogical fear, she admitted, but one too formidable to conquer at her age. She would not hear of Kristy coming home and flying back with her—far too extravagant to consider for a minute. Flora simply coughed again, and said, flatly, "No."

"Flora, have you been sick?' Kristy asked, suddenly aware of the dry cough accompanying Flora's remarks.

"Of course not. I've had a touch of summer flu, and this nagging cough has just hung on, that's all," Flora said.

"You didn't write me about that!"

"Why should I? I'm fine now," said Flora.

After further discussion about the truth of that, Kristy sadly accepted Flora's refusal, and called the airport to make flight reservations for tomorrow morning. Just as she hung up, Meleia came in, and it was galling how quickly her deft fingers created a beautiful garment. The sarong flowed as sweetly as the waterfall when she had finished. She secured the icy blue material over Kristy's breasts and overlapped the two ends, leaving a deep pleat which slowly fanned open above the knee. The silky fabric clung to Kristy's hips, and molded the contours of her bosom. She regarded it distrustfully. Would it stay around her breasts with no other means of support?

Meleia chuckled. "It will stay up, never fear. You have enough to hold it and we will pin it so . . . and so. There! Jason desires your hair down—"

"I can do my own hair, but thank you for your assistance. You look lovely, Meleia," Kristy said, eyeing the gaily colored red and gold piece of tapa cloth that just covered Meleia's curvacious hips and tied in a tantalizingly careless knot at the side.

"*Mahalo*," Meleia said, her hands fluttering in pretty dismissal. "Jason is impatient, he says *wiki-wiki*," she reminded.

Kristy muttered something appropriate under her breath as she looked at Meleia's costume. She wanted, suddenly, a scrap of cloth for her own hips, to have, just once, that sensual, paganistic aura that shimmered around Meleia.

"Tonight, I sing," Meleia gleefully reminded Kristy

before she left.

"And you'll do fine," Kristy promptly assured. Despite her initial antagonistic reaction to Meleia, she found herself liking the young island girl more and more, *and she very nearly had a friend,* she thought. The only thing standing between them was six-foot-three and of dubious conscience. Kristy simply could not believe it of him, and yet, if Jason was capable of seducing a married woman, then Meleia's tender age would not give him pause.

Disgusted at her ugly thoughts, Kristy sat down and copied Meleia's hair-style, which was easy to do; sweeping her hair behind one ear, she allowed it to cascade down her cheek in a mass of soft curls that covered one shoulder and part of her breasts. She picked up the salmon pink flower and regarded it with a frown. How it was worn was significant; tucked behind one ear meant she was available, tucked behind the other, she was taken, but which was which? Oh, what the deuce did it matter since she was neither! Pinning the flower behind her right ear, she stood up and studied the effect.

She looked about as Polynesian as a snow rabbit, she thought sourly. The ice blue fabric accentuated her fairness all the more, but Jason had chosen it, and she was, she supposed, required to wear it. She circled one ankle with a tiny gold chain, clamped a golden serpent band around her upper arm. She looked an utter contrast to last night's chic lady, but hardly heathenish. Kristy thrust the thin white straps of leather between her toes, and headed for the gaiety centered round the pool.

She looked immediately for Jason, and found him in the lobby. He smiled, his eyes flaring over her. "Fire and ice, Mermaid, an impossible combination. It has to be one or the other," he said with his familiar teasing grin. But there was a coldness at the back of his eyes.

Kristy tipped her chin. "Not necessarily. There are some snow-covered volcanoes, aren't there?"

"Extinct ones," Jason lightly agreed.

Feeling herself dismissed when he turned to greet someone, Kristy went out to the terrace. Tonight's affair was open to all the guests, and the evening progressed beautifully. The piece de resistance, a succulent *kulua* pig baked in an underground oven, the elaborate platters of fruits and vegetables and Ben's exotic drinks, and the hula dances performed by strikingly attractive young women, dented the air of bored enjoyment affected by their more prestigious guests. By ten o'clock, everything save the polished *milo* bowls of *poi* were greatly diminished, and they had settled down to enjoy the lively entertainment of limbo dancers, and the excitement of flaming torch artistry.

Jason stood aside, watching with shrewd benevolence, paying scant attention to Kristy as she glided among the celebrants. Shanna was not here tonight, although Meleia was much in evidence. Jason's manner was as brusque with her as it was with Kristy. He made it clear he had no time for either woman.

Taking her cue from this display of indifference, Kristy avoided him altogether, but she could not help stealing glances at the big, handsome man. Tonight's attire was, in some cases, wildly informal. Jason was as immaculately groomed as ever, but looked supremely relaxed in a saffron shirt of loose-weave silk, and dark brown slacks. His long, tanned fingers held a glass of champagne, but rarely did it touch his mouth. Jason was all business tonight.

Meleia's songs were a tremendous hit. Kristy applauded with honest enthusiam for her very fine talent. Jason's protege—if Meleia could be termed that—would not long remain an unknown, not with that velvet-smooth voice.

Kristy turned in time to note Jason's gaze resting on her with disturbing intensity, his eyes dark and troubled. Quick to respond to this, she went to him and lay a hand on his arm. "Jason, is everything alright?" she asked. The tender concern in her voice embarrassed her, but his face softened to the smile she loved.

"Everything's fine, Mermaid. Looks like we'll be in business once we get this crowd of freeloaders cleared out." Jason moved away after this comment, but now and then she sensed his intent gaze upon her, that brooding quality a tenuous thread of hope each time she felt it. She wanted more reaction to her leaving than a handful of glowing references! The strain was beginning to tell on her, but she held her slender body as straight as a reed, her hips swaying gently as she walked, her face creased with an achingly bright smile as she countered furtive passes with a tact she didn't know she possessed.

It was nearly two before the pleasantly and not so pleasantly intoxicated guests began drifting towards their rooms. Feeling lightheaded with fatigue, Kristy grimly saw it through. Before she took her leave, she went to Jason with a diffident question. "Jason, are you going to be here tomorrow?"

"No, I'm leaving for St. Croix tomorrow," he said, tiredly.

"I see. Well, I guess this is goodbye, then, because there's been a change in my plans. Flora isn't coming to Kauai, and I'm going back to Texas tomorrow," she said matter-of-factly.

Jason looked at her sharply. "Flora isn't coming? Why not? Oh, come on, I'll walk you to your door and we can talk on the way," he said, an irritated edge to his voice. Once clear of the hotel, he said, "Now. Why isn't Flora coming?"

"A very simple reason. She's afraid to fly."

"I see. Fear of flying is a very real phobia, but perhaps she's simply afraid of flying alone. You said she hasn't flown before, and first flights can be alarming, especially to an older person. Have you thought about accompanying her?"

"Yes, I suggested it, in fact. I really think she'd be okay if someone was with her, but she was horrified at the idea of me coming home just to accompany her back here. I can afford it, you understand," she quickly assured. "It's just that—well, it's an extravagance, and one Flora won't agree to. So, that's that."

Some of her disappointment escaped into her voice despite her efforts to keep it steady. Jason sat down on the porch steps and reached up a hand to her. Kristy sank down beside him. Their shoulders rubbed, and when he shifted position, his hard thigh set snugly

248

against hers. Disturbed by the contact, she drew away, but the steps were too narrow to affect distance. She loved the smell of him, the sense of unleashed strength that lay coiled in his body. With a soft sigh, she gave in and delicately leaned against his warmth, relishing it, craving more.

"I'm so tired," she said by way of expiation.

"Yes, I know. Tonight was very demanding . . . I have a suggestion which I hope you'll consider on its own merits. I've business in Dallas on the twenty-eighth, which is less than a month from now. I'll be returning to Hawaii alone, and picking up two passengers in Amarillo would be only a minor inconvenience."

"Thank you, Jason, but no."

"I would have bet a hotel on that reply," Jason informed the moon. "Look, give it a moment's thought before you summarily refuse? Perhaps consider your cousin for an instant?" he sarcastically suggested. "The offer was for her benefit, not yours. I'm coming by private plane and there's no extra expense involved beyond a few gallons of fuel."

"My cousin would be the first to agree with me," Kristy said stiffly. "Please don't think I'm ungrateful, Jason, it's a very kind offer. But you've done enough for the Lorings. It's time we got out of your hair and gave you what rightfully belongs to you; this hotel . . . and the waterfall property. I know about my uncle's terms. You were more than generous in accepting them," she said quietly.

"May I ask who told you?"

"That doesn't matter. I only found out recently, or

I'd have—"

"Gone off in a snit of pride?"

"Have immediately released you from such terms!"

"Semantics, Kristy. But it's not important," he conceded, relaxing again. "As I said, no one forces me to do anything; had it not been agreeable to me, that would have been the end of it. But I'm a fair judge of character and yours appealed to me. Besides, how many green-eyed mermaids does a man fish from a ditch, hmm? You've been an experience, Miss Loring, and save for a little distasteful temperament, your performance has been flawless."

"Thank you . . . I think."

He laughed and leaned back on his arms. Stretching out his legs the full length of the steps, he tipped his face to the moon and idly asked, "Eager to get back home?"

"I left many things undone, so yes, I'm . . . eager. And it'll be good to see those I love again," she steadily replied.

"Yes, I guess so. Four months is a long time and the heart grows fonder, etcetcera . . ." Jason stood up with that fascinating display of oiled strength, and again reached out a hand to her. Her fingers wrapped tightly around his for an instant as he drew her up beside him. Long, hard fingers, warm and strong. He dropped her hand.

"Best of luck, Kristy," he said lightly.

"The same to you, Jason. I wish you—and The Blue Pearl—all the best."

"Oh, I'm confident we'll have it. Reservations are

flooding in. Well, it's late and you're exhausted." He kissed her cheek. "Goodbye, take care now. And give Flora my regrets?"

Hurting, she looked up at his dark face. *This had a touch of unrealness about it,* she thought. Last night they had been lovers, tonight they were acquaintances saying a superficial goodbye. But they were still friends, would always be friends, she tried frantically to relieve the pain constricting her throat. He was standing so close she could smell the cologne he used, mixed with that stirring scent that was uniquely Jason. *Rare and unforgettable,* she thought achingly. Her voice was level. "I will. Goodbye, Jason. And thank you for—for everything."

"You're welcome, Kristy," Jason said lightly. He took a step, then stopped, irresolute. The night was suddenly close around them, shimmering with unheard sounds. "Look, do me a favor?" he asked abruptly. "I'll be back in two days time, and we'll make another attempt to get your cousin here. Judging from all you've told me about that little lady, she deserves the vacation you want so much to give her, and I mean to see that she gets it."

He chuckled, self-embarrassed "I'm big on family too, you know. All the things that go with being blessed with people you care about, the giving, the getting, the sharing—I know firsthand how you feel."

Kristy shook her head. "Jason, there's no way anyone can change Flora's mind when she sets it to something. She's as stubborn as I am. To Flora an extravagance is an extravagance and don't be ridiculous," she half-sighed, half-laughed.

"Well now, I'm fairly good at changing stubborn female minds," Jason wickedly reminded.

"Not these female minds," Kristy said. "There's too much Loring-Ramsey mixed up in there."

Jason grinned. "We'll see," he said, and Kristy was again struck by the sense of unreality as his laughter chimed out. Jason touched her nose. "Well, I'd best get on—Melly's waiting for me."

"Melly? Oh, you mean Meleia," Kristy said, her voice flattening.

"Yes. She hasn't found an apartment yet so I've been letting her use mine. 'Night, Mermaid."

Kristy grabbed his arm. *I can't let it end like this,* she thought, *not with all those ugly words between us! I have to tell him.* But precisely what she meant to tell him was unclear, even to Kristy. She placed her hands on his arms.

"Jason, I know you've deliberately avoided discussing last night—"

"Don't, Kristy," Jason said sharply.

"No, please, I have to tell you something. Last night you said some ugly things to me, and they aren't true, Jason. I know you were angry and that you had a perfect right to be angry—"

"I thought so," Jason said, exceedingly dry. His hands curved over her shoulders, lightly. "However, I let it get out of hand. I did get ugly, and I apologize for that, Kristy. Just take it for what it was—things said in the heat of anger."

"Jason, I meant to—to finish what we started, honestly, I did,'' Kristy said urgently. ''You know I wanted you just as much as—but then something went wrong. I couldn't go through with it because I . . . suddenly realized that when you love someone the way I love—''

''Kristy, I'm so beat I'm about to drop in my tracks and I just don't have the patience to stand here and listen to you agonize over love gone sour or sweet or wherever the hell it's gone!'' Jason said roughly. Realizing the tightness of his grip, he dropped his hands. ''I accepted your reason for your actions, I've apologized for mine. Now let's let it go at that.''

His voice gentled. ''You look like you're about to fold at any second. Get yourself to bed, Kristy. I'll see you when I get back. Goodnight.''

Defeated, Kristy bade him goodnight. She watched his tall form until it was swallowed up by the palms. The wind played in their fronds, a soft sighing sound, as formless as tears streaming down a face.

She had carefully made no promises. There was nothing to be gained by staying here any longer than she had to. She would leave the picture she'd made for him in the office tomorrow morning, and then she'd close up Alex's house and go home where she belonged.

Go home with pride and dignity intact. It was cold comfort, but it was something.

Chapter Thirteen

"A touch of flu, Flora?" Kristy exclaimed, aghast at the white-faced woman who greeted her. With those dark circles under her eyes, Flora looked so small and fragile, Kristy could not contain her wrathful concern. "How long were you sick? And how could you not tell me?"

"What would you have done, hopped a plane and come home? Was your dreadful Mr. Thorne that compassionate? I'll hear no more about it," Flora stated.

"The devil you won't! Now take off your clothes and put on a gown. You're staying in bed for a solid week!" Kristy flared.

In between pampering her cousin and forcefully keeping her off her feet, Kristy did a great many other things that first week home. One of them was to answer, steadily and without visible resentment, the avid questions of longtime friends and neighbors. She was kept on edge by their persistance in bringing up Steve's name, in slyly informing her that he was not yet married or engaged, in patting her hand and looking sad and assuring her that things had a way of working out. Killing kindness, Kristy called it.

"Good grief, you'd think I'd been left at the altar!" she told Flora.

"Kristy, everyone in town thought you and Steve were going to be married. Agreed, it was assumption on their part, but it's only natural to . . . they mean well, honey."

"But it's been four months! How long are they going to mourn my terrible, dreadful, *heartbreaking* tragedy!" Kristy began to laugh. "I swear, Flora, it's the craziest thing! I don't even think about Steve anymore. I've been gone four months, I had a fabulous job, I've seen and done things that should have them pea-green with envy—and they're still feeling sorry for me!"

"Perhaps they are pea-green with envy," Flora suggested gently. "A sure cure for envy is feeling sorry for the object of that envy."

"Maybe," Kristy said. Proceeding on that assumption, she adopted a noncommital smile and cheerfully overlooked the comments which annoyed her. There were more important matters to occupy her mind. She was still determined to open her own shop, but the major decision of where to locate kept varying from one day to the next, until she was driven to distraction by this uncharacteristic vacillation.

It was Flora's wistful comment about the nearness of winter and how much she dreaded it, that triggered a new train of thought. Why spend another winter here? *There was Houston, San Antonio, Corpus Christi—the whole golden sunbelt stretched out before them,* Katie thought with rising excitement. They had nothing holding them here. She had been home such a short time, yet already she felt like a caged bird.

Gradually Kristy had come to realize that she had outgrown her environment, that this vague sense of being smothered, both physically and mentally, was directly related to the tight, restrictive, dully sophoric atmosphere of a small town. She would always love it, but she no longer fit into the space she had left four months ago.

A square peg jammed into a round hole, she thought with stale humor, but it was more truth than cliche. The Kristy who came home again was irrevocably altered. She saw it in the eyes which watched her with faint puzzlement. The naive young girl they knew as Kristin Loring had returned a woman.

Kristy had mixed emotions about that. Maturity commanded a painfully high price. But she had both the courage and the confidence to sell this house and start a life for herself and Flora in a strange new city. Armed only with intelligence and a smidgin of practical experience, it wouldn't be the easiest thing she'd ever done, Kristy reflected, but she could do it.

When Flora called her for lunch, she left off scrubbing the bathroom tiles and hastened downstairs, her manner crisp and assured as she related her new idea. Flora was amenable to leaving Rhyland, if that was what Kristy wanted. Kristy faltered for an instant; what did she want? She took no joy in anything, a feeling of deep loss and sadness accompanied her every waking moment and wet her face when she slept. A robot that duty turned on in the morning, turned off at night, Kristy wretchedly admitted, forcing a confident smile.

"I think it would be good for both of us," she said firmly. They talked it through to final agreement, and later that afternoon, Kristy called a realtor friend.

She gave a vexed sigh as she hung up. "He says the market for old houses is extremely depressed, Flora, and that we must have this place in tiptop shape before giving it to him to sell. I guess we'd best get on it."

After a week of rest, Flora was looking and feeling much better, and insistant upon helping. Kristy wasn't too sure that her cousin's malaise did not stem from loneliness. Wrapped in this fine guilt, she gently directed Flora to easy tasks, mainly sorting through the incredible accumulation of nearly three decades of aquisition.

Feeling a sense of racing against time, Kristy painted every room in the house, scoured and waxed the hard-wood floors, and tackled the many, tiny-paned windows. She could not afford to rest on her laurels until the house was sold, but at least she could leave it in the peak of condition. She scrubbed harder, ran faster, worked like one possessed. By the end of the third week, she had the interior of the house glistening with clean. She tackled the yard, the flower beds, painted the peeling picket fence, called the Salvation Army to come haul away usable discards, and Lord, but she was tired!

"Rest awhile, Kristy," Flora urged.

"There's no time to rest," Kristy said impatiently. "The sooner we get resettled, the better."

Time passed in a blur of activity, but by Friday she had run out of things to do and was faced with the next step, the actual move itself. She hadn't thought it would be so painful to arrive at that point. Methodically, she called the realtor and put the house in his hands, arranged with a local used furniture dealer to come on the morrow, then sat down to make a list of orderly departure.

As she picked up her pencil, she glanced at the calendar. Today was the thirtieth. Jason would have already finished his business in Dallas and returned to Hawaii. Strange how distant and remote Kauai had become in just this short time. *Except for the bright warm spot that glowed constant in her heart, the memory of her time on the island receded to a misty once-upon-a-time,* she thought wistfully, *faded to a dream, a beautiful dream . . .*

Blinking at the rush of tears, she put down her list and went outside, looking for something physical to do. The shutters of the downstairs windows were a little dingy, she was relieved to note. She decided to paint them rather than wash them. Clad in a two piece swim suit and a wide brimmed hat to shield her face, she was soon perched on a ladder, painting in mindless dedication, oblivious to everything around her.

"What on earth are you doing!" an incredulous voice inquired. "Get down from there at once!"

Kristy was so astounded she dropped her paintbrush. "Yes, Jason," she said distractedly, and had actually stepped down a rung before a blazing rush of anger supplanted astonishment and raised her voice two full octaves.

"You stop that! You just stop giving me orders! This is my house and my ladder and I will roost on it if I choose!"

"I said at once," Jason repeated.

Kristy's head spun wildly. "Jason, may I remind you that this is my yard and that I no longer work for you. What are you doing in my yard, anyway?" she ended in a squeak as the dazzling wonder of it belatedly hit her. Jason Thorne, positively edible in a crisp white shirt and black slacks and looking exasperated with her as usual, was standing in her yard! Incredible!

Already precariously balanced, she let go of the ladder and threw up her hands. "Damm it, come here!" Jason growled, and plucked her off the ladder. Then he went up it and got her painting equipment, and back down again without mussing a hair on that glossy black head.

Incredible!

"Close your mouth, Mermaid," Jason suggested.

Feeling adrift in a mine field, singingly alive with joy, Kristy closed her mouth with a snap, and immediately reopened it. "I—you—it's just that you're the last person in the world I expected to see here—in Rhyland!" she said wildly. "Why aren't you in Hawaii?"

259

she blurted.

"Because I'm here," Jason said most reasonably. "Now if you're through asking questions? . . ."

Through asking questions Kristy thought incredulously. She had, by actual count, ten-thousand questions swarming around her mind like a flock of maddened butterflies! "No, I've one more. Just what the devil are you doing here?" she heard herself saying coolly. "You've got no business here, standing in my front yard—interrupting my painting!"

He flashed her a toe-tingling grin. "You're very impertinent, Mermaid; anyone ever tell you that?"

"Oh, Jason!" The joyous shout sang through her veins. "I believe you did. Now, why are you—oh! Uh, this is my cousin, Miss Flora Ramsey; Jason Thorne," she gulped, taking note of her cousin materializing out of a pittosporum shrub.

Flora displayed little surprise at the startling presence of this young, handsome, and obviously important visitor. Kristy wished she was as good at concealing hers. "Mr. Thorne, my pleasure," Flora said. "I've heard such a lot about you."

"Ah no, the pleasure is mine, Miss Ramsey," Jason warmly corrected. His eyes crinkled. "I hope what you heard was complimentary?"

Flora looked so embarrassed, he laughed aloud as he cut a glance at Kristy. Flora blushed. "Would you like some refreshments, Mr. Thorne? It's so hot . . ." Turning, she led the way into the cool, shadowed parlor.

Kristy mutely followed, feeling that the whole world had gone mad. Jason Thorne in her parlor. The world had gone mad! Jason looked around with avid interest, noting the family portraits, and the large picture of a young, smug-faced Kristy clad in her Sunday best; a Bible in one hand and a dainty little purse in the other, black patent Mary Janes and lacey white stockings, ruffled pinafore and fat sausage curls tied with a big pink ribbon. Jason's smile spoke volumes. Kristy flushed hotly, her green eyes firing daggers at him. Jason strolled leisurely around the room.

"I must say I agree with you, Kristy, your mother was very beautiful," he said, pausing before the portrait done by a local artist. He laughed softly. "You don't resemble her very much . . . save for the curve of mouth, and that rather stubborn chin."

Amused blue eyes licked her. Suddenly realizing her half-naked state, Kristy leaped to her feet and said, "I'll go bathe and change. Excuse me—" and went flying up the stairs.

After a record-breaking shower, she donned a white cotton sundress and knotted up her hair with a kind of obtuse desire to nullify any natural appeal she possessed. She had a sneaking suspicion why he was here, and she intended cutting him off before he got Flora all stirred up abut something Kristy did not intend to permit. Flora's birthday was past, and she was quite satisfied with the gifts she'd received. They needed nothing from Jason Thorne and if he brought it up, she would tell him, Kristy vowed, courteously, of course, but tell him—No.

That had to be the reason he was here. She could think of no other. None that made a grain of sense.

"We're friends," she desperately reminded her slap-happy self. "It's perfectly natural for friends to . . ." Oh, nothing was perfectly natural. Furiously, she caught back the escaping curls wisping about her cheeks, but they were evidently endowed with a will of their own. Giving it up, she descended the stairs, pausing on the lower landing with an annoyed frown as she heard Flora inviting Jason to stay for supper.

Listening to Jason's happy acceptance, her annoyance increased. Inviting him to supper implied a degree of intimacy she would rather not allow, it was vitally important to keep a wall between this man and her vulnerable self. But how could she retract Flora's invitation without being rude? Hospitality was a proud Texas tradition. Flouting it put her in the same catagory as cattle-rustling!

"Ah, you've joined us at last," Jason approved, rising to his feet as she swept into the room. Flora's eyes rounded at the angry glance flung her way. "Miss Ramsey has invited me to stay for supper," Jason said so innocently, Kristy w. k 1rd put to suppress a caustic retort. He was thoroughly enjoying this.

"Yes, I heard. And of course you're welcome," Kristy said, sinking down on the couch beside Flora. Jason sat at ease in her father's old leather chair, and she would have liked to pinch herself to see if she was hallucinating or not, but Kristy clasped her hands in her lap and gave Jason a commanding look.

Musingly, he gazed around the small, old-fashioned room, and Kristy's discomfort grew apace. Seen through his eyes, everything in it looked shabby and

262

commonplace; which it was. Kristy had replaced none of her parent's furnishings. Her home was comfortable, if inelegant, and she fiercely resented her raw unease. This house did not reflect her personal tastes, but it was her roots, the source of strength that had molded her, and her gaze intercepted his with icy pride.

Girded for battle, she was promptly disarmed by the gentle smile that curved his beautiful mouth. That thick lock of hair fell enchantingly over his brow, and she ached to brush it back, to go to him and kiss the deep cleft in his chin. The room seemed stifling hot to her, the tension knotting her throat a physical pain. Seeing everything in this glaring new light, Kristy noted Flora's hands, so small and finely made, calloused and permanantly reddened from years of gardening and housework, the simple housedress she wore somehow a poignant accusation.

If I had the money, I'd give her anything her heart desires, Kristy thought, aching with nebulous guilts. Contrarily, as soon as her cousin went to check on dinner, Kristy said, "Jason, would you take it dreadfully amiss if I asked precisely what you're doing here? And if it's what I think it is, the answer is a flat no."

Jason smiled into his tea glass as Flora came back into the room. Kristy looked from one face to the other with a sinking heart. How could she have thought that a simple *no* would deter Jason Thorne?

"Jason, you didn't," she groaned.

"Kristy, I did," Jason mimicked. "It's already settled; your cousin thinks it's quite possible she can conquer her fear of flying by taking her first flight in my plane."

263

"Oh Kristy, isn't it wonderful!" Flora burst out. "Mr. Thorne asked me not to say anything until he'd talked with you, but—It's not inconveniencing him at all! He explained to me that he quite often gives people rides in his plane, so it's not as if . . . well, it's simply a friendly gesture, that's all," she assured.

"He assured me you were friends," she added, looking a little anxious as Kristy made a sharp movement.

Kristy subsided. "Yes, I suppose you could say we're friends. I'll have to think about this, Flora," she said. Jason's quick grin did not escape notice.

"Nonsense, nothing to think about, it's all settled," he said. "We'll go into the details later. This is delicious iced tea, Miss Ramsey, may I have some more?" he asked Flora with his most charming smile. Kristy seethed. Flora lit up all over. She bade him wash up for supper, and Kristy to come help her in the kitchen.

Kristy closed her mouth and dutifully followed orders. Once they were alone, Flora chided, "Mr. Thorne seems a lovely man. I can't imagine why you felt compelled to describe him in such derogatory terms, Kristy. I've never met anyone so warm and friendly and easy to talk to."

"May I do something to help, Miss Ramsey?" Jason inquired in an unctuous voice as he strolled into the kitchen and shrunk it to half size.

Flora promptly handed him the heavy tureen of chicken and dumplings. Hot biscuits and fresh garden green beans, her superb sweet and sour pickles, and a spicy spinach salad rounded out the menu. Jason ate with hearty appetite, heaping praise upon Flora until she glowed.

Kristy was bemused at the rapport between those two just-met and totally-dissimilar people. Flora's bubbling questions about the island and his respectful answers, struck her as just another quill of incredulity. Normally shy and self-effacing, Flora bloomed like a rose under his charm, and the kitchen resounded with laughter and chatter.

"I can't believe this," Kristy informed her coffee cup. They stopped and looked at her with identical expressions, then resumed their conversation. With the guilelessness of a child, Flora pried into Jason's background, and despite her air of bored disinterest, Kristy listened eagerly to the precious nuggets of information, helplessly drawn into their enjoyment. Jason adroitly worked in the house he was building. Except for carpets, wall coverings and such, it was nearly completed, and it was a trial for a man to make those kind of decisions, he lamented to Flora.

"Why don't you just turn it over to your personal decorator?" Kristy coldly inquired.

"This is my house, Kristy, naturally I'm interested in the finished creation. Too much so to just turn it over to a decorator, even a personal one who knows my tastes," he said, aiming his remark at Flora, who bobbed her head and gravely agreed.

Kristy lowered her eyes and sipped her coffee, remembering that spacious master bedroom with its banks of windows that could bring the world in, or intimately close it out. He had said nothing about the picture she'd left for him. Well, it was only a blown-up photograph, Kristy bitterly denied its value.

The sunshine pooling on the table had a mellow gold look to it. *Nearly September, and soon the harsh, crying winds of winter would come*, she thought, feeling as if they already had.

If this kept on, she was going to wind up in tears. Kristy got up to fetch the coffee pot. Her hip brushed his arm as she refilled his cup. To be so near him was exquisite torment.

"I feel I must repay the pleasure of such a meal, Miss Ramsey. What are the social facilities in your town?" he asked as he lay down his silverware.

Two helpings of fresh strawberry shortcake had sweetened his voice to a velvety purr. How did he eat like that and still keep his trim figure, Kristy idly wondered. Keeping her eyes and voice the temperature of an icy green river, she said, "We don't require payment. Besides, I'm sure you've something to do—"

"Ah no," Jason smilingly denied. "I'm staying the night at the Rhyland Inn, and frankly, that motel room doesn't tempt. Isn't there some place we can go for some after dinner entertainment?" he asked Flora.

"Well, there's a dance at the Rotary tonight," Flora said.

Kristy's mouth twisted. She could just imagine the urbane Jason Thorne at one of their country music and beer dances. "I'm sure Jason isn't interested in a Rotary dance. There's quite a nice bar in your motel—"

"It would be my pleasure to escort you and your cousin to the Rotary dance," Jason gravely told Flora.

Kristy took a deep breath. She felt explosive with all

the emotions she was holding in tight restraint, and an evening with Jason Thorne was too disturbing to even contemplate.

"Flora, if you and Mr. Thorne wish to attend the dance, then do so, but I have no desire to accompany you," she said with a freezing look for Jason.

"Your cousin is a mulish little thing, isn't she," Jason remarked to Flora. "How did you manage to survive all those years you sacrificed to rearing her to this ungracious state?"

Kristy thought this a very low blow. She didn't hear Flora's reply. Her mind churning, she helped clear the kitchen, so preoccupied she broke a plate. The trip to Kauai was the main culprit. How to refuse Flora this enormous pleasure? Or permit it, and still retain her own integrity? Perhaps in his lifestyle, such extravagant gestures were too commonplace to warrant comment, but she still felt it a lowgrade form of charity, and *the possibility of being unreasonable and selfish did not alter conviction,* she thought grimly. And all this reflection had accomplished nothing but destroying one of her mother's good china plates!

After what seemed an endless time, Jason left, and Kristy turned to her cousin with a wry smile. "Well, Flora, I guess we'd best get dressed. Seems we're attending the Rotary dance. Why don't you wear that pretty red dress I bought you?"

A curious expression flitted across Flora's face before she turned aside. She was a simple, good-natured woman, innocent in many respects, but she was both intelligent and mature, and Kristy had unconsciously

267

relegated her to the role of an overbright child these past weeks. Suddenly, hideously aware of her sin, Kristy caught her arm and said, "Flora, can we talk a minute? You know I'm not against your trip to Kauai. I wanted so much for you to have it! The only reason I couldn't make an instant decision was . . . well, we're right in the middle of . . . we've put the house up for sale and to just drop everything—That's what I've been wrestling with all evening. But of course you have a say in the matter . . . in everything we do, you know that."

Flora's smile was beautifully understanding. "Child, I know what you've been wrestling with, and of course I understand. I freely gave you the right to make the decision about our life, and whatever you decide will be fine with me," she said, leaving Kristy even more undecided.

Sometime later, she got out of the tub without realizing she'd gotten into it. The scent of crushed violets sweetened the steamy little bathroom, so apparently she had remembered to add bath crystals to the water. She splashed cologne over her body and daubed on perfume. Excitement, rich and heady and undeniable, flowed like a winy river as the thought kept slamming her heart; Jason Thorne was here in Rhyland. In her parlor, she amended, as his husky laugh sent her pulses skyrocketing.

She selected a simple lilac frock of summery gauze, styled with a low, rounded neckline and a full, scalloped skirt. After adding high heeled slippers and placing the blue pearl between her breasts, she gave attention to her hair, but her attention kept escaping to the room below. Kristy absently brushed as she listened to sounds as beautiful as any symphony; her cherished cousin's chirping voice blending with Jason's resonant tones. *If she could record it,* she thought wistfully, *she would have no more trouble going to sleep at night.*

Leaving her hair flowing free, she checked herself in the mirror. Radiant green eyes reflected the happiness racing through her blood with wild turbulence. She could not prevent the stupidity of hope. "Twice a fool is twice bitter," she reminded the flushed face in her mirror. "He told you precisely what he wanted from you. Do you need it engraved on stone?"

He laughed again, and Kristy despised herself for this weakening wave of love, but she was powerless to combat it. He would see no sign of it, she vowed. Cool and composed, she joined Jason in the old-fashioned parlor.

Flora was too tired to attend the dance. Successfully controlling her consternation, Kristy looked at the drawn white face and aired her concern, saying that perhaps she too should stay home, but she soon found herself being firmly escorted to Jason's rented car.

When he had settled himself behind the wheel, he turned to her and smiled. "You look lovely, Mermaid, like a flower in that dress."

"Thank you. I do hope you won't use that ridiculous name tonight?" Kristy snapped. She had enough to contend with without giving rise to false speculations.

"Very well. Tonight, we're Kristy and Jason," he said agreeably.

"It will be Kristy and Mr. Thorne," she flatly

corrected.

"If that's what you want," Jason said. For a moment, all the ugly words they had exchanged crowded between them. Jason determinedly banished them with light conversation pertaining to the charm of her town, Cousin Flora, the sky now darkening into pink and gold day's end.

Keeping an icy distance between them, Kristy stared blindly ahead. She was too sensitive to miss the tension in Jason. Beneath that easy manner coiled an anger he could not totally conceal. They were each acting a part in a play she did not comprehend, but she was grimly resolved to play it through.

Disregarding the curious stares which followed them, Jason took her arm and jauntily escorted her into the big, barnlike hall. It was Friday night, and not only the local people but all the nearby towns had turned out in force. Kristy felt giddy with the ordeal of facing all the inquisitive eyes taking note of their entrance.

How could they not take note? Clad in a cerulean blue shirt, superbly tailored slacks and an aura of power that practically screamed his importance, Jason detained her at the entrance while he lazily scanned the room. His suntanned skin glowed against the blue shirt, and his glossy hair refracted the rays from overhead lights. Tall and proud, he stood beside her, his head erect and shoulders back in unconscious response to that frank appraisal.

As Kristy glanced up at him, her heart performed a series of aerial leaps that threatened to fold her legs. He was commandingly attractive, and her chin came up in prideful acceptance of the respect accorded her. Jason laughed softly at the haughty tilt of head. "It's your show, Mermaid," he reminded in a husky whisper.

Grimly at ease, Kristy led the way to a table occupied by several schoolchums and their husbands. It was impossible not to relish the look in feminine eyes as she carelessly performed introductions. Throughout the evening Jason was enduringly good natured and overflowing with such charm, he had them eating from his hand, *especially the female contingent,* she thought, watching him with feigned amusement. With Kristy, he was impeccably circumspect, and she gave to him a carefully structured indifference. However, cynical blue eyes informed her he knew as well as she that her social status in Rhyland had been elevated to staggering heights, simply because he was escorting her.

Everyone knew, of course, that she was leaving town again, and everyone had something to say about it. She could not take anymore of this. "Let's go now, please?" she whispered to Jason.

Jason drove her home without attempting conversation, his mood chill and withdrawn. When he stopped the car in front of her house, they sat in silence for a time. The tension mounted until her neck ached from the strain of holding her head erect. Whatever was coming was not going to be pleasant. Jason fairly crackled with anger. Well, she was ready, even eager for it. Anger would fill this aching void, this hurting, wanting, aching void!

The attack began on a totally unexpected front. "Why didn't you tell me about your ankle?"

he burst out.

"My ankle?" Kristy echoed. "Why I—I just didn't. How did you . . . oh, Flora told you."

"Yes, Flora told me," he mocked harshly. "You have a serious handicap and yet you let me stand there and call you the clumsiest woman I've ever known!"

"It isn't a serious handicap, just a trivial defect that I've had all my life. I pay no attention to it, so why should I go round telling people about it? And as for what you said, you merely spoke the truth. I'm not all that graceful, with or without a weak ankle," she said. "Jason, why did you come here? It wasn't just for Flora, was it?"

"Not entirely, no. I didn't conclude my business in Dallas until this afternoon, too late to start home, so I decided to come meet Flora." He shrugged, knowing how flimsy that sounded. "And too, we have some unfinished business ourselves, don't we?"

"Not to my knowledge—"

Razor-edge, Jason's voice slashed across her disclaimer. "You give me a beautiful gift, but instead of actually giving it to me so I could express my appreciation, you leave it in the hotel office with a cute little note. *I thought you might like this for your study*," he mimicked. "I return from my trip expecting you to be there, only to find that you'd run back to Texas the very next morning—"

"I did not run back to Texas. I made it very clear that I was leaving that next morning. If you thought differently, it was because you wanted to! I made you no promises, Jason. If you hadn't been in such a hurry to

272

get back to Meleia, maybe you'd have realized that!''

"Get back to Meleia?'' Jason echoed. He turned sharply to face her. "You thought I was sleeping with Melly?'' he asked incredulously.

"What's so astounding about that? You said she was staying at your apartment—and she is a very desirable woman,'' Kristy defied that black scowl.

"Melly's a child—a voluptuous, loveable *child!*'' Jason exploded. His hands clamped around the steering wheel. "I taught her to ride her first bicycle, for God's sake! She's had a girlish crush on me since she was sixteen, but what in hell is so unusual about that! It thrills me that you think so highly of me, Kristy,'' he said acidly.

Aching with regret, Kristy touched his hand. "I'm sorry, Jason.'' She withdrew her hand as he stared stonily ahead. "Seems I'm always the one saying I'm sorry,'' she said bitterly. "Don't men know how to pronounce those two simple words?''

Jason gave a short, ugly laugh, and got out of the car. "Come on, it's late—I've had a long day,'' he said curtly.

Kristy slid across the seat and came up in the circle of his arm. His cologne slammed her senses, and she went weak with longing. "Oh, Jason,'' she whispered. Mindlessly she lifted her face to his kiss. His fingers digging into her soft shoulders, Jason roughly pulled her to him, his mouth crushing her lips against her teeth. He was hard and tight with fury. His mouth ground down, savagely bruising.

There was no pleasure in it. He set her aside with a

273

mutter of disgust, and closed the car door.

Blankfaced, Kristy preceded him up the walk. *It was like a chess game,* she thought forlornly, *and she was a terrible player.* Her stiff back taunted him, rebuffed him. She heard him swear softly, softly.

"Do you want to talk about it, or shall I assume we leave tomorrow for Kauai?" he asked as they stood on the porch.

"Jason, I know you mean well, and as much as I appreciate—"

"Oh stop it, Kristy! I was not at all inconvenienced by coming here, and I happened to enjoy the evening, as well as the dinner. And as to my motives for disregarding your expressed wishes, after hearing so much about Flora, I took a personal interest in her birthday gift—is that so damned odd? I'm not entirely without feelings, you now. It's possible that I might have a normal desire now and then," he said scathingly.

"Possible, but I can't accept your reasoning—"

"Accept it or not, it's true. This has nothing to do with you, it's entirely between Miss Ramsey and myself. However, I realize that unless *you* wholeheartedly agree, *she* won't. And I hope to hell you're not that pridefully selfish!"

"We're arguing about a woman you met for the first time this evening," Kristy said faintly. Eyeing his clenched jaw, she knew they were arguing about something far deeper than that, but just what escaped her. She didn't care any more. He was only fighting her, she was fighting both of them, and she'd run out of ammunition.

274

"However, you're right, I'm not that selfish. Very well. Ten o'clock tomorrow? That will give me time to make a few arrangements. Goodnight, and thank you for the evening."

"My pleasure," came Jason's sardonic response. "Ten tomorrow is fine with me. Goodnight."

Watching that tall figure stride down the sidewalk, Kristy stopped trying to delude herself any longer. Nothing could have prevented her from going with him tomorrow—to Kauai or Timbuktu, it didn't matter, just as long as it was with him. She rubbed her bruised mouth. Illogical, but when had love ever been logical?

Chapter Fourteen

The California coastline dropped away as the sleek Lear jet again climbed above the clouds after their brief refueling stop. Stupid of her to have dreaded this flight, Kristy reflected. Jason was positively a knight in shining armor. Seeing that he had Flora well in hand, she curled up in the gray velvet seat and drifted off to sleep.

When she awoke feeling rumpled and befuddled, she found it hard to sort out her realities. This time yesterday she was perched on a ladder painting shutters; today she was somewhere over the Pacific in a private jet with a big genial Sir Galahad in attendance. She felt idiotically happy. *Just watching Jason's unaffected smile was worth all the torment to come*, she thought, returning it as she yawned and flexed her arms.

His eyes were impossibly blue, and warm as a summer morning. Half convinced that she was certifiably insane, Kristy stretched her travel-cramped legs, then began to search for her shoes. The long trip was coming to an end and she couldn't wait to bathe and change this wrinkled dress. *Jason looked as fresh as when he got out of the shower this morning,* she thought, eyeing the neat red shirt and gray slacks.

As they neared the island, towering white clouds banked the eastern sky, but Kauai itself lay like a jewel in the sunlight. Flora's excitement spilled over like drops of sparkling water. Jason chuckled at her gasp as the plane descended lower and lower over a sugarcane field, giving every appearance of landing in that deep green sward. "I assure you there's a runway down there," he said, laughing again at her dubious look. When the silver ribbon of concrete miraculously emerged, Flora heaved such a sigh, he was tickled anew.

That gentleness she loved in him was never more evident to Kristy. Suffused with affection, she watched him with her beloved cousin. They appeared to have known each other all their lives and were the best of friends. Kristy shook her head with a wry smile, but she was profoundly moved. However conflicted her own emotions at returning to Kauai, Flora's open delight was everything she had imagined. Flora trusted Jason implicitly. So did Kristy, implicitly.

As soon as the plane rolled to a stop, Jason was on his feet. A car bearing the hotel's insignia waited on the runway. Taking one of the leis the driver carried over,

Jason dropped it around Flora's neck and kissed her cheek. "Welcome to Kauai, Miss Ramsey," he said gently.

"An old Thorne tradition," Kristy murmured. She knew enough about Island customs to realize that Flora's lei was created from the rare *ilima*, and her own from *maile*, which were bestowed only upon very special people. Her smile romped out of control as Jason carefully drew the lei over her curly head and settled it in place, then ceremoniously kissed her cheek.

Naturally he took command of their luggage and getting them settled into the car. Kristy derided her enjoyment of this; modern day women were not supposed to enjoy dominant males. *But since she was hopelessly out of date in every other way, she might as well admit this too,* she thought, curiously unbothered by it.

The air sang with the perfume of *piake* and gingers and a thousand other flowers, and gaily colored birds flitted through the enormous bouquets that were poinciana trees. Kristy's heartbeat cadenced the words flowing unceasingly through her mind. *Home again!* There was the hotel looking impossibly lovely in the afternoon sunlight, and Meleia, looking even more so, flinging her arms around Kristy the moment she exited the car.

"Oh, Kristy, I'm so glad you're back—I've missed you!" she cried in a lilting voice.

Surprised at this warm greeting, and at how much it meant to her, Kristy hugged her, swimming with guilt, saying, "Meleia, I've missed you too!—Oh, Ben!" she wailed as the big man scooped her up with a gravelly roar of welcome. *It was like a homecoming,* Kristy tearfully thought, and when she heard Jason directing the bellboy to cottage number ten, she could scarcely contain the flood behind her eyelids.

There was chilled champagne and an outrageous basket of the most exotic fruits on the coffee table, butterfly orchids in the bathroom and a dozen white roses in the bedroom. Twin beds had replaced the king-sized bed, temporarily, Kristy supposed. She felt relieved at that. She could not have borne to sleep in the bed where he had lain with her.

Laughter and chatter filled the cottage as they sipped champagne and everyone spoke at once, with too much to tell and not enough time to tell it. Jason sat at ease in one of the green velvet chairs. Each time Kristy looked at him, yesterday telescoped into now, until her voice grew tremulous, until her heart was physically hurting.

In her yellow sarong, Meleia flitted about like a honeybird, her melodious voice rising and falling with excitement, a lovely, joyous child. Watching her, Kristy bitterly regretted her former aloofness. And the ugly reason for it. How could she have mistaken Jason's brotherly manner with Meleia!

Flat blue eyes asked the same bitter question. Kristy's mute apology collided with a stone wall.

They were Jason's guests for dinner that night, Flora looking astonishingly young and pretty in Kristy's white crepe with its flatteringly draped neckline, clinging to Ben's strong arm, and Kristy in strapless lavendar gauze, clinging to nothing but pride.

After a delicious dinner, they went to the club to listen to Meliea's beautiful songs. They stayed quite late. Jason was a marvelous host, and by midnight, Kristy had melted into a puddle of love that absolutely must not be given expression. She refused to meet his gaze, fearful that hers would betray her powerful longing to be the one who shared his bed tonight.

Jason escorted them to the cottage and bid Flora a warm goodnight, but detained Kristy when she started in the door. "Are you too tired to join me for a nightcap?" he politely inquired.

"No, not at all. You go on to bed, Flora, I'll be just awhile," Kristy said.

Jason absently took her hand as they walked through the moon-dappled night. He suddenly stopped to face her, and he was too near; Kristy ordered her body to move, but nothing obeyed. Jason stood looking down into her face for a long moment. Unable to bear the silence, she asked quietly, "What is it, Jason?"

"I have a question or two. Everything might as well be open and honest between us, don't you agree? I'm referring, of course, to your little ultimatum. Are the rules still in effect, Mermaid?"

Resenting that light, teasing voice, Kristy said evenly, "Still in effect. And still adverse to a night or two of meaningless pleasure . . . and I'd appreciate it if you'd turn off the charm, it gets irksome after awhile." Instantly contrite at her pettiness, she touched his arm. "I'm sorry, that was uncalled for. But I really would prefer this impersonal relationship to the rather uncomfortable one we had before."

"Alright," he lightly agreed. "Nothing like being honest, hmm?"

Thinking of the lie she was living, Kristy smothered a laugh. "Honesty is the best policy, so they say," she murmured. "And while we're being so terribly honest, let me tell you, please, why I acted so stupidly about Meleia. She told me that you were very old and good friends, but I—took it the wrong way. And she never, not once, clarified your relationship. I . . . the main reason for my blindness was jealousy. She's just so naturally beautiful. . ." Kristy shrugged, hoping her explanation would suffice.

"Alright, we'll forget it," Jason said with his usual insouciance, but she knew it wasn't going to be that easy to forget. She had cast some very ugly aspersions on his character, maligned someone he loved, a sin in itself to a man so fiercely loyal to those he cared about.

"Did you see him while you were home?" Jason abruptly asked.

Groping to follow, Kristy shook her head. "Him? Oh, you mean Steve. Yes, I saw him once or twice, accidental meetings."

Irony thinned his voice. "Ah. And did love bloom anew?"

"Does love bloom? I wonder where they got that frivolous term?" she returned with a chuckle to show how absurd he was being. Turning, Kristy placed a hand on the bole of a palm and tipped her face to the moon. She was literally aching with love, but not for Steve. She didn't want to talk about him, and she especially didn't want to stay here in the perfumed darkness

281

with Jason. Last night, laying in her own bed in a fever of anguish, she had made a firm decision. As much as she wanted sex with Jason, she had to have it all, and that all included his love. *All or nothing*, she thought bleakly, there was no in-between for Kristin Loring.

When she sensed a sharp movement behind her, she asked gaily, "Shall we have that nightcap now?"

"One nightcap, coming up." Jason took her arm and steered her back onto the brick path. Ben had left them at ten to resume his bar duty. Jason signaled to him as they moved through the crowded room and out to the new open-air section of the bar. They chatted idly about its effectiveness until the attractive waitress brought their drinks; a brandy for Jason, and a splashy rum and citrus juice for Kristy.

"Well, when do you intend finishing up that new house?" Kristy asked with artificial brightness.

He gave her a sour look. "I'm too busy to fool with houses. Look, I want Flora to have a good time while she's here, and I have to leave tomorrow, so I've placed a car and driver at your disposal. Have you anything to say to that?" he challenged.

"No. Except that such extravagant gestures leave me a little breathless. Private planes and cars with drivers are a bit outside my experience, we live a little more simpler lives," she wryly confessed. "However, I will make no more trouble about anything you want to do for Flora."

Jason grunted. "See that you remember that. While you're here, you're guests of the hotel—"

"Oh no we are not!"

"You have an exceedingly short memory, Kristy!"

"My memory is impeccable, Jason! I said for Flora, not me. We are paying guests, I'll bear the expense of room and meals while we're here. If I couldn't, we'd have gone to Alex's house," she ended vehemently.

"Damn it, Kristy, this is for Flora! Look, this is her first visit to a hotel that has been in your family for nearly two decades, it's perfectly normal to extend my hospitality. At least give me credit for being civilized!"

Kristy wilted under the lash of anger, but not for long. "While I admit to the possibility of your being civilized, I don't see that it logically follows that we should sponge off you any more than we have already! You know—"

"I know one blasted thing! That you're so damned muleheaded I'd like to shake you!"

"And you're so arrogant I'd like to slap you!"

Taken aback at having become embroiled in a quarrel so quickly, they glared at each other until Ben suddenly appeared with two fresh drinks. "Thought you might be needing these," came his laconic opinion. He set the drinks before them, scooped up the empties, and sauntered off. Jason touched her hand, then quickly drew back. She knew he felt the tingling electricity too, the sexual awareness surging between them stronger than their barbed anger.

Jason sighed. "Oh hell, Mermaid . . . let's dance."

"The band has already quit for the night."

"Yea, so they have." He lifted his glass and regarded her over the rim. "Then let's drink—anything but talk."

Kristy suddenly laughed, green eyes sparkling on that moody face. "It's probably just as well you're leaving. One day back on the island, and we're going at it hammer and tongs."

Jason grinned and raised his glass to hers. "Here's to calm, pleasant, peaceful relationships, Kristy. I sincerely doubt we'll ever have such."

"Wouldn't you find it a bit boring?"

"Maybe. But I'd sure like a chance to find out," he said so glumly, she laughed again. Jason drained his glass and set it down sharply. "Well, I have an early flight in the morning. I'll walk you back to the cottage."

"I don't want to go back yet. I haven't finished my drink."

"Then would you take it dreadfully amiss if I left you to enjoy your drink alone?"

"Of course not. I'd find it delightfully in character," Kristy quipped, wrinkling her nose at him. She wanted desperately to ask where he was going and when he would return. "Good night, Jason," she said lightly.

Jason stood up and ruffled her hair. "Good night, Kristy, enjoy your vacation," he said sternly. "Oh, one thing—"

"No more interference, Jason. If you decide to give Flora the whole darn island, I shall swallow hard and say thank you so sweetly, I'll attract bees."

Jason threw back his head and laughed. "Goodnight, Mermaid," he said naturally.

"Goodnight, Jason. Have a nice trip." As she watched him walk lithely out into the night, Kristy gave herself some orders. "Get your priorities in perspective, Kristy; this is a vacation for Flora, nothing else."

The next two days passed gloriously. Flora adored her special status, and even Kristy had to admit to being thrilled at such special treatment. As they skimmed along in the luxurious car, stopping at a whim, lunching when and where they pleased while the driver patiently waited their pleasure, she reflectively decided that if this was what it was like to be rich, one could certainly get used to it in a hurry.

In late afternoon, they returned to the hotel, and Flora rested while Kristy swam or lazily sunned, or chatted with Meleia. Their evenings were given to enjoying whatever live entertainment the hotel offered, usually in the lively bar, under Ben's eagle eye.

The third evening, Kristy was contentedly lounging by the pool waiting out Flora's rest, when Shanna Bouchard appeared at her side. "Miss Loring! How nice to see you again. Jason told me you were back; vacationing this time," she said with a warm smile.

Kristy sat up in blinking surprise. Womanlike, she bridled at the trace of condescension in Shanna's sultry voice. "Are you a guest here, Miss Bouchard?" she asked pleasantly.

Along with her warm smile, Shanna wore a short cotton shift, with extravagantly heeled clogs. She kicked them off and began to unbutton the shift as she gaily replied, "Oh, no, I'm just here for a swim. I do adore this pool, don't you? Jason left this afternoon for San Francisco, and I found myself at loose ends, so I decided a little physical exercise was in order," she said, examining one svelte thigh for muscle tone.

"Oh, I didn't know he was back from his last trip," Kristy said inanely.

Shanna gave her a brief glance. "Why should you? Unfortunately, his pool is being chlorinated today. . . join me?" she invited, peeling off the shift to reveal a stunningly brief bikini.

She could have been a model with those elegantly boyish hips and tiny breasts, Kristy thought. And how generous Jason was with his apartment. Meleia moves out, Shanna moves in. "I think not," Kristy said. She came to her feet. Flora should be up and about, she abruptly decided; calling a casual goodbye to Shanna, she walked swiftly to the cottage.

The evening wasn't much fun, nor was the late night swim all that soothing. Kristy had doggedly blocked all thoughts of Jason and Shanna's relationship, but Shanna's unexpected appearance and her careless words destroyed fragile defenses. Kristy lay in bed and perversely tormented herself with erotic images, imagining Shanna taking possession of that beautiful house and the man who owned it, Shanna in his arms as he explored every inch of that honeygold skin with his mouth and hands. . .

Why was she such a fool when it came to men? A tear trickled down her cheek, and she irritably wiped it away. Self-pity was so stupid! Kristy got up and huddled in the green velvet chair to avoid waking her cousin.

When she went to bed, it was nearly dawn, and she overslept the next morning. Since they were getting a late start for the beach, Kristy ordered breakfast sent to the cottage while she bathed and put on her bikini. Ben was there when she emerged from the bathroom. When he made a teasing remark about breakfasting at ten o'clock, Kristy gave him a brief smile and poured herself a cup of coffee. She didn't want to go anywhere today. *Some time alone would be a blessing,* she thought tiredly, maybe she could unravel some of the tension tightening her chest. But her cousin's wishes took precedence. . .

As if sensing her dilemma, Ben cheerily offered to accompany Flora, and Kristy had miserably few compunctions about taking him up on it, especially since her cousin was so quickly agreeable. After they left, Kristy lounged around the cottage for awhile, but her own company was flatly boring. Alone in these beautiful rooms, she was assailed by memories. Serious words, teasing words, husky love and stingingly contemptous words swirled together in a mad cacophony of sound as she wandered from room to room, remembering a joyous incident here, a bitter hurt there.

She went to Alex's house with vague thoughts of cleaning it just for something to occupy her nervous hands. It was neat as a pin inside and out, but it smelled musty, neglected, too lonely to endure. Feeling like a helpless leaf caught in a turbulent wind, Kristy closed the house. She had not been to the waterfall yet, and dreaded going, but found herself there anyway. A charming wooden bridge spanned the ravine where Jason had fished out a mermaid; people frolicked in the deep green waters of the pool, sunned themselves on the shiny black stones, trampled the ferns. Too many memories here. Kristy went back to the hotel pool.

At five, Flora and Ben still hadn't shown up. Kristy changed into a skirt and white peasant blouse, and went to the lobby. To do what? Tears itched her nose as she walked into the empty office and sat down behind Alex's old desk. It was dusty, evidently not much used now that the managerial staff had moved to handsome new quarters behind the dining room. She cradled her head in her arms and closed her eyes.

"Well, hello, Mermaid!"

Her heart had stopped. In dazzling slow motion, Kristy raised her head at the husky greeting, her eyes suddenly filled with the tall slimness of Jason Thorne. He lounged against the doorframe, a jacket nonchalantly slung over his shoulder, looking tanned and fit in a cream shirt and dove gray slacks.

Kristy busied herself smoothing her skirt. "Hi, Jason. How was your trip?" she asked, relieved at her casual tone.

"My trip was fine." He hung up his jacket and turned to her again, frowning as he commented, "Doesn't look like you're having too good a time."

"Oh, I was just taking a nostalgia break. Ben and Flora went to the beach this morning, and from there is anybody's guess, since they're not back yet. I can't imagine what they're doing," she said worriedly.

"Having fun, I imagine. Come have a drink with me and we'll discuss it," Jason suggested.

Ordered was more like it, thought Kristy, her eyes sparkling again. All it took was his smile to set the sun in place again.

Once they were seated in the pleasant open-air bar, Jason continued the conversation with a preoccupied manner. Eyeing the fingers drumming on the table, Kristy asked, "Is anything wrong, Jason?"

Jason's gaze was on the palm fronds snapping in the wind. "No, of course not. Anyway, nothing that's your concern." He smiled to take the sting out of it. "You're here on vacation, remember? By the way, I'm free tomorrow, so please inform Flora that I intend to monopolize her entire day. I thought we'd go up into the Kokee region. Did you get that far?"

"No, we didn't," Kristy said. Feeling fevered with delight, she listened as he outlined their excursion, and the thought kept pace with her heartbeat; an entire day with Jason! A person ought not be so easily transported, she scolded, and raised shining eyes to his with a disgustingly radiant smile.

A gust of wind snatched napkins off their table. Frowning, Jason said, "There's a storm building up out there. It might get a little windy tomorrow, and it's naturally cool where we're going, so you and Flora bring sweaters."

"A storm? What kind of storm?" Kristy asked sharply.

An eyebrow tilted. "I believe they call them tropical disturbances until they reach hurricane force," Jason said dryly. "Oh, don't look so anxious, Kristy, it's miles away, and it's doubtful we'll even get a whiff of it." He looked at his watch. "Well, I've got a very important date, so I'll have to leave you to drink alone again. Sorry," he smiled, ruefully.

"Quite all right, I've become accustomed to being deserted," Kristy said, excruciatingly gay. Her gaze slithered over his shoulder to the fairly attractive man sitting alone at the bar. "Perhaps I'll find someone who'll stay through an entire drink, who knows!"

Jason had risen to his feet as she gamely carried on. "Perhaps you will," he gently agreed. He half-turned to leave, then swerved back to her. "Today is Meleia's grandmother's seventy-fifth birthday, and cause for gala celebration, since she practically raised the three Thorne scalawags, as she calls us." His wicked grin flashed all over Kristy. "Everyone else got her practical gifts—like warm socks. I got her a flask of Arpege and one of apricot brandy!" he confided, looking highly pleased at his cleverness.

Oh Jason, my darling Jason! Kristy reached up and kissed him with a loud *Umm-ma!* smack of delight. "Give her that from me—for doing such a splendid job with at least one of those scalawags!" she breathlessly commanded.

"If I hadn't already promised to escort a young lady to the party, I'd let you give her that in person, but Meleia's dreadfully jealous—just refuses to share me!" he teased, one big hand ruffling her hair. "See you tomorrow morning—ten o'clock okay?"

"Ten o'clock is fine. Have a good time, Jason," Kristy said with heartfelt sincerity. She yearned intensely to be a part of that intimate celebration.

Jason left, then, and she watched him to the last possible second. How could she have confused an adolescent infatuation with this profound emotion! No matter what its surface disturbances, love flowed as deep and steady as the sea, and with the same implacable power.

Broodingly, she watched the scene around her, the women who sat and waited, the men who roved, and sought. She thought she knew what the women hoped to find here on this sun-gilded isle, but the men puzzled her. Casual pleasure, passion, also casual, no commitments, no constancy, no love; in a month's time they would forget names, faces, the color of eyes and the intimate taste and smell of a particular woman. What had they gained? And what memories did the women who permitted themselves to be used take back with them?

Depression engulfed her. Kristy got up and went back to the cottage.

His hip warmly touching hers, Kristy sat between them in the car, with Jason driving and Flora glued to the window as they wound up and around the Waimea Canyon road. When they reached the *Puu Ka Pele Lookout,* they got out of the car and stood looking at the spectacular view in speechless awe.

"The Grand Canyon of the Pacific," Jason said, gesturing at the mile-wide gorge below. Rainbows danced in glorious profusion through the misty maze of peaks, and the keening wind created a mosaic of shifting grey shadows alternately striped with sunlight.

"It's magnificent," Kristy said, feeling choked with

it. She looked up at him, and became even more so. Disordered black hair, smiling mouth, deep blue eyes as mysterious as the awesome Waimea Valley falling away at their feet. Kristy shivered. She had seen to Flora's sweater but hadn't minded her own, and it was crisply cool, with a touch of moisture in the wind. A distant bank of clouds gave hint of the storm which was, as yet, still milling around in the sea. Frowning, Jason glanced at the tremor rippling her shoulders, and Kristy hurriedly turned from his sardonic gaze.

"Oh, alright, you were right, I should have brought a sweater," she conceded.

He laughed and put an arm around her, which warmed her much more effectively than any sweater could have done. They got back into the car and followed the winding road to its end, then got out again to look down upon the cliffs four thousand feet below. The Pacific hurled itself soundlessly on distant beaches, and a jet left twin white ribbons disintegrating in the milky sky. The old and the new, the temporary and the eternal, she reflected. Such a philosophical line of thought washed away petty differences. As naturally as she breathed, Kristy smiled at him and took his hand in a gesture of sharing.

But when his warm, hard fingers enfolded hers, she felt too nakedly vulnerable. Kristy took back her hand. Jason didn't seem to notice.

After a leisurely lunch at the Kokee Lodge, they retraced their torturous trail back down to the valley, and stopped at the Menehune Garden to enjoy ancient Kauai chants and dances, and a prolonged tour of the beautiful gardens. It was after four when they arrived back at the hotel. As Kristy got out of the car, her hangbag fell to the ground, spilling its contents in one of those embarrassing revelations of the junk a woman carries with her.

Kristy knelt to gather it up, aided by a resignedly smiling Jason. She had just crammed everything back inside her bag when Shanna Bouchard's clear voice rang out. Kristy came out of her crouch with all the grace of a three-legged cow.

Shanna casually kissed Jason on the mouth, then hooked her hands to his arm. Her long, lissome body was sheathed in a white jumpsuit, halter-styled, her back and shoulders beautifully bare, her hair swaying gently in the wind. She greeted the two cousins with poisonous sweetness, looking vastly amused as she took in Kristy's rumpled, wind-blown appearance.

"You must have given them the full treatment, Jason! Heavens, darling, did you get rained on?" she trilled eyeing Kristy with a malicious chuckle.

"No, we didn't get rained on, but it was very windy," Kristy said evenly. Livid at being caught at such disadvantage, she shoved back her hair with unmistakable annoyance. "Thank you for the lovely day, Jason. Come on, Flora, let's go collapse!" she gaily suggested. Icy green eyes shot to Jason's unperturbed face. "And leave Jason to his own affairs—"

Or affair, Kristy bitterly corrected. "We've taken up enough of his time," she laughed. *God she was hurting!* And hating. All her soft intimacies given him this day were stinging little slaps in the face. Kristy reached deep for the airy farewells she exchanged with Jason and his women, but she could not totally conceal the contempt that sheened her hard green eyes. His face perceptibly darkened as they exchanged warring glances. Shanna stood close beside him, still locked onto his arm. *It was all so casual, so contemporary*, Kristy thought, her aching heart a sting of tears she fought with bitter valor. Taking Flora's arm, she walked blindly to the cottage, waving to the first faceless person they met with extravagant gaiety.

If Flora noted anything amiss, she gave no sign of it. The wind had stiffened, and twilight was cloudy and wet, but there was an aching lushness to that warm, moist fragrance filling the deepening night.

"Only two more days of vacation left," she sighed.

"A person could cry on that thought," Kristy wryly told her cousin.

After Flora slept, Kristy did just that for awhile, soundlessly, messily. Sleep was out of the question. The cottage seemed inordinately close and stuffy, and she tossed and turned in a welter of torment. *What were they doing now, Jason and his honeyskinned, black-eyed woman?* Kristy crammed a knuckle in her mouth. If only she hadn't started trusting him again! Another night without sleep would leave her looking a wreck, Kristy grimly warned herself, but warning did not suffice; when an angry dawn finally drifted in, she was awake to greet it.

The morning was glowering, with off and on showers. Flora slept until ten-thirty and Kristy restlessly prowled the cottage, wishing she would awaken, but loathe to disturb what was obviously needed sleep.

When she finally did stir, Flora decided on a day of rest after yesterday's exertions, and Kristy ordered breakfast and a newspaper sent to her, than left for the hotel.

The gauzy scarf that kept her hair in place sailed off across the grass with Kristy in hot pursuit. She stuffed it in her pocket and skirted the agitated papaya trees, and once in the open again, paused to cast an anxious look at the sky. Mountainous clouds blotted out the sun, boiling up and collapsing in upon themselves, thick and gray and ominous. The tropical storm had begun churning towards the jewel-like cluster of islands at a furious speed.

Chapter Fifteen

The television set in the lobby had a group of interested guests encircling it. Kristy shouldered in and watched the weather reports for a time, then hurried to the manager's office. As she expected, Jason was there, talking on the telephone, his glance towards her decidedly unfriendly. The pale-faced man standing beside his desk gave her an unhappy look.

"Yes?" Jason barked as he put down the receiver.

"I—the storm—what do we do?" she blurted.

"*We* do nothing," he said sharply. "You're a guest, so like all the other guests, you will remain calm and stay out of the way. There's nothing to get upset about, we're too far inland—excuse me." He picked up the ringing telephone and sourly listened. Kristy waited out the call.

"I'm not just a guest and I want to help," she persisted despite his vexed scowl. "After all, this was my uncle's hotel before it became yours."

Coldly surveying her, he sighed, an infuriated sound. "Oh, very well. Tell her what to do, Jim," he wearily instructed the manager. "I've got some other things requiring attention, but I'll be back here before . . . I'll be back." Pushing to his feet, Jason walked past her. "Will you stop looking so scared?" he growled.

Of course she was scared, *anyone in their right mind would be scared*, Kristy thought. "I'm not scared, just concerned," she snapped. Why was he so cold and impatient with her? Was she being a nuisance? "Jason, I really do want to help, but if I'm being a nuisance, I'll back off," she said, matching his icy manner.

He paused at the door with a remote smile. "At times you can be something of a nuisance, I admit. However, you're good with people, and some of our guests will undoubtedly be uneasy. Do what you can. Oh, you might remember to check Alex's house," he said. Inclining his head, Jason walked out the door.

"Alex's house," Kristy repeated. She smiled at the manager. "I'll do that and then I'll come right back," she promised. Why was he looking so nervous? He was supposed to give her an encouraging smile! Right out of Hotel Management, she bet, a New Yorker, from the sound of that accent. They didn't have tropical storms in New York. Nor in Texas.

By five o'clock, the sky was inky black, and palm fronds lashed the air with sharp snaps of sound. Kristy had kept so busy she'd not had time to keep personal tabs on the storm's progress, but everyone she met was chock full of information; the storm was bypassing them. Flora had taken refuge in the bar, as had a goodly number of hotel guests. Kristy paused to check on her, certain she would be anxious. Instead, the lively little woman looked as if she was enjoying the excitement, and was helping clear the outside area of potentially dangerous objects.

Ben was conspicuously absent the last time Kristy stopped by, but Meleia was there. Leaving Flora in her care, Kristy rushed on to the manager's office. She had just raised her hand to knock on the door when Ben's voice, rich with amused sympathy, riveted her attention.

"Jason, I'm trying to appreciate your dilemma, but frankly, what I'm actually doing is stifling an urge to laugh," he drawled, a chuckle behind every word. "For Pete's sake, stop this hopping back and forth like an indecisive rabbit. If you want to marry the woman, then do it!"

"Damn it, Ben, marriage isn't something a man jumps into as easy as he jumps in and out of beds!" Jason hotly retorted. "It's a big step and I don't mind admitting it scares hell out of me! Particularly with this woman! Everytime I get near her, I have to stop and test the air to see if I'm going to get my head snapped off . . . most evil-natured woman I've ever met," he ended so aggrievedly, Ben went off again.

"And besides, there is a little matter of love, you know. I hear that's important," Jason added with satiric ill humor.

"So you're not sure about love—maybe it'll come after the honeymoon, who knows?" Ben merrily countered. "You're two of a kind, Jason, very well suited, I think. Besides, you can't hold off that contractor forever. Personally I think an oyster grey bedroom would be like sleeping in a rain barrel, but everyman to his taste!" he chortled.

Jason began to laugh. "I do think I'm man enough to change a woman's mind about a bedroom, Ben, at least the color of it!"

"Appears to me that that woman has a mind like a steel trap under all that softness. Wouldn't count too much on changing her mind if she's not ready to have it changed," Ben jeered.

Jason muttered something Kristy could not make out, but it contained Shanna's name. She dropped her hands to her sides and stepped backwards until she bumped the wall. Her face felt so tight-skinned, she touched it with testing fingertips. "A grey bedroom," she muttered dazedly, totally illogical words—who would want an oyster grey bedroom?

Someone chic, sophisticated, utterly self assured. Deep down, she had never really believed Jason would marry Shanna Bouchard but that he would eventually see Kristy's love, would eventually come to love her in return, a happy ending just like in all good stories. *Incredible,* she thought, *incredible how a person could delude herself!* Savagely it beat at her. *The storm—I'm here to find out . . .* Why was she here? It was Jason's hotel, let the damn thing rot!

With abstracted clarity, Kristy discovered she was wandering around the lobby. Catching the desk clerk's puzzled look, she smiled and walked steadily back to the office. Ben and Jason were still laughing and talking. Weren't they concerned about the storm? Feeling oddly lightheaded, she knocked on the door, and entered at his command.

Ben stood up, but Jason remained seated behind the desk as his gaze lazily played over her coral slack suit. The crisp fabric was no longer crisp, it was every bit as weary as Kristy. Both men had drinks in hand and looked none too fresh themselves. She pushed at her hair, smiling at Ben.

"Hi, Ben. You've got a bar full of uneasy people looking for succor," she chided.

His faced suddenly blurred as she swayed like a tulip at the end of its stem. Jason shot to his feet. "Are you ill? You're white as a sheet!" he angrily accused.

When he reached for her, she recoiled. Sending Ben a look, she said sharply, "I'm fine. Just a little tired, that's all. Tell me—I've been so busy, I haven't heard the latest—but is it true the storm won't hit Kauai?"

"Yes, it's true. It's going to miss the islands by a good distance. We'll get rain and wind, but hopefully, it won't be too bad," Jason said, studying her with a trace of confusion.

There was a childish tremor in her voice as she asked, "It really won't be too bad?"

"No, just wind and rain, that's all," he repeated gently.

"Hey, honey, you're not scared, are you?" Ben

asked, startled.

"Yes, a little. I've never seen a tropical storm. We don't get them at home. Just tornadoes," she said a little sheepishly.

Ben laughed and tweaked her hair. "*Just* tornadoes?" He laughed again, then said to Jason, "Well, I'd best get back to my bar. Got all those uneasy people waiting for me," he ended with a teasing grin for Kristy.

"Flora is there too, Ben. You'll watch out for her till I get there?" Kristy called as he walked to the door.

"I'll watch out for her," he promised.

"I think it would be best to close the bar," Jason said.

Ben nodded. "I'll keep Flora with me."

"Alright. Enjoyed the drink, Ben—and that sage advice," Jason said, grinning. He stepped towards Kristy, and she recoiled again. He gave a short laugh at her involuntary reaction, but suddenly the air between them was charged with something that dismayed her. His face was utterly expressionless, his eyes flat and opaque, yet she felt a tremble of alarm.

"Don't look so alarmed, Kristy, I rarely assault women in an office," he drawled. "Why don't you run along now, there's nothing else to do but wait it out—and since it's so unpleasant, we needn't do it together."

Kristy stared at him, too unsettled to react. Fragments of thought skittered across her mind, none making sense, and none willing to remain long enough to catch their meaning. "I didn't . . . I heard you laughing and I—" She dug at her burning eyes. "Well, I guess I'll go see about Flora then, and maybe check on 202—a widow lady—she's terribly afraid."

"Forget 202, you're going to bed—you look like hell," Jason said roughly.

"But it's just five o'clock. And Flora—"

Jason's hand hit the desk in a sharp slap. "Damn it!" he swore lustily. "Would you stop arguing with me— just this once! Flora will be in the hotel, well looked after, and a few hours rest will not endanger anyone!" he sarcastically assured her. Taking her arm firmly in hand, he towed her out the side entrance and down the path to her cottage. Kristy followed as docilely as a farm animal. He was right, of course, she did need some rest.

They ran the last few steps through pelting rain. Jason closed the door, but not before he noted her furtive check of the sky. "I told you there's nothing to be afraid of, it's just a little wind and rain," he impatiently repeated. "These cottages are strong enough to withstand a hurricane—you'll be quite safe here."

Stung by his annoyance at her timidity, she raised her chin and coldy replied, "I'm not afraid. Just—just concerned for the hotel, that's all. And about that woman— she's all alone and she's in her sixties, Jason."

Jason shot her a skeptical look, his mouth thinning when her eyes dropped. "I will check on 202, I promise. Now get yourself in bed and rest awhile. I'll call you if we need you," he said gruffly.

Kristy turned to obey, but he made a groaning sound and caught her in his arms, pulling her fiercely against him. Murmuring something inaudible, he buried his face in her hair and held her tightly, tightly.

His body was warm and hard and inexpressibly dear,

302

and she closed her eyes to the sweet, sweet rapture of closeness. Jason held her locked to him as he began a tantalizing tease of her senses, brushing her ear, her temple, her cheek with soft, hungry kisses. Eagerly she waited for his rough, hot mouth to reach hers. The smell of him, the feel of his body, aroused and straining, demanding as he would always demand what she would give, would so willingly give! Love surged and flamed and she had a sensation of melting under the bliss of those searching hands. *Oh my darling,* she thought yearningly, caressing through his silky hair.

And then she remembered.

Kristy twisted her face aside before he could kiss her. Just a short time ago, he was agonizing over marrying Shanna and now he was beginning this beautiful love-making with her! Sickened by such duplicity, she turned wooden in his arms, his caresses, his attempted kiss a shudder of repugnance.

Jason dropped his arms and stepped away from her as swiftly as if she'd struck him again. His fingers bit deep into her upper arms, shaking her with his thick, grating, "*Damn* you!"

She refused to look at him. Her body trembled under his smoldering gaze. "Please, Jason," she whispered.

Jason let go of her. An eyebrow arched with his sardonic laugh. "Sorry," he said. He walked out the door and slammed it resoundingly behind him.

She longed desperately to call him back, but if she did, her defenses would collapse completely. "You're leaving tomorrow," she reminded. Stumbling to the bathroom, she took a long shower and gave her tired body a brisk rubdown, then redressed in slacks and shirt. It seemed she ought to be doing something, but she couldn't think what. At least she was thinking with clarity. Before she left tomorrow, this stupid charade she'd been living was going to end, and she was going to stop behaving like a moonstruck idiot. Her giggle sounded a little hysterical, but the relief of her decision was immense.

"I will simply say to him, Jason, thank you so much for this lovely vacation and for all your kindnesses. I have loved you from the first time I saw you and that's why I've behaved like a silly little fool," she said aloud. It sounded wonderful! What he would reply didn't enter into it, at least she would be acting like a mature, intelligent woman; Kristin Loring again, calm, easy, predictable as rain, something she had not been for a long, long time.

Knowing she could not possibly sleep, she lay down atop the bedspread and shut her eyes. *The wind cried around the windows like a lost child,* she thought . . .

The crash of breaking glass jolted her awake. Bolting upright in bed, Kristy sought to orient herself, but the manical howl of wind further distorted her senses. She had left the lights on, yet it was pitch black in the cottage. *The power must have failed,* she thought distractedly; didn't the hotel have an emergency generator? She scrambled across the bed and stared with disbelief at the luminous face of her alarm clock. She had slept nearly four hours!

Her legs were entangled with a blanket she didn't remember getting. Fumbling for the small flashlight she kept on the night table, she switched on the narrow beam and followed it to the living room, to the appalling hole in the window.

Wind-blown rain had already soaked the carpet. Stumbling over the fat green coconut that had smashed the pane, she sped to a drawer for masking tape—*oh blast, where was it!* She knew she'd left some here somewhere. Locating it by touch, she grabbed up the large sheet of cardboard Flora had placed at the door for a footwiper. The pretty gingerjar lamp crashed to the floor. Kristy found it and set it upright, then returned to the window.

Pleased at how well she was functioning, she set to work with single-minded dedication. After a long, fumbly fingered time, she had secured the cardboard over the hole, and covered the cracked panes with a solid layer of tape. *It would surely hold against the wind,* she thought, nodding vigorous agreement. Finding towels by flashlight, she sopped up the excess water and threw the sodden linens in the tub.

The wind's fury shuddered her with anxiety. She jumped as something struck the door a heavy fisted blow. It was very hard to remain calm, but she knew she was perfectly safe; Jason said so.

She sat down on the couch, but the desperate need for lights and people grew to strangling force. The lights came on, flickered, dimmed, went off again. Were they off in the hotel? Was Flora all right? *Of course she was; Jason said so.* Instinctively, she placed complete faith in his assurance. She turned off the flashlight to save batteries, and sat stolidly in the dark.

305

A rain of coconuts thundering across the porch brought her to her feet with a sharp gasp. Staying here took more courage than she possessed! She snapped on the flashlight, opened the door and plunged out into the savage night.

Stygian blackness swallowed her up in a nightmare of blinding rain and insanely howling wind. Struggling to keep her feet on the brick path, she wrapped her arms around her head and forged ahead, only to be sent sprawling by the tree that blocked her path. Unreasoning panic overwhelmed her as she fought free of its clawing branches. She had lost the path, but there was nothing to do except go blindly on.

When the flashlight picked out the familiar outline of the bar, Kristy edged around the wall until she came to the covered entrance. An uprooted palm blocked it. She crawled over it and recklessly plunged into the debris of shredded fronds to reach the door.

The flashlight went out. The door was locked. It couldn't be locked! She could see the bright orange sign for *Bacardi* rum glowing through the window. Kristy's voice rose to a shrill scream. Mindlessly she hammered on the door until a tiny shred of logic invaded her anger. Everyone would be in the main building, of course. She wheeled and fought her way to open ground again, but she was hopelessly disoriented. The wall of rain effectively masked the hotel lights, and there was nothing but the agony of windlashed trees to guide her.

Standing very still, using every last shred of control, she sought to determine in which direction the hotel lay. Something large and heavy whipping by her face threw her into panic, and she began running wildly until she slammed into the twisted bole of a palm. Clasping her arms around it, she battled for control of herself. It was totally unlike her to go to pieces like this, but oh God, it was frightening!

It took forever to associate the flickering beam of light with reality. Kristy lunged towards it, and fell heavily into the tree that blocked the entrance. Jason's voice penetrated like a shard of fire. The light was coming closer and she was stumbling to meet it, falling and staggering to her feet again and then his hand touched her shoulder and she lunged into his chest and clung frantically to the powerful body shielding hers!

Jason curved an arm around her and half dragged her into the undamaged portance of the covered entrance. He set the flashlight on end, and caught her in his arms. Burying her face in the solid haven of his chest, Kristy clung to him and sobbed with utter abandon.

"It's alright, baby, it's alright, I'm here," Jason said huskily. "Don't cry, darling, you're alright now." His lips moved over her sodden hair in self-assurance. "Are you hurt?" she heard him asking insistantly.

"No—no, I'm not hurt. Just so scared. Oh, Jason, don't leave me alone ever again!" she choked.

Blindly she lifted her tear drenched face to his. Their lips met with bruising force as weeks of pent-up hunger surged wild and free. His arms tightened until she thought he'd crush her, but even as she thought it, she was frenziedly trying to get into his skin with him.

This onslaught of emotion was nearly as terrifying as

the storm raging around them. She gave him everything in her frantic kisses. The scalding torrent of love pouring through her, the wild, primitive feelings released by the fury of the elements, scorched his mouth with passion.

They came apart to gasp for air, and a second later, his mouth reclaimed hers with savage hunger. As if they could not get enough of each other, their flaming kisses went on and on. Kristy groaned his name over and over. Their soaked bodies fused together, and there was nothing—nothing but this mutual outpouring of fierce, elemental need.

Jason released her lips with a groaning sigh. His ragged breaths burned her skin as he dug his face into the curve of her neck and head, burrowing deep under her hair with rough kisses.

"Why! Why isn't this enough for you?" he asked fiercely. "Why do you continue to love a piece of scum not worth the tip of your finger!"

Kristy's mind was utter chaos. Mistaking his meaning, she stared at the shadowed face in confusion, which swiftly changed to outrage. "Don't you ever say that again, do you hear? I will not have anyone, not even you, talk about Jason Thorne that way!" she hissed, shaking him with every word.

"Me?" Jason echoed. "I was talking about Steve . . . you thought—*me?*"

She was infuriated and he was too damn bit to shake effectively! "Yes, you. I wasn't talking about Steve, I was never talking about Steve Brady when I spoke of love! It was you, you big, dumb—*jackass!*" Blazing with love, she grabbed his head and shook it, then kissed him furiously.

"Jackass!" His voice cracked. *"Jackass?"*

"Yes, jackass! I have never in my life met such a dense, muleheaded—"

"Will you for God's sake stop hissing at me and say whatever the hell you're trying to say!" Jason roared.

"I was never in love with Steve! I love you, blast it!"

"Me!" Jason echoed incredulously, exultantly! His kisses rained over her face and he grabbed her so tight she was being squashed, but she clung to him with all her might.

"I love you." she screeched above the wind's howl. "I don't want to leave here ever! I want to marry you and have fifteen or twenty kids all with blue eyes and black hair. Is that clear enough for you?"

"Oh God!" Jason groaned, strangling with laughter. "Yes, it's clear enough! Do you realize we're standing here in a raging storm kissing like two idiots? Come on, woman, let's get you back to the hotel, where I'm going to tell you exactly what I—what the devil were you doing out in this storm?" he roared furiously.

"The window broke—it was so dark," she stammered.

He swore mightily. "I asked you if you were afraid and you said no! You would have been perfectly safe in the cottage, I checked on you and you were sleeping. I couldn't believe it when I went back and found it empty and you out somewhere in this storm, falling over everything as usual! Kristy, I am dangerously near to spanking you! Also close to loving you—"

Kristy stilled. "You don't love me?"

"Oh for—do I go running off to Texas with kidnapping in mind—or go out in howling storms to check on a small woman who is all alone in a cottage!" he roared again. "Of course I love you! Now put your arms around my waist and hang on!"

"Yes, darling."

"And say that again!" he ordered furiously.

"Yes, darling!" Kristy happily obeyed. "Isn't it a lovely storm, Jason?"

He laughed and squeezed her before picking up the flashlight. "The loveliest storm I've ever had the pleasure to drown in. All right, here we go. Hang on tight, baby."

A wild time later, they stumbled in the side entrance of the hotel with mutual gasps of relief. "Jason, Cousin Flora," she began as he towed her to the elevator.

"Ben's taking care of Flora. We'll go to my suite and get you out of those wet clothes and into a hot bath," he said testily as he caught her long shiver. Despite her blissful inner warmth, Kristy was blue-lipped with cold. Once inside the suite, Jason wasted no time setting this aright. He guided her into the wine and cream bathroom and started the water as he said, "You strip and climb into this. I'll put a robe outside the door. Stay in the water until you're thoroughly warmed."

A little hurt at his sharp tone, Kristy said, "But you need to shower too, Jason, you're soaked."

His name came from her lips with such melting love, he smiled. "There's another bathroom in the spare bedroom, sweetheart, I'll use it." Jason bent his rain-soaked head and kissed her. "Now get into the tub . . ." An eyebrow tilted as he kissed her again, and raised his head with a wicked grin. "Before I'm tempted to get in there with you! Oh Kristy, Kristy, I love you . . . my little drowned Mermaid, I love you," he whispered. "When do you plan to ask me to marry you?" he growled when he could.

Blinking at rivulets of water streaming from her hair, Kristy said, "Jason, will you marry me?"

He laughed and squeezed the breath out of her. "As soon as possible. Now into the tub. There's a hairbrush and comb over there—if you don't mind using mine?"

Kristy lost no time obeying his command when he left the room. She floated down into the heavenly warmth with a sigh of content. She felt no urgency to hasten her bath; what would come would come in the fullness of time. Tonight's experience was savored to the fullest before she left the tub and reached for the heavy white terrycloth robe just outside the door. It smelled of Jason and was ten sizes too big. Dreamily she cuddled into its soft folds.

She had washed her hair and toweled it to a damp fluff. His hairbrush, and a small hand dryer, completed the job. The feathery curls hugging her face were especially dear tonight. Jason had said she had lovely hair. Still brushing, she went back into the bedroom. Jason tapped and entered at her invitation. Kristy's heartbeat escalated to a wild paean of love. He wore a midnight blue silk robe over pajamas and houseslippers and his hair was still damp, and he was too beloved to bear it!

His handsome face wreathed in a smile as he studied

311

her. "You certainly look different than that little drowned kitten I left awhile ago."

She smiled radiantly, but her eyes clouded as she saw what he held. "Where did you get those?" she asked evenly.

Jason grinned. "I made 'em open the shop downstairs. Here you go, a robe, a gown, and, ah, these," he murmured, placing the garments in her hands one by one, the tiny pair of black lace briefs last of all. A gust of wind shook the windows. When Kristy flinched, he caught her in his arms. "Darling, don't be afraid, it's nearly over now," he said so tenderly, tears pricked her eyes.

"No, I'm not afraid, not with you," Kristy said softly. "Oh Jason, there's so many things to be cleared up, so many things I'd like to unsay," she whispered. His mouth touched over her face, then settled on her lips in a long, sweetly gentle kiss totally unlike any other. When it would deepen, he drew back to look into her eyes.

"We'll clear them up, Kristy, never fear. My lover, will you be uneasy sharing the rest of the night with me?"

"No, Jason, I won't be uneasy. I love you. I told you it was all right when there's love." She grinned, self consciously. "I've never slept with a man, Jason. Believe it or not, you've a twenty-three-year-old novice on your hands."

He laughed softly. "I knew that—I always knew that, Mermaid. But I meant share my suite, not my bed."

She blushed, her eyes widening, her mouth curving

into a startled little "Oh!" Jason kissed it with exultant joy. She was flamingly aware of his thighs pressing against her yielding body. All resistance flowed from her as she kissed him with the fire of total surrender. She was trembling when his lips left hers. Jason was trembling too, she delightedly noted. He cupped her face and looked at her searchingly.

"You would love me now?" he asked huskily.

"Yes I would—now and forevermore, Jason."

Jason lay his cheek against hers and held her. "I will teach you of love, my darling, but at the proper time," he whispered, kissing her softly. "Do you remember the time at my house, when I asked you to let me teach you love? I meant it then as much as I do now. My lovely Mermaid, I think I must have loved you since the day I saved you from drowning—" he laughed joyously and shut her mouth with his. "From the moment you cuddled in my arms like a soft little kitten and looked up at me and said, 'If you don't stop laughing, I'm going to tear your throat out'—or something to that effect!"

"I *cuddled* up in your arms?" Kristy's incredulous expression evoked another deep laugh. *I was right,* she thought, I'll never grow tired of hearing that laugh! Jason swept her up and carried her to the bed. Ignoring her gasp, he stood her beside it and matter-of-factly began turning down the heavy spread to expose pale blue sheets.

"Go put on your nightgown, you've had a terrible fright, and you're exhausted," he commanded.

Inwardly amused at his sternness, she took up the

313

filmy garments and carried them to the bathroom. When she came out, Jason was not in sight. She got into bed and pulled the sheet up to her scantily covered breasts. When Jason strolled back into the room, she held out her arms. "Come here, darling," she said, eagerly drawing him down beside her. Jason stretched out on his stomach. Glowing blue eyes roamed over the gossamer black gown, the seductive golden hair fanning over his blue satin pillow, and his voice deepened to unbearable huskiness.

"Do you know how many times I've imagined you like this? I love you, Kristy, more than I've ever loved anything or anyone in my life."

"Why couldn't you have told me that before?" she asked with sudden desolation.

"Because I didn't know it before, I guess. I knew I wanted you—wanted you in a special way, more than anything I've ever wanted in my life, but love? Not an easy word to tackle, Kristy." A long finger traced her collarbone, the curve of her jaw, then moved to the rounds of her breasts with beautiful right-ness. The taut nipples poking the thin black nylon arrested his progress. His head dipped, and he kissed them. "I love you. And I want you."

"But when I came back this time, you were so indifferent to me," she said, looking woefully confused.

"And how were you to me, Kristy? I felt like an interloper every time I got around you and Flora. That night we went to the bar for a nightcap, I meant to tell you I loved you, but—" The spreading fans of his lashes concealed his eyes. "You made it so plain you were uninterested."

"Not uninterested, just trying to keep myself from begging you to stay with me," Kristy dryly interrupted. "It strikes me that we were both rather stupid, Jason."

"Um, I've been struck by the same notion, Mermaid!" he grinned.

"Shanna told me that you two had an understanding, that you would be married someday," she said quietly.

Jason smoothed back the curls clinging to her cheeks. "Any idea of marriage between Shanna and myself was soley a creation of her imagination. I never spoke of marriage, nor encouraged her in any way. She was an amusement, nothing more.

"And her feelings for me are about as deep as that ditch you fell into," he added dryly. Kristy's lashes drifted down. "What else, Kristy?" Jason sighed.

"She also told me that you—that she was comfortably married when you—well, seduced her, is what she implied. That's why I thought—" she stopped, awkward now.

"Why you thought I could seduce someone as young and innocent as Melly?" Jason finished for her. "All right, let me tell you about Shanna. We met in our teens, but since she's three years older, we had little to do with each other until we, in our early twenties, drifted into an affair. She was interested in marriage, I wasn't. We broke up, not too pleasantly, as I recall. She married an Englishman some twenty years her senior. The marriage broke up months before we met again. Then, well, she was still very attractive and we found it mutual. We each knew exactly what we wanted from the other–I spelled it out, in fact."

Jason sighed. "But Shanna is too spoiled and willful to even consider not getting what she wants, and after a time, she decided she wanted me, the Thorne name, whatever."

"She intimated that she was staying at your apartment this week," Kristy said.

"She was not. She has her own apartment in that complex. When she met us here yesterday evening after our excursion, I was furious. We had an ugly scene and she left—for where, I neither know or care," Jason said flatly.

Kristy smiled, trustingly. "Was she the one going to give you that oyster grey bedroom?" she asked impishly. Jason looked startled. "I overheard you and Ben talking tonight," she explained.

"Talking about you, as it happened. I finally unloaded some of my misery on him. Kristy, I think every thought I put into that new house was for you. I started it long before I met you, but after that, it was always yours." He stopped, looking sheepish. "I had to practice a lot of self-deception, you know. It isn't easy to build a house for a particular woman and pretend you don't know it!"

"Why did you have to pretend, Jason?"

Jason looked into wide green eyes and helplessly shook his head. "Because you were such an interference. I'm a normal, self-centered, thirty-three-year-old-male who's lived a full and active life. You know that, Kristy, I've never denied myself the pleasures so easily available to me. You were supposed to be just another

316

delicious bit of fun, but I found I couldn't get you out of my mind—no matter what I was doing or who I was with, something of you would come creeping in, the way you laugh, the way you felt in my arms, even just some saucy remark you'd made that utterly delighted me. Then I'd come to you and you'd give me that slanted, green-eyed look and I'd—I'm not accustomed to being treated like an adolescent fumbling around in the dark," he said dryly. "You can't imagine how that pricked!"

Jason kissed her, a touch of hard, possessive anger in it. "Besides, I thought you were still hung up on Steve, and that irritated hell out of me. Frankly, Miss Loring darling, I was quite certain I could seduce you anytime I pleased, but I wasn't sure you wouldn't end up hating me."

"And when did you decide you loved me, Mr. Thorne darling?" Kristy teased.

Jason laid his face on her breasts and curved his arms under her in fierce possession. "When I began work on the waterfall, I guess. It was then that I realized what a fool I'd been, my darling."

Sapphire eyes met hers. "There were too many memories there—I kept seeing you at every turn, standing there on the ledge with your hair blowing in the wind, lying on one of those black stones sleeping in the sun . . . So I decided to come get you. Bring you back where you belonged—by damn I would. On the flimsiest excuses, as you well knew. I didn't know what kind of a reception I'd get when I showed up unannounced at your door, but I tell you truly, Kristin had

317

you refused to return peacefully, I fully intended to kidnap you!''

They laughed, joyous and free of dark restraint. ''But when we got back, you made it bitterly clear you didn't want me and I—'' he shrugged, and for an instant, the familiar hard, cold mask flowed over his features.

''Don't ever look at me like that again, Jason. There was never a time I didn't want you, but I've got pride too . . . maybe a little overmuch,'' she sighed.

''Maybe a little, but I love it too.'' Jason smiled at her badly concealed yawn. ''Go to sleep now, love. We've got years and years to learn everything we need to know about each other.'' He kissed her, then tucked the covers around her shoulders. ''Goodnight, Mermaid,'' Jason said, and walked swiftly from the room.

Kristy cuddled into the sheets with his husky whisper to warm her. The smell of him was sweetly thick around her, on the sheet, on her. Convinced that she could not possibly sleep with this rapturous happiness expanding her heart, she nonetheless drifted deeper and deeper into the velvet mists of slumber.

When she awoke, sunlight illumined the room, the deep blue eyes illumined her face. Jason sat quietly in a chair beside her bed, contentedly watching her sleep. Kristy blushed at the smile spreading over his face.

''Good morning, Kristy.''

''Good morning, Jason darling!'' she laughed with lilting happiness. ''Why are you sitting here spying on my sleep?'' she asked, wrinkling her nose. He leaned down to kiss it, then her lips in possessive delight. Kristy drew him down onto the bed with her and lustily kissed him.

There was no frantic sense of urgency in their kisses, in the hands moving over her with sweet intimacy. That joyous current of sexual awareness pulsed within them like an extra heart-beat, but surety muted it, and made of it a tantalizing pleasure. *There was all the time in the world,* she thought joyously, exuberantly, laughing and kissing and nipping at him with small, sharp teeth.

"Now, why were you spying on me, I asked!" she hissed.

"I wanted to see what you looked like in the morning . . . see just what I'm getting into in this temporary madness that has befallen me," Jason groaned.

Her hands slid into his hair. "Temporary?"

"Yes, temporary. I doubt it will last over fifty years— a hundred at the most," he said so hopefully, she began tickling him. How beautiful, how glorious, how incredible it all was! In a dream, she said, "I love you, Jason Thorne."

"Say it again," he whispered. She laughed and kissed his hair and said it again and again and again . . .

"Someone's knocking on the door, Jason," she nudged him.

"Yes. Probably Flora. I suppose we're hopelessly compromised—not a chance of getting out of marriage now, is there," he sighed, walking to the door. Crystal blue eyes danced over his shoulder.

Kristy sat up and tried to look compromised. "Not a chance, Jason."

He paused, a hand at the knob. *"Fifteen or twenty kids?"* Jason suddenly, incredulously remembered.

Slanting green eyes lazily crossed his. "Well, maybe

319

we'll stop at ten, Jason. I would like some time for gardening, you know,'' Kristy said.